i choose you
xoxo

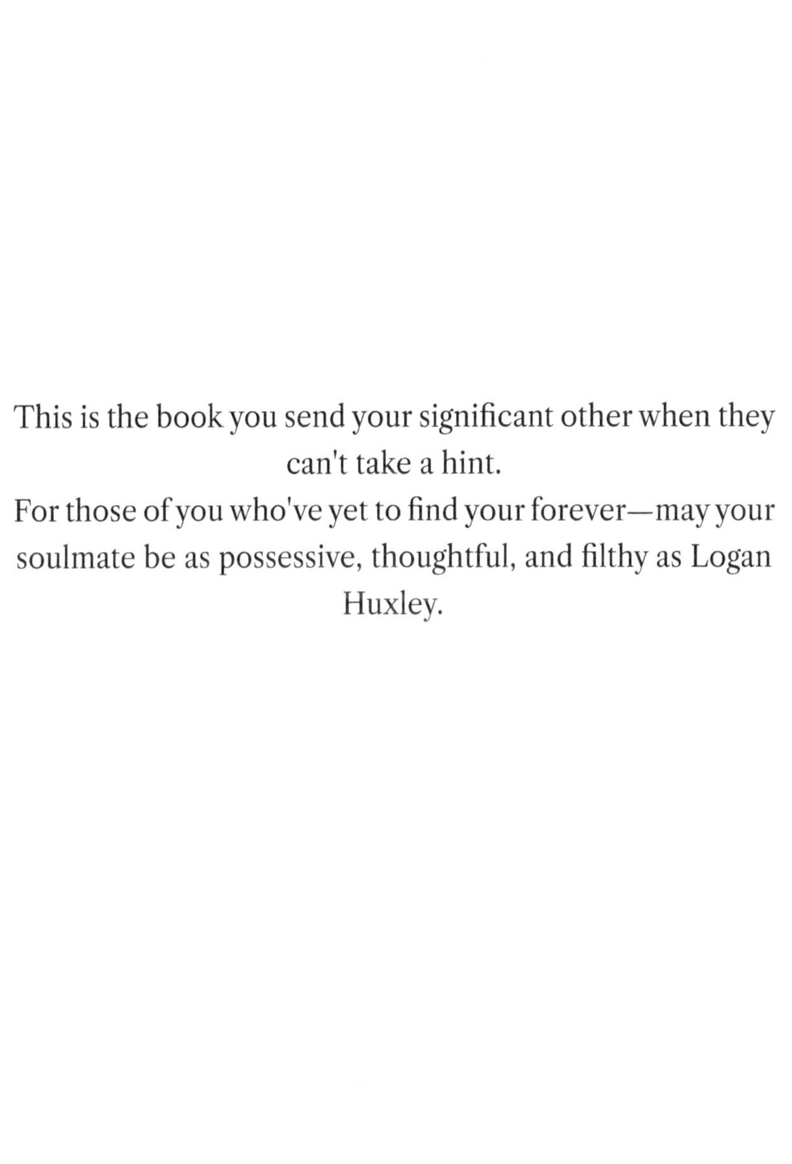

This is the book you send your significant other when they can't take a hint.
For those of you who've yet to find your forever—may your soulmate be as possessive, thoughtful, and filthy as Logan Huxley.

Trigger Warnings

Proceed with caution and remember to practice self-care before, during, and after reading this series. Enjoy!

This is a.....low angst, instalove/instalust, OTT-possessive Hero, healing heart divorced plus-size heroine, medium-length, sweet, SPICY book with a LOT of talk about babies, including but not limited to: descriptive memory of miscarriage/pregnancy loss (13 weeks), infertility/treatments, PCOS, breeding, knotting, stuffing/stretching, LOTS of jizz, and eventually, pregnancy. PTSD from the military. Loss of a family member (memory)

There are omegaverse themes in this book but it's contemporary, NOT PNR! Enjoy a regular couple with the added bonus of knotting, breeding, nesting, "slick", "heat", attempted pregnancy, alpha/omega talk, growling, and more.

The infertility story in this book is my own, so I understand how triggering these topics can be for those who have experienced them. If you'd like to read the book but skip the 'loss talk,' please skip the scene in chapters 1-2 where the FMC discusses her past. Other than that, it's glossed over and not detailed.

If you have a specific trigger and are unsure if it's in this book or one of my others, please do not hesitate to reach out and ask. The best way is through email or Instagram.

Foreward

There is a lot of talk of infertility struggles and miscarriage in this book. As I said before, it's my story.

So, I understand how difficult trying to conceive is. How hard it is to want a baby so bad that you'd do anything. I understand the heartache of trying and being unsuccessful. I understand how much the losses hurt. I understand.

It's a journey, and it's hard as hell. If this is something you've struggled with or currently are, my heart goes out to you. Just know the TTC community is vast. More women than you can even wrap your mind around are going through the same thing, and you are not alone.

Hopefully, this story can bring you some hope and peace. Writing this book was cathartic, leaving me feeling even more hopeful for my future than ever.

However, you come first. So take care of yourself and proceed with caution.

This special edition not only includes a new Daddy Logan cover, but you'll also find that the interior has also undergone some changes. Each chapter includes an image of real-life women living unabashedly in their bodies, as they should. I also spoke to readers who've contacted me over the months since this book was released. Women who've shared their incredible stories with me and, with their permission, borrowed words and phrases that stood out, creating a tapestry of empowerment.

The first time I saw it all come together, I cried like a baby. I hope you enjoy it as much as I do, but above all else, I hope you feel seen.

You are perfect in your existence, exactly as is.

You are enough.

XOXO

Bex

Playlist

This book was written with
My Best Friend by George Strait
in mind.

CRACKED FOUNDATION

BEX DAWN

Prologue

I had dreams.

Plans.

Things I had hoped to do, to accomplish. No. More than hoped. I had expected.

Now, look at me. I'm nowhere near where I thought I would be. I am nothing like the person I dreamed I would become, and the life... the *vision*, I had for myself, is dead.

As dead as my marriage.

As dead as a lot of things.

Death. It's a funny concept, isn't it? You live your life to the best of your ability. Well, sometimes. Some people just float through life, hoping for the living to come to them. Too petrified to meet their untimely end. Too afraid of all that could go wrong if they seek out the things they truly want. So instead, they just stay stagnant, waiting for some sort of blip in their world to jolt them out of their monotony. They wait and wait for the perfect time to start really living.

And then—they die.

Others, the brave ones; actively seek out the living part of their life. They take what they want, do what they want, and achieve what they want. Like the time-old mantra, they *live life to the fullest,* and then, they might even welcome death when it comes. They've done the whole life thing, probably even made it their bitch, so why would they be afraid for it to come to an end?

Me? I'm somewhere in the middle.

I'm not a lump on a log, waiting for life to smack me upside the head, demanding I hop to. I'm not terrified of living. Quite the opposite actually. I want to live life to the fullest. I want to achieve things, make my dreams come true, see the world, and make incredible memories. Does that mean I'm going to go out and live as though I'm invincible? Indestructible and resilient to the bitter end? No. No, it does not.

Because, like many others, I've learned I'm not invincible, indestructible, or resilient to the bitter end.

I am breakable. I am perishable. I am only human, and I do, in fact, have an expiration date.

What I do between now and then? Well, that's not completely up to me, now, is it?

I used to think it was. I used to think I was the master of my life and my future. I used to think my dreams, goals, and aspirations were mine, and mine alone, to do with what I wanted. I used to think I had the ability to make my visions a reality, that nothing, and no one, would or could come between me and my future. As though it was some sort of foregone conclusion.

Pfft. Right.

Maybe that would have been the case if the future I saw for myself was a solo one. An existence that only depended on me, myself, and I. Unfortunately, it wasn't. *It's not.* Nope. I'm the dumbass who decided to go and dream up a whole-ass future that is solely dependent on other people. I dreamt up grand plans of a future that included me surrounded by people I could love, that would love me back.

The problem with dreams like that is: the only thing in life that you can control is yourself, and your own actions. Sometimes, we even get ourselves wrong. Sometimes, we fuck up our own lives.

However, when you dream about living a life full of love and companionship, you put your faith and trust in another human being. Therefore your future plans, dreams, and visions are reliant on something and someone completely and utterly out of your control. Sometimes that goes great. Sometimes, people really do find their happily ever after with another human who wants the same things, who chooses the same path, who works for the same end goal.

But—what happens when that person decides to take your life, your dreams, your everything....

And crushes it to all hell?

IT'S MY CHOICE

BE PATIENT WITH YOURSELF

Unapologetica MYSELF!

ST posi

BE bold

ALL BODIES are GOOD BODIES

beautiful

Fearless

be happy

HERE TO STAY

IN CONTROL

LOVE yourse

be kind to yourself

I am enough

FEEL DEEPLY

YOUR POTENTI is choic

brave

be

IT'S my CHOICE

Yo pre

I am exactly where I need to be

I am capable

POWER you are strong

love you

YOU ARE enoug

beautiful

breathe

Perfect

Shiloh

One

"I 'll take another, Jeeves," I demand, tongue flopping haphazardly around my drunken mouth. The bartender, most definitely not named Jeeves, chuckles, and shakes his head, but does indeed make me another martini. "Extra olives, please. I require *sustenationess*." I emphasize the s's, making sure to really drive the point home.

He glances up at me with wide eyes full of laughter, if I'm not mistaken. It could be dread. Irritation. Possibly distaste. It's really difficult to tell when there are currently two of him. Four sets of eyes, two wide noses, two pouty-lipped mouths. Makes distinguishing subtle expressions quite difficult.

Although, that could also be the four vodka martinis sitting heavily in my very empty stomach. As in, I haven't eaten for like a solid ten hours. All because I wanted to make a good impression tonight. I didn't want to look all bloaty in my skanky red wrap dress, that fits my curves like a second skin. Spanx can only do so much for a girl.

Jeeves grins, and slides my drink in front of me. Swapping out my empty glass for a full one. He's smiling. With both mouths. Must mean his eyes were in fact, filled with laughter, and mirth, and not all the other crap I'd imagined. Cool, cool, cool. Dragging my sluggish gaze from his, my eyes connect with my new drink. Instead of one olive, it has two. *Yay me.*

Clearly, he assumed the fat girl didn't need any more snacks than necessary. "Hey! Jeeves!" I snap. Irritation, drunkenness, and hunger consuming me at once. "I said *extra* olives. Remember the whole sustenationess thing we talked about?"

"Sustenationess is not a word. My name is not Jeeves, it's Dom. I'm well aware of your demand for food, but olives won't do shit. Especially not to soak up all that alcohol." Wow. Jeeves—nope, that's wrong. *Dom* is sort of a dick.

He smiles brightly.

Okay, not a dick.

I smile back.

He grimaces.

Dick.

Frowning, I pick up my drink and take a healthy swig, washing all my worries away. Except my worries actually amount to the size of Texas, and all the vodka in the world couldn't get rid of them, or make me feel better. At this point, I think I'm drinking in excess in hopes that I will just pass the hell out, forgetting my problems existed in the first place.

Sticking my fingers into the dainty glass, I fish out an olive and pop it into my mouth, just in time for Dom to return with a glass of water and a delightfully surprising treat. A big ass plate of fries, and a burger that is filled to the brim with juicy deliciousness.

My head swivels in his direction so quickly that I almost fall off the barstool my ass has been perched on for the last hour and a half. Prior to this chair, my ass was sitting at a table in the fancy dining room of the high-end restaurant for an additional 45 minutes, waiting for a blind date that never showed.

Third one this month. Awesome.

"Oh my god, you shouldn't have, Dom! This is the sweetest gift I've ever been given!" I gush, only half joking. I almost want to cry at how thoughtful he is, but then I force those bitch ass tears down because the last thing I need is for this cute bartender to think I'm a straight nutjob, crying over french fries.

Digging into the fry pile, I hand him one with all of the gratitude in the world, and the grace of a bull in a china shop. He barks out a laugh and reaches for the fry. I drop it because I overshoot where his hand actually is. He laughs again, bats my hand away, and grabs a fry straight off my plate like we're besties or something. Awww, cute. I made a friend. Now I really might cry.

Dom leans on the bar right across from me, a dirty white towel tossed over his shoulder, a button-up black shirt lacking a few at the top, and exposing his hairless tan chest. A bit thin and narrow for my taste. I prefer my men manly, rugged, and hairy. His chest reminds me of a naked mole rat, but his face is pretty. I can bet he's got a killer six-pack and cut Adonis' belt. My eyes trail down his body in an attempt to do a slow, sly perusal, but of course, my drunk self fails epically.

"Not that I would ever tell a pretty girl not to check me out, but it would be fruitless for ya, Sweetheart. My heart's already taken by another." *Ouch, rejected again.* Dom sighs dramatically, as though he's actively picturing his beloved right here and now. His golden-brown cheeks turn a little pink, and it softens his rejection, but I can't fight the scowl from appearing on my face. He snags another fry, and forcibly shakes his wistful expression away, before booping me on the nose with the offending carb.

Well fuck. "That's adorable, and all, Jeeves, but I have to tell you, if you can't control your loved-up self, I'm gonna have to ask you to kindly fuck off. I'm pretty sure my horrible love life has the potential to rub off on unsuspecting people in my near vicinity, and I would hate to deprive you of your happiness." My deadpanned declaration may seem heartless and sardonic, and maybe it is, but beneath it is an insanely large chasm of deep, soul-wrenching pain.

Usually, I can hide that shit like some sort of professional spy, but right now, I'm drunk as hell, and nursing yet another brush-off by a man who didn't think I was worthy. So excuse the fuck out of me if I can't tamp down my emotions tonight.

The pink-cheeked, giddy expression on Dom's face falls completely, and I steel myself for the tirade that's likely to come. The rude comments. The yell. The slap in the face. Metaphorical or otherwise, but it never does.

Dom nods knowingly and grabs another fry. He bites down on it and tilts his head to the side like he's trying to get into my brain to figure me all out. Good luck. I can't even figure my own shit out.

He gives one decisive nod like he's come to a conclusion. I take a big bite of my burger, stuffing my mouth so I can't say something or respond to whatever wise words he's about to throw my way. With the mood I'm in right now, I'm liable to eat his heart for dinner instead of this burger if he really pisses me off.

"So, Stephen is the head chef here. He's 6'3, has bright curly red hair, freckles, muscles for days, an ass that doesn't quit, a dick that could make you fall over and cry to the Gods in appreciation. Not to mention, as you can tell, he's gifted in the kitchen." My eyes narrow in confusion, then widen in understanding, then narrow again as a fresh wave of confusion fills me.

"Huh?" I mumble, washing down my bite of delicious, savory bacon cheeseburger with a sip of my drink. "Uhh, are you trying to set me up with the chef? Because I mean, he sounds hot and all but I don—"

His eyes grow comically large before he begins to shake his head rapidly, effectively cutting me off. Just watching him makes me dizzy. I have to close my eyes against the instant wave of nausea. Hell, maybe it is time to switch to water.

"No, no, no. Do *not* get any ideas. That one is mine." His quick and adamant admission takes me a minute to process, but then clarity washes over me. Ahhhh.... so Stephen the Chef is Dom the Bartender's lover. Or boyfriend. Maybe my husband. Except, the forlorn look on his face tells me that maybe Stephen is none of the above. "As I was saying, Stephen is the chef here. He's beautiful, amazing, and confusing as fuck."

"Uh oh. Spill the tea, Jeeves. What did Stephen the Chef do?" Leaning in, I push my plate between the two of us so he can access my fries easier before sliding my water glass in front of me. I clumsily latch onto the straw, and rest my elbows on the bar, giving him my full attention. Talking about someone else's fucked-up love life is way, *way* easier than discussing mine.

"Right, so, Stephen and I both got hired here three years ago when *Pietro's* first opened. We went through training together, menu preparations, early morning openings, and late-night closings. All of it. For three damn years. The very first time I saw him, I knew. Something in my gut just told me, *it's him.* Like this guy, he's meant to be my forever, ya know?" I nod, completely invested in his drama.

Dom opens his mouth, but a customer calls out for the bartender. He tosses a finger in my direction, pauses his story, and jogs over to help the woman.

My mind goes back to the few things he's already said, and I can't help but wonder about my own love life. Was there anyone I've ever felt that way about? Someone who I just looked at and *knew*? Someone that made me say 'damn, you're my forever'? My other piece? My soulmate?

I immediately know the answer.

No.

That realization hits me deep in the gut. Like, way deep down inside of me. Holy shit.

Considering I'm semi-freshly divorced from a man I spent ten years with, I'm beyond shocked at the realization that I didn't look at my ex and just know. I didn't look at him, and tell myself he was *the one, my forever, my soulmate.*

I looked at Cole and said, 'yeah, I love you, let's do this whole future thing'.

I was 30, my High School and even some of my College friends had more than paired off to get married and have babies. I wanted that. I was ready. My career was in a good place, my finances were solid-*ish*, I owned a car, and my credit score was respectable. Why hadn't it been my turn yet? Why was everyone finding their HEAs while I was still working on my HFN?

One of my good friends had just gotten engaged to a guy she'd barely been dating for a year. She was giddy and falling all over herself with joy, as she asked me to be her Maid of Honor before going on and on about their plans: a home, their wedding, *babies,* the cribs, the nursery theme, her baby shower. She wasn't even pregnant yet, and here she was, shoving her Happily Ever Pinterest board in my fucking face.

I was happy for her, I really was, but here's the thing; you can be happy for someone, downright elated, and still be sad for yourself, which I was. Completely and utterly wrecked.

Everything crashed in on me at once. I saw my time-line slipping away before my eyes. My life, which up until then, had gone according to plan. I graduated High School with good grades. Not enough to land me Valedictorian or anything crazy, but enough to get me into a good college. I did the dorm thing, the college job thing, the good grades-make friends-gain the freshman 15(okay 20)-thing. I did it all. I graduated with my teaching degree as my plan told me to. I did my work-study, internship, the whole nine. Landed a good job and *wa-la*. I was a self-made, a whole-ass grown-up.

Even though my 'plan' dictated I do all those things, that was never my *dream.* I did those things because that's what society told me to do. In order to succeed in life, you must follow the path. You must grow up and adult. Contribute to the world. Pay your taxes. Work your ass off until you're old enough to finally be granted a life of freedom based on minimal wages and exhaustion. By that point, your knees hurt too bad to explore. Your energy levels suck too much to travel and enjoy shit the way you want to. But, hark, that's what society deems the acceptable humany level of humaning is, so, I did it.

However, my dream, my personal timeline, and buck-etlist were so, *so,* much simpler than all of that. It still is.

Yet, I am so past every single self-imposed deadline, I've basically given up on the whole concept altogether.

Some children dream grand dreams about going to the moon or being the first doctor to cure some sort of horrific illness. Some want to be something sweet and lovely, like a veterinarian or a nurse. Some dream of wilder things full of spunk and bravery, like professional bullfighters and ninjas. And some dream of pursuing the arts, like being dancers, authors, or painters.

Me? My dreams are as basic as they come.

1.   Fall in love with a good man.
2.   Live in a comfortable, modest home with space for a large Christmas Tree that always feels warm, safe, and welcoming.
3.   Have a double-door stainless steel refrigerator that is always packed full of fresh fruit and vegetables. (Clearly, this was before I knew what a bitch to clean stainless steel really is.)
4.   Have a partnership, friendship, and genuine connection with my husband.
5.   Fill my home with lots and lots of babies, and never let them know what being unloved or unwanted feels like.
6.   Grow old and be happy with my family.

That's it. That's the whole damn thing. The whole she-bang. The entire list of dreams for myself. I never dreamt of grandeur. I never wanted ridiculous amounts of money. Just enough to make sure that my family was content,

well-cared for, and comfortable. As a kid, I didn't realize why my life goals were about safety, full fridges, and
Christmas trees. When all of my friends were talking about
rocket ships and ballerinas, I was dreaming of a home that
never felt cold and I never questioned that. It just made
sense.

Now, as an adult, I get it. I dreamt of what I lacked, and
what I needed. Even as an adult, who has made sure she
is safe, comfortable, and taken care of by her own self, I
still want those things. I want them with a gut-wrenching,
soul-deep need. I crave and ache for them to the point that
it genuinely hurts.

So yeah, when Cole came along, I saw potential instead
of reality. We were similar in a lot of ways. We wanted the
same things, or so I thought, and things just progressed.
Before I knew it, time was flying by. I was wasting away
precious days, having a boyfriend instead of a husband, a
'kinda' relationship instead of a marriage. I was ready for
the next step. So, fucking ready. When Cole asked me to
marry him, my brain said 'finally' even as my heart said
'shit'. But, I had timelines and dreams.

I tried to squeeze him into all those boxes, making him
fit into dreams he wasn't shaped for.

I never knew that uttering the word 'yes' was the same as
throwing in the towel. I never knew that three tiny little
letters would equate to my downfall. I never knew that by
agreeing to marry him, I was giving up on all my hopes and
dreams for the future.

I never knew that I would be signing up for years of pain, longing, and heartbreak because settling for the wrong future is just as bad as not having one at all.

IT'S MY CHOICE

patient with yourself

love

ALL BODIES are GOD BODIES

be happy

yes you can

Fearless

IN CONTROL

LOVE yourself

are to STAY

I am enough

FEEL DEEPLY

YOUR POTENTIAL IS ENDL...

be kind to yourself

it's my choice

be brave

I am exactly where I need to be

You are worthy

I am capable

love you

YOU ARE enough

glow

breathe   Perfect

Shiloh

Two

"**W**oman!" Snapping fingers directly in front of my face pull me back from the dark melancholy that I had fallen into. My eyes focus and connect with Dom's big honey-browns.

"Huh?" I murmur, forcing the messy ball of emotions in my throat back down to my stomach, hoping that the alcohol there will kill the pesky bastards.

The thought reminds me, once again, of why I generally avoid alcohol in public. One too many brushes with embarrassment, litter my memory. Alcohol and I are not friends. In fact, we are downright enemies since it either turns me into a blathering, sobbing wreck, or an angry raging bull. Shaking my head, I force myself to meet Dom's eyes and stay in the present.

"Welcome back," I murmur with a smile that feels as fake as I'm sure it looks.

Dom considers me in a way that would make even sober me feel uncomfortable. He's not leering at me, just studying me, which is almost worse. I can deal with gross, or random men, checking me out and devouring me with their eyes like I'm some sort of turkey dinner. It's basically a part of all women's lives that we've just become accustomed to.

At one point or another, we will no doubt be checked out and/or catcalled. Don't forget about the kissy lips, ass slaps, and repulsive comments. Don't *even* get me started on the unsolicited dick pics. Who in their right mind wants to stare at a random photo of your cock and balls? They aren't cute. Really and truly unattractive, and staring at them in full technicolor while they stand at attention does absolutely nothing for our lady bits. Zilch.

A word from the wise, guys...video cum shots *with sound* is one hundred percent where it's at. Talk about giving lady boners. I almost have to fan myself at the thought.

I digress.

The point is, women as a whole have been unfortunately taught to expect and ignore unwanted advances and salacious perusals from creepy members of the opposite sex. That is not to say that all genders don't deal with unwanted advances from other people. I'm sure that they do. However, I can only speak as a woman who has been hit on, perused, catcalled, touched, *groped* and so much more, basically since my boobs made themselves known to the world.

It's not a great fucking feeling, but I don't think I'm alone in saying that I've learned how to ignore it. Yet, I'd rather put up with those types of looks than the one Dom is giving me now. He's looking at me like he's trying to find my damn soul.

"Let's just scrap the entire Stephen story, and head straight into why you've been sitting here all night dressed to kill, drunk off your ass, and hanging out with little old me, hmm?" he coos, blinking at me innocently as if to soften his demand.

"No, no. That's okay. Let's talk about Ste—" I start, shaking my head adamantly.

"Nope. Not happening. I'll spill the Stephen tea after you spill the, wait, shit. What's your name?" he asks, pausing mid-passioned rant. The twists and turns of our conversation threaten to give me whiplash.

"Shiloh," I mumble, latching onto my straw once again only to realize my water glass is now empty. Dom rolls his eyes, but smirks at me before snagging my glass and quickly swapping it for a full one.

"Shiloh's a beautiful name for a beautiful woman," he smiles softly, but I see the calm calculation behind it. "Now that we've gotten that out of the way, *spill.*"

Sighing heavily, I drop my head onto the bar as I resign myself to my current fate. Maybe I should just tell him everything. Get it off my chest like some sort of barside confessional. He's a stranger who probably hears people whine about their sad lives all day. He knows what to expect from depressed drunks who sit by themselves, and I'm pretty sure he already knows that I was stood up. It's not hard to guess.

Fuck it.

Rolling my head to the side, I lock eyes with Dom and let him have it. All of it.

"A little over a year ago, my ex-husband, Cole, and I divorced. We were together for almost ten years but only married for two." At that, we both grimace, Dom, knowing as well as I do that someone who waits almost eight years to propose probably didn't want to be married in the first place. I know that now, but hindsight is 20/20 and all that. "Just wait. It gets worse."

"Aww, shit. This is going to make me want to get drunk, isn't it?" he groans, running a hand through his hair and mussing it up. I nod stoically, because yes, my story is enough to drive a sober person to drink. Hence the reason I am where I am, drunk as hell.

"Right, so Cole and I met after college. I'd had quite a few relationships before him. I guess you could say I'm a serial monogamous. I love being in a relationship, and I liked all of the boyfriends that I had, but nothing ever took, ya know?" Dom says nothing, and I realize that I've already deviated from my original thought. Sitting up, I finish off my martini, needing the hit of alcohol for the conversation, before continuing. "Anyways, I met Cole when I was 22, at the school I was hired at after finishing my teaching degree. He was the principal there."

"No!" Dom smacks a hand down on the bar, making me jump. "He was your boss? Damn girl, get it!"

Shaking my head, I can't help but bark out a laugh at his dramatics. "Yes and no. He was technically one of my bosses, but it wasn't as taboo as you think. A lot of teachers had relationships with other staff members. It just happens when you spend so much time together, especially in such a stressful environment."

"Stressful? You make it sound like you were working on a battlefield," he jokes.

"I was a kindergarten teacher, Dom," I deadpan. "It was absolutely a fucking battlefield." His eyes widen in understanding before he crosses himself, muttering some sort of prayer. My eyes roll, but I smile at him just the same as he darts away to quickly refill my martini, probably sensing that I'm about to get to the good part. He gets pulled away once again while finishing my drink.

Dom rings up one more customer, settling his tab and making small talk. I peer around the restaurant, noticing I'm now the last one sitting at the bar and everything's pretty much cleared out. Glancing down at my watch, I see it's after eleven, and I'm guessing that an upscale place like this probably doesn't stay open past midnight. Just my luck. My night finally turned around with Dom's easy company, and he's going to have to kick me out soon.

Jogging back to me, Dom slides me my drink before setting a second glass in front of himself. When I arch a brow at him in question, he grins and shrugs. "Bar closed six minutes ago. I'm off the clock."

Fuck. Pulling out my wallet, I quickly fish out my credit card and pass it over to him. "Shit, sorry! Didn't mean to keep you here past closing."

Dom takes my card and drops it next to my drink, completely dismissing it. "For one, I'm exactly where I want to be. Everyone still has to close down their sections. We don't normally leave till after one in the morning so it's fine. For two, put your money away. I don't want it."

Feeling a wave of his pity wash over me, my body tenses, and I fight the urge to take off before I can embarrass myself further

"Stop it! I don't feel sorry for you. I didn't put your meal into the computer system, I just grabbed it from Stephen in the kitchen, and you deserve the drinks as payment for having to sit on the shitty, uncomfortable barstool for half the night, so stop with your pity party and finish telling me your story so I can get to mine." He finishes with a wink before blowing me a kiss, effectively breaking the tension. We both fall into a fit of giggles before taking healthy swigs of our drinks.

"Kindergarten," Dom gestures to me as he reminds me where I left off. "Why did you say where you *used* to work? You also said you were a kindergarten teacher. Past tense. Are you no longer?"

Sighing, I shake my head and swallow deeply. This is where everything gets painful. More painful than the divorce and leaving Cole. Not knowing where to start without giving some sort of background for reference, I make the sudden and rash decision to just go all in with Dom. Maybe it's because I don't really have any friends besides Rayvn, my bestie from college, or maybe it's just because he's easy to talk to. Either way, we're about to get a whole hell of a lot closer.

Whatever. If it ends badly, I'll blame it on the vodka.

"When I was younger, I had really heavy, bad periods." Dom immediately chokes on his drink making me chuckle. "Sorry, but this is relevant, I swear." He composes himself once more before giving me a firm, albeit cringy, nod. "Yeah, so I went to the doctor when I was 16 and was put on birth control to regulate everything, with no other information than to take it regularly. Unfortunately, it didn't help and only ended up making me really sick. I tried a few different kinds, but it was all the same, so I was just told that I either put up with the side effects or abstain from sex. I even ended up with a blood clot after taking a certain brand."

"What? That's awful, and you were so young." Shaking his head, he reaches out and gives my hand a squeeze. "My little sister dealt with something similar but luckily, the pills helped regulate things for her, and she felt a lot better. It's terrible that doctors just push a prescription on you instead of actually looking for the cause though, especially for such young women."

Dom's compassionate, heartfelt response instantly makes my eyes water. He unknowingly just showed more compassion on the topic than any other man I've ever met, including my ex.

Sniffling, I squeeze his hand in thanks. "Yeah, I agree. So, long story short, I chose to skip the chemicals and just deal with the shitty cycle and pain. There was never any point since I wasn't actually having sex at the time, and if and when I eventually did, condoms were available. Flash forward to my twenties. I started noticing other hormonal issues, so I consulted a specialist and discovered I have PCOS."

"Oh, shit. What's that?"

Grunting in annoyance, not at Dom, but at my stupid health issue, I gesture to my body as if that explains everything before realizing that it explains nothing.

"Basically, it means that my ovaries are dysfunctional, I grow hair in weird places, I gain weight easily and struggle to lose it as well as a myriad of other crap. The biggest one is that it will be difficult for me to conceive naturally, if at all. Which is where shit gets real."

Dom's face takes on a look of understanding and sympathy that I appreciate, but can't currently handle right now. I take another drink of my martini, having lost count of what number I'm at by now, but not having the energy to care at the moment. Staring into the half-empty glass, I watch as the blue lights from above the bar reflect on the shiny crystal glass and clear liquid.

"I've always wanted to be a mother. It's inherent for me. Deep in my bones, I know that it's part of my journey. I know in my soul that if I leave this life without ever having experienced motherhood, it will break my heart. So, because of that, I've also always known that whoever I end up with someday, will need to have that desire as well. It was so extremely important to me, ya know?" I murmur the last part, my words barely audible over the low jazz music playing above us. Dom squeezes my hand in comfort.

"When I met Cole, we got along really well. We were like instant best friends. We had a lot of the same views and similar personalities. We clicked. When things started moving from friendship to relationship, it was slow and natural. But I still had dreams, and I made sure to have a serious conversation with him. I had to confirm that we wanted the same things out of life because, in my head, there is no point in pursuing something serious with someone if it's going to be a dead-end relationship.

"Cole swore up and down that he wanted a family someday. That being a father was important to him. He also told me that for him, that dream was years down the road. He asked for time, and I gave it to him. As long as it would happen eventually, I was fine with waiting. For the first few years of our relationship, we used protection, but the conversation naturally came up for us to stop since we were committed and monogamous. I explained my fertility issues and the likelihood of needing medical assistance someday, and he understood. He was supportive."

Tears rapidly fill my eyes the more I think back to the progression of my relationship with Cole. The many, *many* conversations we had about the future. He didn't quite get the whole PCOS and infertility issues, nor did he pay them much attention. He wasn't callous about it, but he wasn't overwhelmingly there for me, either. I just chalked it up to him being a man who was uncomfortable with female topics. When I brought up treatments, and even possibly IVF, he didn't balk, he didn't panic, he just said *okay.*

That was that. I never looked back. I accepted every-thing, and we went forward. Things progressed, or so I thought.

"A few years passed, and despite not using any protec-tion, I never became pregnant. We never even had a blip. So, we both just assumed that all the doctors were right. I brought up seeking further assistance from doctors or even starting treatments because I knew it would be a lengthy and pricey process. Cole responded by asking for more time. There was always something. A new car, a new house, a vacation, or a certain position he wanted to get to in his career. All of his reasons made sense. I was able to justify his requests because he always placated me by saying, *soon.*

I know I pushed him for marriage, but I was 29, he still hadn't proposed, and I was beginning to feel like he just didn't want it. He proposed on my 30th birthday, and even though my gut told me that things didn't feel right, I said yes. Looking back, I know there are a hundred reasons why I said yes, but there were a lot of reasons why I should have said no. I ignored them all because there my future was just waiting for me. I jumped, we got married, and then I fell pregnant."

Dom grins, immediately excited for me, but the tears streaming down my face rapidly tell him without words that it's not a happy ending. "Fuck," he whispers.

"Yeah, *fuck.*" Chugging the remainder of my drink, I push my glass away and shake my head when he moves to refill it again. "I was so damn excited, Dom. Like, seriously, a sobbing, excited mess. I had peed on hundreds of sticks before that one. Every time my period was late, I was nauseous or bloated, or tired. Even though those are all side effects of my illness, I never lost hope. That was the only time the stick ever turned pink."

"What did Cole say?" The innocent question makes me cry harder. Now that the floodgates are open, I can't seem to stop. Gasping, Dom darts away before quickly returning with a stack of cocktail napkins. Giving him a watery smile in thanks, I dry my eyes the best I can before blowing my nose. It's undignified and gross, but necessary.

"He was so mad," I whimper. "He wasn't happy. He went on a rant about how it wasn't time, and he had just gotten put up for a promotion, and blah, blah, blah. For the next few weeks he treated me like shit. Every time I had morning sickness, threw up, got tired, dizzy, and felt like shit, he ignored me. I was beyond happy for every symptom, thankful for the life inside of me that was making me sick. It didn't bother me. I was grateful, but Cole ignored it all. If I said I didn't feel well, he nodded and walked away. If I threw up, he put his headphones on. If I said I was tired, he told me to go to bed. It was miserable.

When I finally went to the first doctor's appointment, he came, but didn't speak the whole time. I got an ultrasound, and I knew right away that something was wrong. I cried, and still, Cole was cold and uncaring. I finally broke down and told him he was ruining the pregnancy for me. That we were given a miracle, and that based on what the doctor had said it was a good chance our baby wouldn't survive, but I wanted to love that baby the entire time I had her. I didn't want him to waste that time."

Looking up, I see Dom's face now covered in tears, and I fight the urge to throw myself into his arms. *It's been so long since anyone's hugged me.*

"Cole didn't say anything. I had weekly scans and was diagnosed with Intrauterine Growth Restriction and told that our baby wouldn't make it. I lost her at 13 weeks while I was at home. Cole just sat and watched. After that, I went through a significant depression. The only thing Cole ever said was *when are we going to start having sex again.* I knew then that our marriage was over. Up until that point, I was able to justify all of his actions. He wasn't ready, he was nervous, he wanted to be set financially, and with his career, he didn't know how to handle pregnancy and loss. I made excuses for all of it, for him, because I loved him."

"Oh, honey." Dom sniffs and grunts before quickly darting out from behind the bar. Before I even realize what's happening, I'm wrapped in his arms. "Fuck him. Seriously, *mija*, fuck him. Not all men are like him, and I get why you made excuses, we all do that for those we love, but seriously, no. Just no."

Soaking in his words and embrace, I lean into him, allowing this random human to give me comfort where no one else has. I have no family, besides a sister who lives in another state. No one else was with me when I lost the baby besides Cole, and it's been a hell of a year since our divorce. This surprising interaction with Dom is wildly cathartic and all too meaningful.

Finally finding the strength, I pull away and kiss his cheek. "Thank you," I murmur. "And I know, fuck him. He's a prick who has deep, *deep* issues and I see all of them now."

Dom wipes the tears from my cheeks in an incredibly intimate gesture, and I decide right then that we're now friends. Clucking, he wipes his own cheeks before dropping onto the barstool next to me. "What happened next?"

Groaning, I prop my elbow on the counter and lean my head on my hand as I turn to face him. "I was done after that. I couldn't trust him, couldn't bring myself to be intimate with him anymore. Two years into our marriage, everything fell apart. We went to therapy as a last-ditch effort. He eventually came out and said that he never wanted kids. He had assumed that because of my infertility issues, I'd never be able to conceive and that we would just be happy without them."

Dom slaps an open palm on his forehead and mutters a string of words in Spanish that I don't understand, but I can only assume are curses in Cole's direction. "What a fucking piece of garbage. Please tell me you left his ass after that?"

"Yep, and then I quit working at the school. At first, it was because I couldn't be around him and he made it very clear that because of his 'high ranking position'," I scoff out the words and roll my eyes, "he couldn't be the one to quit. Realistically, I could have fought it, but after losing the baby, I just didn't have the heart to be around small children anymore. I took some substitute jobs as a teacher with older kids for a while but found it just as difficult. So, now, I'm a 33-year-old, jobless divorcee with a broken uterus who can't get a date to save her life. No, correction. I can get them, but I apparently can't keep them."

Dropping my head onto the bar with a *thunk*, I groan, allowing myself to wallow in the sea of my shitty circumstances, if only just for tonight.

Dom laughs and rubs my back in a sweet gesture befitting my new bestie. "About that. Did you get stood up tonight, sweetness?"

Making a gagging noise, I tilt my head to look up at him with my nose scrunched up in displeasure. "Rule number one of this new friendship, Jeeves. Don't ever call me sweetness again."

His lips purse and his hand on my back stills as he considers my words. "Don't call me Jeeves and I won't call you sweetness, deal?"

Sticking my tongue out at him, I'm thankful for the moment of distraction from the heaviness of my story. "Fine."

"Fine." Grinning, he leans over to mirror my position, with his head on the bar. "Maybe the guy had an emergency or got into a wreck or something."

"One can only hope," I mumble, before slapping my hand across my mouth in a vain attempt to erase the horrible thing I just said. Dom's eyes widen before he starts obnoxiously cackling. The sound is so loud in the quiet room that I fall into a fit of giggles with him. When we finally come down from the obligatory drunken laugh-fest, I sigh, suddenly feeling exhausted. "I wish I could say that's the case but it's unlikely. That's the third time I've been stood up this month, so I've come to an unhappy conclusion."

"And what's that, oh genius one?" he grumbles sarcastically.

Not bothering to move from my prone position, I gesture toward my body once more. "That they are walking in, taking one look at me, and walking out."

Dom stares at me silently for a few moments. I find that I'm far too tired and confused to know what he's doing. Finally, his eyes widen, "oh, you were serious?"

"Obviously. What other explanation is there? How can three men have catastrophic events rendering their cellphones useless, in one month? It's highly improbable. Nope. The only common factor is me."

Sitting up, a look of utter outrage fills his face. "That is just plain bullshit. What on God's green earth do those men have against a stunning, curvalicious babe like you? That's horseshit, and I refuse to believe it." Crossing his arms, he juts his chin out defiantly.

Rolling my eyes, I finally sit up. Slowly and with my eyes closed so as not to make the room spin. "Look, I'm not saying I hate my body or my curves. I've dealt with being a big girl my entire life. Somewhere around the age of ten, my body went from slim to not. Yeah, I got bullied and picked on and that definitely affected my outlook on myself and my appearance, but I embraced my size. I had friends, boyfriends, and things I was good at. It wasn't a big deal."

Sighing, I shrug. "It just takes its toll is all that I'm saying. After the shit show that my relationship became, it's hard to not feel insecure. As a human, I come with these handy dandy things called hormones. They do all sorts of neat tricks, including, but not limited to, making you emotional, giving you adult acne, and even controlling your weight. Seems no matter how much I work out, those little fuckers are hellbent on keeping me fluffy."

Dom busts out laughing, but quickly tries to smother the sound with his hand. "Fucking bastards," he agrees with a falsely stoic nod.

"Anyways, it's been a journey, but I'm learning to love my body. Not just because I'm fat, but because it's controlled so much of my life. No matter how well I attempt to take care of it, it fucks me at every corner. Wouldn't be a stretch to assume that now includes dating."

Dom tosses back the rest of his drink that I figured out is a Tequila Highball, which is my mom's favorite drink. "Okay, so here's the game plan. We are going to forget about all the sad, sorry fuckers, that may or may not have ditched you because honey, trust me. If they bailed before ever meeting you, they ain't worth a second of your time. Next, we are going to forget about the ex-douche-face. Just completely forget about him, and move forward because, as far as I'm concerned, he doesn't deserve your brain space."

Giggling at his antics, I feel another layer of pent-up stress leave my body.

"Fourth, or wait, third?" He thinks for a second before nodding, "yes, third. If your heart doesn't want to teach anymore, then don't teach, and don't feel guilty about it. Maybe you'll go back to it someday. Maybe you won't. But you're single, you're accomplished, you're a badass bitch, and it's time to go after your dreams. Take no prisoners, honey. If the next guy isn't right, don't try to change yourself to be with him. The right guy will come along. You got me?"

Tugging my lower lip into my mouth, I bite down before nodding.

"Good. Okay, so I think I have a solution to help with all of your problems." Grinning like the Cheshire Cat, Dom stares at me with a look that has me backing up as much as I can, without falling out of the tall chair.

"Do I want to know?" I mutter.

"Oh definitely," clapping his hands together in glee, his smile widens to a point that actually looks painful. I grimace. "*Stephen.*"

IT'S MY CHOICE
BE PATIENT WITH YOURSELF
Unapologetically MYSELF!
Love YOURSELF
BE Bold
ALL BODIES are GOOD BODIES
beautiful
Yes
fearless
IN CONTROL
be happy
LOVE yourself
FEEL DEEPLY
YOUR POTENTIAL IS ENDLESS
Brave
to find yourself
IT'S my CHOICE
I am exactly where I need to be
I am capable
Love you
YOU ARE enough
beautiful
breathe
Perfect

Shiloh

THREE

"Stephen?" Sighing, I shake my head. "We've already been over this. Stephen is *your* man Dom, remember? I don't see how he is the answer to *my* anything."

"Oh, sweet girl, ye have but little faith." Standing, he leans over and kisses my forehead before smacking my cheek softly a few times. "Be right back."

Before I can ever protest, Dom is dashing away in the direction of what I can only assume is the kitchen. My heart begins to palpate in my chest at a tempo that's basically burning off all of the alcohol I've consumed. What in the world could the chef have to do with this, and why am I suddenly filled with ridiculous amounts of nervous anticipation?

It's one thing to show my craziness to a random bartender who no doubt deals with drunks all day, but I draw the line at bringing more people in to witness my mental spiral like some sort of circus freak. Nope. Not happening.

Jumping to stand, I quickly grab the edge of the counter for balance, preparing to fall on my ass, either due to the booze, or the stupid stilettos I chose to wear tonight. Closing my eyes, I hold the bar with more force as a wave of dizziness washes over me.

"I don't even freaking like heels. I'd much rather wear my Birks, but *nooo,* society would balk at my hippie attire in such a classy restaurant. Stupid heels. Stupid dates. Stupid fucking men—"

"Are you talking to yourself?" Dom shouts, making me jump.

My eyes spring open, and I spin to face him which is completely and utterly the wrong move because seconds later, I'm on my ass with no solid understanding as to how I got here.

"Oh, fuck!" he cries at the same time another voice, a *deeper* voice, yells, "Are you okay, ma'am?"

My head snaps in the second man's direction, as indignation rapidly fills me. "Do *not* call me ma'am!"

They both skid to a halt only steps before colliding with me. Dom chuckles and reaches a hand down to help me up. The other man follows suit, grasping my other arm and yanking me upright. The two men quickly deposit me back on my feet before giving me space to compose myself, which is a move I am both thankful for, and mortified by.

Thankful to be standing, mortified to have made such a humiliating first impression. I have no doubt my dress was displaying all sorts of everything when I was on the ground. Subtly and quickly, I smooth the material down and make sure that all of my nooks and crannies are tucked away where they belong. As I fix myself, I take in the newcomer.

My eyes track up his wide, muscular, and very tall frame. It's a long, slow perusal that I can later blame on the alcohol or possible concussion from my fall. Either way, it's so worth the embarrassment of getting caught checking him out. When I finally land on his face, I find the man grinning down at me with a knowing expression. Red curls flop haphazardly over his piercing green eyes, and I instantly realize who the man is.

Stephen. Stephen is the Chef, and Dom the Bartenders maybe, sort of boyfriend or more, possibly less. We never did get to his story, did we?

"Are you okay, *miss?"* Stephen asks, his smooth, deep voice full of mirth. If I'm not entirely mistaken, I would venture to say he's holding in a laugh, and what a beautiful sound I would imagine that to be.

"A beautiful man with a beautiful voice," I mumble absent-mindedly. My eyes widen in horror as it dawns on me that I just said that last sentence out loud. My hand flies up to cover my mouth as I take a quick step back, and then another. Stephen and Dom both bark out loud, boisterous laughs, and oh, I was so right. Stephens' laugh is soulful and warm like a hug. It's almost pretty enough to wash away the embarrassment from my verbal slip-up.

What the hell is wrong with me? Yes, he is incredibly handsome. Gorgeous, actually. Tall, well-built, masculine.

He's got a touch of metro-chic to him and he's a little less rugged than I usually prefer, but it works for him.

Wait. Why am I even thinking about what *I* like? This is Dom's man for shit's sake.

"Christ on a cracker. I think I'm drunker than I thought," I groan, scrubbing my flaming hot face with my hands. The men's laughter finally comes to an end, just as I feel a hand land on top of mine.

"Girl, it's fine. We've all been there, and you definitely deserved every single drop of alcohol tonight. Come, I want you to meet Stephen. *The beautiful man with a beautiful voice*," he cackles as his voice takes on a female quality in his attempt to quote me.

Flicking his hand away, I push his shoulder, feigning irritation, yet I can't help but laugh at him. I really like Dom. "Well, since I'm putting my foot in my mouth and making a disaster of myself, I might as well add to it."

Dom grabs my hand and tugs me toward Stephen, as he arches a brow in my direction.

"I've decided we're now besties so be prepared. I'm just as much of a clutz sober, as I am drunk."

Dom grins and squeezes my hand. "I've been in the market for a new best friend so consider your application officially accepted."

We both laugh but it dies on my tongue as we step in front of Stephen who has his large arms wrapped over his broad chest, as he watches the two of us with a look of amusement. He's wearing tight, dark wash jeans and a grey, form-fitting v-neck shirt. I assume he's changed out of his chefy attire, and his current look is both casual and hot as hell.

He may be taken but I still have eyes and I can appreciate a good-looking man when I see one. Hell, I can appreciate a good-looking female when I see one. Hot people are hot. Not that I would ever act on my physical attraction to Stephen, obviously, since he's my new besties man and all.

"Stephen, this is Shiloh. Shiloh, this is Stephen. He's the head chef here and my—" Dom breaks off, and swallows thickly, his mouth opening and closing at an obvious loss for words.

"Friend," Stephen interjects, shoving his hand out for me to shake.

My eyes instantly dart toward Dom's, and I don't miss the pained expression that crosses his face. Trying not to draw attention to him or his feelings, I place my hand in Stephens with a small smile. Not going to lie. The chef's hotness factor just went down a peg based on the fact that he hurt my friend's feelings

"Nice to meet you, Stephen," I say before pulling my hand back and stepping discreetly in Dom's direction. I wind my arm through his, offering him my silent support. My guess is that there is a lengthy and possibly quite painful story behind all of this. I have a feeling that many a drunken bitch-fests are in our future.

Dom pats my arm, and regains his composure in a way that I envy. I've always worn my expressions openly, and have a difficult time hiding what I'm feeling. My mamma's the same way, and she always blames it on our mixed

Italian-Portuguese household. Growing up, she used to say that there was nothing wrong with being loud and wearing your feelings proudly.

Dom smiles his cheerful mask firmly back in place. "Right, so, like I said, Shiloh. Stephen is the answer to all of your prayers. You need a job, and he has one for you."

Stephen's eyes widen in Dom's direction, before quickly darting to me then back to Dom, then back to me. Clearly, he's just as confused as I am. "What?"

"Yeah, what?" I echo. Sliding my arm from Dom's, I step away, planting my hands on my hips before declaring, "I may love to eat, but I don't know anything about working in a kitchen!"

"*Obviously.*" He rolls his eyes, and shakes his head at the pair of us like we're naughty children. "Stephen doesn't need any help in the kitchen. His brother, however, is looking to hire someone."

Understanding washes over Stephen's features. "Yeah, he is." Stephen nods, and reaches up to rub his large hand across the back of his neck, suddenly looking uncomfortable as he glances in my direction. His eyes track down my body, taking in my form-fitting wrap dress, high heels, and curled hair before turning back to Dom. "I don't know."

A look that I can't quite make out takes over Stephen's face immediately following his appraisal of me, as though he finds me lacking. *Oh, fuck no.* "What the hell was that look for?" I bark out, unable to hold myself back.

His head rears back and a look of surprise replaces his distaste. "What look?"

"*You.* You just looked me up and down and then decided that what? I'm not *good enough* for whatever job your brother is hiring for? Do I not meet your high standards?" My hands flail about as I stomp toward this judgmental prick. "Am I not the right type of person for the job? Do I not appear physically capable?" Poking a finger into his chest, I growl, "Whatever it is, I can do it. Don't dismiss me based on my looks."

Stephen has the decency to look ashamed and thoroughly chastised, as he peers down at me. He stares for what feels like forever before his lip tips up in a smirk. "Yeah, I think she'll do just fine."

Dom claps his hands; the loud sound jolts me out of my angry tirade. Giving him an apologetic pat on his chest, I smile at Stephen before putting some distance between us once again.

Did I forget to mention that I'm also a hothead? And what the hell did I just sign up for?

"Uh, thanks, I guess," I shrug, "but what job is this exactly?"

Stephen chuckles and gestures toward a high-top table next to us with three stools. Nodding, I move to the table and take a seat between the men. I don't miss the way Stephen subtly scoots closer to Dom, leaning his large arm into the other man's side.

"Do you have any computer or organizational skills? Do you feel like you'd be comfortable in an office setting?" Stephen asks. My brows furrow, not missing that he hasn't stated what the job is yet.

I open my mouth to respond, but Dom quickly jumps in. "Of course, she does. She was a teacher, which means she at least has what, a bachelor's degree?"

Swallowing, I nod. "I was a dual major in English and Business Communications, and I have a minor in Early Childhood Education."

"See! She's brilliant, and she's more than likely excellent with organization, paperwork, and probably even computers."

Stephen snickers and places his hand on Dom's before squeezing it gently. "Let her talk," he murmurs. Looking between the two of them, it's clear to see they both harbor feelings for one another, and it makes my heart squeeze. I want someone to look at me that way. Cole never looked at me adoringly.

Stop feeling sorry for yourself, Shiloh, Jesus.

Turning back toward me, Stephen smiles and juts his chin out, signaling me to continue. Clearing my throat, I give him my list of qualifications for an unknown job at a random, surprise interview. By the time we're done discussing my past work experience, I'm beyond impressed with myself. I can't believe I was able to hold an intelligent conversation after so much vodka.

"My brothers and I own a construction company called Huxley Homes. It was our father's, and he passed it down to my brothers and me. Logan is the only one who works there, day in and day out, managing everything. Charlie does construction and works on the build sites. I help manage the finances, but I'm unable to be there for the company as much as I should be."

"You're doing what you love, and Logan understands that," Dom says softly, noticing the guilty expression on Stephen's face. The latter smiles softly but doesn't agree with him.

"Anyways, Logan is the oldest out of the three of us, and as I said, he manages everything. It's a lot of work, and I've been telling him for years that he needs to hire an office assistant. He's had a few, but they were all just temporary, and we really need someone stable. It would be a lot of filing, inputting data, answering phones," he pauses with a grimace, "maybe even some light cleaning up around the office at the beginning."

"Cleaning?" Not that I mind cleaning, but the way Stephen says it has me thinking there's some sort of unspoken information there.

Nodding, he grunts, "Yep."

Dom slaps Stephen on the arm and rolls his eyes. "What he means is that Logan is sort of a tornado."

"Tornado?" I deadpan. "What the hell does that mean? Like he's messy?"

Stephen and Dom share a conspiratorial grin that has my hackles rising. "Yes? No?" he shrugs. "He's just a very busy man who really needs help. He cares more about projects, deadlines, and making sure that everyone is happy and taken care of, than he does about anything else. The office desperately needs some TLC, and Logan is *not* the man for the job."

My brows lift to my hairline. "You've been there?"

Dom cackles and raises his hand in the air. "Meet temporary office assistants numbers one through three."

Now it's my turn to laugh. "What does that mean, and how does that happen?"

He shrugs again, looking completely unphased. Meanwhile, Stephen has his hand covering his mouth, holding his laughter back, while staring down at the table like it holds all of life's answers. Smart man.

"It means, I worked there for a day, then quit. Went back the next week, lasted two days, and then quit again. Came back a few hours later that same day to try again, and quit thirty minutes later."

"You do understand that all of that information does not bode well for this job. You're not exactly painting an inviting picture to a prospective employee," I state, pointing out the obvious.

"It had nothing to do with the job and everything to do with me." Dom sighs in exasperation. "I'm not made for office life, honey. Look at me. I'm meant to be out in the world, being seen and enjoyed. I like loud atmospheres where I get to talk to people and hang out with drunks. It suits me. What does not suit me is a quiet office, where I'm left to nothing but my thoughts and the voices in my head."

Stephen and I both burst out laughing at that, but I have a feeling Dom's declaration was 100% honest. While I totally cannot picture him in the environment that he described, I can picture myself there. In fact, it sounds completely perfect. My OCD is already panting at the idea of organizing an office, and getting it in running order.

There could be sticky notes, tabs, files, color coding. Don't even get me started on what I can do with a label maker. The idea of having some peace and quiet after the chaos of my life the last few years sounds kind of wonderful.

Am I actually going to do this?

"So, what do you think, Miss Shiloh? Does that sound like something you'd be interested in?" Stephen asks, tossing a wink in my direction that would make me swoon in literally any other circumstance.

Grinning, I nod and thrust my hand out, "What the hell? I'm in."

Stephen's brows raise in surprise, but he places his hand in mine, giving me a firm shake. "Don't you want to talk hours and pay? Benefits? Vacation?"

Pulling my hand back, I shake my head. "Just tell me when I start, and we can figure out the rest."

"Wow, you're easy," Dom mutters. Stephen and I both reach out, slapping him on the back of his head. "Ow! What and the fuck!"

"My mother would have smacked you so much harder for that comment," I snap, though it lacks any real heat.

"My mother *will* smack you harder than that when I tell her what you said," Stephen adds, snorting at Dom's look of panic. Turning to me he gives me an approving nod.

"You're hired. You start Monday.

IT'S MY
CHOICE

BE PATIENT
WITH
YOURSELF

Unapologe
MYSELF

BE
Bold

ALL BODIES
are
GOOD BODIES

YOURSELF

beautiful

be
happy

yes you can

Fearless

IN CONTROL

LOVE
yourself

HERE
TO STAY

I am
enough

FEEL
DEEPLY

YOUR
POTENTI
IS ENDL

be kind
to yourself

IT'S MY CHOICE

be
Brave

I am exactly
where I need to be

you
are
worthy

I am
capable

love you

YOU ARE
enough

breathe

Perfect

Logan

Four

This entire day has gone to shit, and it's not even 9:00 AM.

The Nelson project is going to put me into an early grave, and there's not a damn thing I can do about it. I've decided to just accept my fate, here and now. My guys have been trying to make progress on the build site, but the out-of-date zoning issues and the constant pushback we're getting from the city are making it nearly impossible. At this rate, there is no way in fuck we'll reach our deadline.

When I took over Huxley Homes for my father, I knew running the company wasn't going to be a walk in the park. I knew it, yet every day, something still manages to knock me on my ass.

As the oldest of four boys, I've always been aware this was my future. Even when we were kids, my father prattled on about how one day it would all be mine.

I swear to God, at ten years old, I equated that speech to the scene in the Lion King when Mufasa showed Simba Pride Rock. The way the light looked shining down on the grassy valley as the antelope majestically hurdled over bushes made me excited for my own future.

To me, Huxley Homes was better than Pride Rock.

Everything was so amazing and new. The construction trailer had a little golden halo permanently suspended over it. My father's hammer was equivalent to a magic wand as it sat in his fairy tool belt. Job sites were places where we made dreams come true. We built people the homes they'd always wanted. They cried and thanked us, blubbering on and on about all the babies that would grow up there, the memories that would be made, the holidays, *etc.*

As a child, I believed the fairytale. *The lie.* I was so fucking excited to be old enough to run Huxley Homes. To take over the family business and carry on the tradition. To be successful. To have a job my future wife and kids would be proud of. Someone who built beautiful things and made dreams come true. I was so excited that one day, I would become a man they looked up to, the way I had my father.

But then, everything went to shit.

Now, here I am—38 years old, single, never been married, no kids, and a family legacy I can barely keep above water. A company that is by no means magic and rainbows. Instead of making people cry because they get to live in their dream homes, I make them cry because I rage out over deadlines and lumber costs. Let's not forget about the two brothers and retired parents who are depending on me to make sure this ship doesn't sink.

Like I said, an early grave.

The only thing that could possibly make this day any worse, is the knowledge that in just a few short minutes, I'll have to enter my own personal Hell.

My office. *The real one.*

The one I try to avoid with every single fiber of my being, preferring to work out of the trailers we set up at each of our job sites. Unfortunately, my office is in our company building where we hold official meetings, house our records and blueprints, as well as a bunch of other random shit a low-tech trailer can't accommodate.

However, it's also a cesspit of memories I'd rather forget. Big, painful fucking memories.

So, I avoid it. I don't stay to clean or sort through paper-work, afraid of what I might stumble upon. I don't relax in my office, kick my feet up on the desk and admire the award-winning views. I just flat-out avoid it. Now, the place is a wreck, which only aids in worsening my overall anxiety and further solidifying my early grave theory.

Unfortunately, today, I don't have a goddamned choice. Stephen, my younger brother by two years and unofficial accountant, called me first thing this morning, demanding I pick up files for him. He claimed they're urgent, but that he's too busy to drive down here and pick them up him-self. As if I'm not already drowning in checklists, errands, meetings, and phone calls. I told him just as much, lacing my rebuttal with a thinly veiled threat.

As I pull into my assigned parking spot, I roll my eyes. Yeah, my threats were apparently ineffective.

I fight the urge to sit in my truck and talk myself out of going inside. I know if I allow myself even a moment to think twice, I'll throw my truck in reverse and high tail it out of here. Rolling my neck side to side, I release an audible exhale, shove my door open and jump out, pocketing my phone as I go.

"Fuck," I grunt, eyeing the large post-and-beam building. It's gorgeous. Even I'm not so jaded that I can't admit that. It's a testament to our craftsmanship abilities and a prime example of our work. It's also the last thing I built with my father, and three brothers, before everything got fucked up.

It's basically a log cabin, with a modern twist. One story with a high peaked a-frame. The façade is a mixture of natural stone, pine, and forest green slatting. At over 2000 square feet, it houses four offices with individual bathrooms, each containing a shower in case we come for a meeting straight from a job site. There's a large break room for all the staff we never hired, a waiting area with a reception desk, and two meeting rooms. All were built with the intention of Huxley Homes growing once it was passed down. It's an iconic building in the town of Blue River.

A memory of the five of us surfaces so quickly and intensely that I almost stagger backward. I can see it clear as day, like it's happening right in front of me. My father, on his ladder, barking orders left and right. Stephen, running to do his bidding like the good son he's always been. Charlie fucking around, throwing scraps of wood in a makeshift game of baseball with—

Nope. Not today, Satan.

Swallowing down a lump in my throat, I push back the emotions that hit every single time I come here and unlock the front door, letting myself in. I'm greeted with silence. Though we built it in a way to support high amounts of daily foot traffic, it sits empty. Like always.

My eyes take in the beautiful entryway and front desk, designed to impress potential clients. My fingers swipe through the fine layer of dust coating the counter and I barely contain a growl of irritation. There's never been a need for a receptionist because we don't come here unless necessary, so the only person to blame for the shitty condition of the place is me.

Pushing through the door that separates the front end from the back, I flick on the hall light, illuminating the row of office doors. Stephen's only ever here when he's not working at the restaurant, but he's a clean freak so his office, is pristine. Charlie prefers physical labor over office work so his office sits completely untouched but just as dusty as the reception area.

The last door remains closed, as always. It's never been used, nor will it ever be.

The anger that had finally calmed, makes a reappearance as I storm past it toward my office. Correction, *my father's office,* because no matter how much time passes since I've taken over, it will never feel like mine.

It sits at the end of the lengthy, well-lit hall, in a position of importance and respect. It's the largest of the four and is the only one with a killer view of the Colorado River, but even that's not enough to draw me in.

Pulling out my office key, I stop short when I find it already unlocked and slightly open, which is odd since I'm anal as hell about keeping the damn thing bolted.

Muscles tense and ready for a fight, I throw the door open. It bounces uselessly off the wall protector and slams back into me just as I step through the threshold. My nose takes the brunt of the injury, sending a sharp pain through my skull and pissing me the hell off.

"God fucking damnit!" I shout, resisting the need to punch something.

A scream pierces the air, making me stumble backward in shock. My head damn near slams into the wall in my rush to avoid the shrill sound.

My brain momentarily goes offline as I take in the scene before me. Confusion, irritation, panic, and anger swirl within me at a speed so quick, that I can't process what's happening. It's a fucked up side-effect of two tours in the military. You'd think it would make my instincts sharper, and maybe at one point they were, but not so much any-more.

As I reign in the emotions flying through me, I focus on the room in an attempt to gain some clarity. My eyes zero in on the intruder, sitting on the floor, surrounded by piles of paperwork.

A woman.

There is a woman in my office, going through my shit.

A strange, random woman, wearing a dress that's so god-damned tight, I can see every single spectacular curve and dip of her lush body. *It's red.* My brain decides to zero in on that fact for some reason, negating everything else.

Red. The color of strawberries and sin, because with a body like hers, there's no way the Devil wasn't involved in its creation.

I force myself to focus once more, letting go of the ridiculous infatuation with her dress. My eyes trail up her body, taking in every fucking tantalizing inch of her. She's sitting on her knees, her thick thighs spread wide, causing her dress to ride up just below her pussy. The tight, red material clings to her wide hips, rounded belly, and perfect tits. I think it has sleeves, though, I couldn't give a single fuck either way, especially when my eyes catch on her long, silky brown hair pulled up into a ponytail that resembles a leash far too closely.

God, the things I could do with that hair. And that body, fucking hell.

Her thick thighs could snap my neck while I ate her sweet cunt, and I honest to God cannot think of a better way to go. I could wrap that long hair around my fist while I pounded into her wet cunt, forcing her to take every inch of me until I came deep inside her. Her wide hips and rounded belly bring forth images of her knocked up and heavy with my kid.

Holy shit, where did that thought come from?

"Oh my god! You almost gave me a heart attack!" the woman cries, yanking me from my obvious perusal of her body. My eyes snap up at the sound of her voice, and for the first time, I meet her eyes.

Fuck.

Her eyes are chocolate. Pure molten chocolate. Her heart-shaped face with rounded cheeks, a sharp nose, and dimpled chin should be illegal. She's perfect. Utterly fucking intoxicating. Her golden tanned skin is pink with irritation or embarrassment. I don't know, don't care. All I can think is *I wonder if the rest of her looks just as pretty pink.*

Against my will, my eyes rake back down her body, homing in on her spread thighs. If she'd shift, even just an inch or two, her pussy would be exposed. Would she be wearing a thong? Boy shorts? Is her pussy bare or does she have dark curls that would look so beautiful coated in her cum.

No, in my cum.

Who is this woman and why is she in my office, looking like a fuckin' gift laid out for me?

"You know, I can see you staring, right?" she drawls, as she snaps her thighs closed. A surge of anger washes through me at the fact that she just took away *my* view.

My lip curls and my eyes shoot to meet her pissed-off gaze. She yanks her dress down and uses the edge of my desk to climb to her feet. If I was a gentleman, I'd help her up, and maybe any other day, any other situation, I might. Unfortunately, I'm too busy trying to figure out how to both speak and hide my thoroughly impressed cock before she sees it.

God, I can't even remember the last time my dick was this interested in anything.

When I don't respond, my mouth too dry to form words, she mutters something under her breath. It sounds a lot like, *'I can't believe my new boss just saw my fat thighs.'* Her words, quiet as they were, snap me out of my lust paralysis. I don't know what part of her statement enrages me more. The word boss, or her referring to her incredible legs as fat.

But, if what she said is true…Yeah, better skip over the obvious ogling of her delicious body for now.

Clearing my throat, I step into my office, making a bee-line for one of the chairs that sit opposite the desk and stand behind it, hoping it'll cover the very thick erection in my jeans.

"Boss?" I grunt, crossing my arms over my chest. "Who the hell are you and why are you in my office?" I ignore the stab in my gut over using the word *my* as I wait for the beauty's response.

Her dark, thick brows dip in confusion as she mirrors my stance. Her arms folding over her chest causes her tits to thrust upwards, creating the perfect amount of cleavage for my eyes to feast on. I barely, just *barely* catch myself before doing just that, forcing myself to focus on her chocolatey eyes instead.

Focus, Logan, Fuck. You're almost 40. You fought in a war. You can resist this siren.

But then, she drags her juicy pink lip between her teeth, and my already aching cock throbs in response. "I'm your new assistant," she says softly.

Though her voice is like silken honey, her statement is ice-cold water, washing over me and dousing my arousal. My teeth grind together so harshly, my jaw instantly aches. "Excuse me?" I grit out as my heart pounds in my chest. No, this can't be happening.

She drops her arms, taking a step back. Suddenly, she looks afraid, and I find that I hate the look on her. What's she afraid of? Me? Her fingers begin to tug and pull on the fabric of her dress nervously, but her spine never loses its stiffness, and her shoulders remain pulled back. She's tough. I like it.

"Stephen hired me to be your new assistant. Well, Logan's assistant. That's you, I presume?" Her eyes roam over my body, homing in on the white-knuckle grip I have on the back of the chair. She flinches, and I immediately let go, stretching my fingers out to relieve the tension.

Stephen? *Fuck.*

Of course, that bastard had something to do with this. It's just like him to hire someone behind my back. He's been on me for years to bring someone in to help out. He's even gone as far as to send Dom, his on-again, off-again boyfriend, to work here. Dom's a nice guy, don't get me wrong, but there's no way in hell I could stand to have him in my office all day. He's too fuckin' chatty. I like silence.

The stunning woman huffs a sound of frustration, reminding me that she'd spoken. She asked me a question, I think.

"What's your name?" I blurt, instead of the twenty other things circling through my brain. For some reason, that seems like the most important one.

She can't work for me. Point blank. I'd die from blood loss. She's too beautiful, too perfect. I'd never be able to leave her alone, or I'd end up fucking her on my father's desk and wind up sued for malpractice or some shit.

Absolutely no way is that happening, but the idea of kicking her out right now without even knowing her name makes my stomach clench uncomfortably.

"I'm Shiloh?" she drags out her name, saying it like a question and giving away her confusion.

Shiloh.

Somehow, she makes that one word sound like a sensual caress. It gives way to visions of me fucking her juicy ass, shouting her name to the heavens as I unload deep inside her.

"You don't work here!" I bark out, irritated with the random sexual fantasies that keep penetrating every single rational thought in my brain. Why do I keep picturing myself filling her with cum? Shit. My heart is hammering in my chest, a dull ache is forming behind my eyes. Anxiety, confusion, lust, and some other unknown emotion are filling me rapidly, causing me to lash out.

Goddamnit. Get a hold of yourself, Logan.

"I'm sorry, but I'm confused. Are you or are you not Logan Huxley, the owner of Huxley Homes?" she snaps, cocking a hip and planting her fist on the luscious curve. I open my mouth, an argument already sitting on my tongue, but Shiloh tuts, reprimanding me like a small child. "Don't argue! Just answer the question!"

My head jolts back, and my eyes widen in shock. No one talks to me like that. *No one.* I should shout at her, tell her to get the fuck out. If she's really my employee, that alone could get her ass fired. But, for some reason, I do none of those things. Instead, I find myself gritting my teeth and nodding at her question.

A small smile grows on her cherub-like face, causing a tiny dimple to form on her right cheek. My stomach clenches again. *What's wrong with me? Am I getting sick?*

"Good, now that we've gotten that all cleared up, it's nice to meet you, Mr. Huxley," she says sweetly, her tone much gentler than it had been just seconds before. Stepping forward, she extends her dainty hand. My eyes drop down, and a brow kicks up in question. "This is the part where you'd politely shake my hand."

Again, without my permission, my body reacts. My hand darts out, clasping her much smaller one in a firm, yet soft shake. Her skin is so damn smooth and delicate against my rough calloused fingers. Her nails are long and red, matching her dress. They look like little claws that I can easily imagine raking down my back. My hand flexes, as though it wants to pull her in, never releasing her again. I force myself to let go and shove the fucker in my pocket before it gets any more stupid ideas.

Clearing my throat, I shake my head. "No, there's gotta be some kind of misunderstanding. I didn't hire you, and Stephen shouldn't have. I don't need an assistant."

She barks out a laugh, then quickly covers her mouth like she's trying to hide the sound. She shouldn't. I want to hear it again and again and again. It's throaty, bordering on sultry. Her voice is how I imagine phone sex operators to sound.

"Clearly, you need me," she giggles, gesturing to the piles upon piles of paperwork covering every surface of my office. A tick in my jaw forms as my stress ratchets up. Sighing, she steps back, putting distance between us. My body leans forward as if to erase the space she just created. "Look, I don't know what happened, or how I ended up in a job that wasn't available for hire, but I'm here now, and you definitely need the help. I've already made a ton of progress, and it's been less than two days."

Two days? She must have started Monday. Fuck, my brother's in for the ass-kicking of his life when I get done here.

Looking over the stacks of papers, I notice the wide variety of sticky notes, folders, and highlighters set up in a neat row where she'd been working. There's even a little machine with a tiny keyboard on it. On closer inspection, I realize the piles of crap aren't random at all. She's organized everything by some system I would have never thought to create, complete with sticky notes and labels.

I glance back at Shiloh, finding her already watching me, waiting for my decision. I don't know a single fucking thing about her, other than the fact that she's beautiful beyond words and she's got a body I'd happily kill to worship. She obviously knows what she's doing.

Stephen must have a good reason for hiring her. He may be a dick, but he's business savvy, and he cares about Huxley Homes. He wouldn't hire just anyone off the streets.

I don't like to spend time in this building, nor do I like people in my space or business, but I can admit Shiloh would probably be helpful to have around. There's no doubt the office needs a massive amount of organization to get back in working order, and the entire building could do with some TLC. But, as my eyes rake down her perfect, thick body once more, I know damn well that's not why I answer the way I do.

"Fine, you can stay."

IT'S MY CHOICE
BE PATIENT WITH YOURSELF
Unapologetic MYSELF
love YOURSELF
beautiful
BE Bold
ALL BODIES ARE GOOD BODIES
be happy
yes you can
Fearless
HERE TO STAY
iN CONTROL
LOVE yours
I am enough
FEEL DEEPLY
YOUR POTENT IS ENOU
be kind to yourself
IT'S my CHOICE
Brave be
I am exactly where I need to be
you are worthy
YOU AR enoug
I am capable
love you
glow
breathe
Perfect

Shiloh

Five

This isn't how I thought my second day at my new job was going to go and I've yet to decide if the change in direction is good, or bad.

When Stephen brought me to the beautiful Huxley Homes building yesterday, I'd been impressed to say the least. I've only lived in Blue River for a few years, having moved here to be closer to the school, but even in that short time, I'd heard about the infamous Huxley Homes masterpiece. It far exceeded any preconceived ideas I'd had.

Stephen was as sweet and easygoing as he'd been the other night as he introduced me to their world. He told me how everything in the business runs, gave me a tour, and outlined my duties. I was excited to get started and I'd prepared for just about anything that could be thrown my way.

Or so I had thought.

Yesterday, Stephen explained that Logan spends most of his time at the job sites and that he wouldn't be in the office this week. So, when a hulking, bearded mountain man threw the door open, his body poised and ready for a fight, I genuinely thought I was being attacked. It didn't help that he immediately, and openly, devoured my body before even having the decency to introduce himself.

After he'd decided I could stay, he barely spoke. I honestly thought he would leave or call and tell Stephen to handle me. I wouldn't put it past the grumpy bastard honestly. Surprisingly, he stayed, asked me what I needed help with, gave a curt nod, and then went to work. That was six hours ago, and the man's barely said more than a handful of words beyond grunts and growls since.

On more than one occasion, I've caught him checking me out. Openly and unabashedly. Every single time, my body heats up in a way I've never felt before. I should be embarrassed that he clearly saw all my goodies on display this morning. Maybe even angry that he stared for so long, but I feel neither of those things. I don't know what it is about him, but I find his apparent appreciation for the way I look satisfying.

Maybe it's because I can't stop checking him out either. He's just so...so...

So fucking hot.

Logan Huxley is hands down, the most attractive man I have ever met in my life. There's no other way to describe him. Well, that's not true. There are lots of ways I could describe the man: asshole, prick, short-tempered, growly, gorgeous, *flannel wearing-buff-bearded-lumbersnack…*

At the thought, I sneak another peek at him while his back is to me. He's wearing well-worn jeans that fit him like a glove, hiding nothing and showing off his thick thighs and bubble butt. He has an ass that no man has any right to have, and any woman would kill for. Every time he bends over to pick something up, a wave of arousal pools low in my belly. My pussy has been wet and achy all day and I honestly don't know what to do with myself at this point. The feeling only gets worse as I continue to stare.

Logan is tall, towering well over my 5'7 frame. If I had to guess, I'd say he's at least 6'3, if not taller. His frame is wide, and I can tell, even through his thick flannel, that he's built and muscular. Much like Stephen, Logan has bright red hair that has a slight curl to it, but beyond that, the two men couldn't be more different.

With just one look at Logan, it's obvious that he's used to being outside and doesn't shy away from a hard day's work. He's rugged, buff, and his overall appearance borders on unkempt. His hair is wild and messy, his beard is thick and overgrown, his hands are calloused, and his clothing is wrinkled.

Logan is all man. Every single delicious inch of him is a treat to look at. From his bright green eyes, freckled cheeks, and nose, down to his huge, boot-clad feet that for some odd reason, make me think very inappropriate thoughts. His whole body is large and every time I see his boots, all I can think is, *I wonder if a man's shoe size really matches his dick.*

My ex isn't the only man I've ever been with. I've seen my fair share of cocks, but something about Logan screams that sex with him would be different. Better. More intense.

"Here," he grunts, as he drops another stack of folders next to my makeshift work area, sending my color-coordinated highlighters flying. I barely contain a screech of irritation.

My gaze darts up to meet his, ready to tell him off, but when our eyes meet, my heart stutters in my chest and my angry words die on my tongue. I'd barely just gotten control of my sweaty palms in the last ten minutes, but one uttered word and access to his intense green eyes, has the nasty habit starting up again.

Clearing my throat, I rack my brain for any sensible, intelligent thing to say, but come up with nothing. It makes no sense. This is so unlike me. One of the things Cole complained about most was how much I talk. It annoyed him that I could, and often did, spark up conversations with any and everyone. However, apparently that skill has completely left the building because right now, I can barely form more than two syllables.

Groaning internally, I glance down at the progress I've made with past contracts and work orders and decide to call it a day. A quick look at the clock on the wall solidifies the decision. I've been here for over ten hours, and not only am I exhausted, but starving. I skipped lunch, too nervous to bring it up in Logan's presence. Not because

I'm afraid to eat in front of the man, but because speaking sentences seemed completely impossible at the time. How he worked straight through lunch, and now dinner, I have no idea. The man looks like he lives off an IV drip of protein powder.

As if to agree with my decision, my stomach lets out an embarrassingly loud growl. Logan's head shoots in my direction and I wince under his scrutiny. His eyes track down my body, homing in on my stomach, as though he's checking to see where the sound came from.

"Hungry?" he snaps like he finds my lack of food offensive. My head rears back and I suddenly despise the fact that I'm still sitting on the floor below him.

Gritting my teeth, I adjust my dress and as classily as one can, I crawl to my knees in an effort to rise without flashing my new, sexy boss, my panties. Logan watches me like a predator hunting for his next meal. Instead of helping me up as a gentleman should, he tilts his head like he's trying to catch a peek at my panties.

"Oh, don't worry, I'm fine." I drawl, my voice thick with sarcasm.

Logan's brows arch and the corner of his lip tips up in a cocky smirk. "You sure are," he murmurs.

My stomach does a flip, my cheeks heat.

He chuckles.

I scoff.

He may be ungodly attractive, but he's a grade-A prick.

Finally on two feet, I yank my dress down, subtly make sure the girls are tucked away, and dust off my ass. "Starving," I respond curtly, now that we were at similar heights, though, I still have to crane my neck back to see his face. "Not everyone can go all day without eating like some sort of robot." Gesturing to the organized chaos surrounding us, I say, "I'm done for the day. I'll finish this up by Friday."

Turning my back on him feels akin to looking away from a beast ready to pounce, but I need the reprieve from his penetrating stare. Making my way toward the corner of the room where I've stashed my belongings, I throw my heavy peacoat over my red wrap dress and curse the fact that I thought heels would be a good idea in the dead of Colorado winter as I slide my feet back into them.

"Why were you barefoot?" he growls, ignoring my statement about lack of nourishment. My head swings in his direction, causing my long ponytail to whip me in the face. I quirk a brow in question and tip my head in the direction of my 'workstation'. His lip curls in distaste or disapproval, an expression I've seen him make far too many times for my liking today.

A culmination of my exhaustion, irritation, hunger, sexual frustration, and unwanted pervy thoughts about my asshole boss fill me in an instant and I *snap.*

Stepping forward into his personal space, my hands find my hips, and I barely contain the urge to stomp my foot as I glower at the dickwad. "Look, I don't know what your problem is, or why you were so against me working here, but you didn't need to stay all day, grunting and growling like a pissed-off bear. If you don't want an assistant, you should have fired me and if you don't want to be here, then leave me to my job and go bark at someone else!"

Logan's eyes widen, then narrow. His jaw begins to tick, and his pale skin turns a nice shade of red. "And another thing," I tack on, finally finding all the words I'd stifled today. "If you don't like the fact that I *have* to work on the floor, give me a damn desk like a normal boss, you insensitive prick!"

His mouth opens and then snaps shut again. He leans forward and from the corner of my vision, I can see his left-hand twitch and flex like he's restraining himself. From what? Hitting me? A lump forms in my throat. He wouldn't, right? It dawns on me then that other than the fact that Logan Huxley is my extremely hot new boss, I don't know him whatsoever.

But then, my eyes meet his and what I see in them erases every single one of my concerns.

Lust. So much lust. *Need.* Fiery hot and burning. His bright green eyes reflect exactly what I'm sure he sees in my own eyes. How can I be so attracted to a stranger and want him this badly, even after the silent, tense day we've shared?

Logan swallows deeply, his adam's apple bobs with the movement. His thick, pink lips part beneath his beard, and one word leaves his mouth on a breathy grunt.

"*Fuck.*"

A rough exhale escapes me and my eyes close of their own will. My body sways, moving toward him without my permission. The heat from his body only inches from my own sears into every available inch of my skin. I feel him lean in, his face nearing mine. His hot breath wafts across my face, smelling sweet, like mints and candy. My hands dart out as if to grab him, pull him in, *touch him.*

Finally.

They meet...nothing.

Nothing but air.

My eyes snap open just as the office door slams shut.

IT'S MY CHOICE
be patient with yourself
Unapologetically MYSELF!
stay positive
BE Bold
ALL BODIES are GOOD BODIES
be happy
beautiful
love yourself
yes you can
Fearless
HERE to STAY
IN CONTROL
LOVE yourself
be kind to yourself
I am enough
FEEL DEEPLY
YOUR POTENTIAL IS ENDLESS
It's my choice
I am exactly where I need to be
be Brave
you are worthy
I am capable
love you
breathe
Perfect
YOU ARE enough

Shiloh

Six

"What do you mean, you can't fix it?" I cry out, pointing at the destruction that was my living room like my landlord can actually see it through the phone. "This is insane!" The useless jerk continues to prattle on, as though I hadn't spoken at all. Giving me twenty ridiculous, and likely illegal reasons, as to why the busted pipe can't be replaced until next week.

"How can you say this isn't a priority? I don't understand," I say, trying for calm and reasonable, instead of screaming like a banshee the way I want to. "How do you expect anyone to live like this? My living room literally has multiple inches of water in it, and all of my belongings are ruined. This *is* an emergency."

Stepping to the left, my sock-clad foot narrowly misses another puddle. Not that it would matter, the bottoms of my pajamas and feet are soaked through already. My landlord once again ignores me, sounding far less awake than I am right now. Granted, it is the middle of the night, but still, I'm pretty sure this situation warrants getting the hell out of bed and joining the land of the living.

Let me tell you, nothing wakes a person up quite like the sound of your two-hundred-pound dog jumping off your furniture and diving into the lake that used to be your living room. My armchair went flying as she dove from chair to table, barking and howling with glee.

I genuinely thought someone was breaking into my house. I tumbled out of bed and sprinted for my life, wielding nothing but a slipper I'd picked up on the way, only to come quite literally *sliding* to a halt as I took in the destruction of my house. Water was trickling through a rather large hole in the wall, opposite my bathroom, which brought on all sorts of freakish questions.

The main one being: *"Is it poo water?"*

Porkchop couldn't be bothered by my shouts of panic as she continued to pounce and roll in the questionable water, from an unknown source, before I tossed her outside. If possible, my landlord Harold cared even less. So far, the best solution he can come up with is to just simply *turn off my water* until he can get someone out here to fix the damage which apparently, won't be until next week.

So now, I have a filthy house, where all of my belongings are possibly contaminated with sewer water. An even filthier long-haired, soaking wet dog, who decided to roll around in the dirt outside to cover up her poo-watered coat, and no place to go until things can be repaired.

Sighing, I toss my phone onto the kitchen table, and finally, the tears of frustration spill out onto my cheeks. Dropping down into one of the chairs, I fight the urge to full-on sob. No, I can't. I have to be smart about this. I have to think, plan, and figure out my next steps, one soaking wet foot in front of the other.

Though I've lived in Blue River for a few years, I don't have many friends here. Cole and I had moved here together, and when we split I lost most of my friends in the divorce. My sister lives in Illinois, my best friend lives in Denver, which is two hours away, and the rest of my family is scattered across the Midwest.

I suppose there is Dom, but we've only hung out once since I met him two weeks ago, and I'd hate to inconvenience him. Not to mention, wherever I go would have to accept Porkchop, because I'm sure as hell not leaving her behind. That means a hotel is out of the running as well.

Maybe I should call Ray. I can't stay with her, she's too far away but she's a lawyer. I'm sure she'd probably be able to work her lawyer-y magic on my landlord. Groaning, I drop my head on the table. She can't do a damn this at this hour.

At first thought, the obvious answer would be to call Logan. Especially since he more than likely knows how to fix busted pipes and water damage. However, after that day two weeks ago when we'd nearly kissed, things have gone from tense, to downright *weird*.

For whatever reason, Logan has insisted on showing up at the Huxley Homes building almost every single day that

I work. I don't exactly understand why, because as far as I can see, he's not getting much work done when he's shadowing me. And that's exactly what he's doing. *Shadowing me.*

He tries to pretend that he's busy. Doing menial tasks around the office. One day, I even caught him dusting the reception area, which is still going unused, despite my best effort to convince him to hire someone. He ignored me, of course, and continued to observe me while I worked. Whether it's because he doesn't know me, trust me, or flat out just doesn't like me I'm not sure, but every time he comes in he remains silent, all the while keeping me in his line of sight.

It's weird, to say the least. Not quite uncomfortable, but definitely odd. Logan is a people watcher, I've noticed. He pays attention to things and though he's not big with words, he is sweet, if not in his own way. Ever since that first day meeting him, he hasn't allowed me to miss a single break or meal.

Every day, Logan makes sure that I take breaks regularly by grunting and pointing at the breakroom. The second day we'd worked together, he watched as I prepared my coffee, and now, he brings me a cup in the morning, exactly how I like it. He orders lunch, deposits it on the breakroom table, and barks at me to eat before dropping down across from me and doing the same. Staring at me the whole time. I have no idea why he's doing any of these sweet things, but every time he does, I internally die a little bit more.

Logan's made no effort to get to know me and despite my best efforts, I haven't been able to get to know him either. Neither of us has spoken about the near kiss, nor have there been any more close calls, much to my irritation.

Every single day, my crush on my silent, grumpy boss grows and another pair of panties gets ruined. The tension between us, both sexual and not, gets worse by the hour. I'm in a constant state of shaky, sweaty lust and frustration that I have absolutely no cure for. So, the idea of calling him now, in the middle of the night to come rescue me, is completely out of the question.

I would die. Hands down, dead on the spot.

Just the thought of seeing him right now has my sweaty palms returning with vengeance.

Glancing down at the time on my phone, I see it's after 2:00 am and realize that my choices are pretty damn limited. Technically, I could stay here, but then Porky would have to sleep outside and I wouldn't be able to shower in the morning for work. Not to mention, if I had to stay in this leaky, creaky, smelly house overnight I doubt I'd be able to get any sleep.

After considering my limited options for countless minutes, I come to a decision that I'll probably regret later. Before I can talk myself out of it, I run to my room and pack all of my necessities, for the next few days just in case. I pack a few changes of clothes, fresh pjs, my cosmetics and toiletries, towels, pillows, and blankets. I make sure to grab my phone and Kindle charger, before tucking the e-reader into my bag. I also pack up everything my dog will need, including her shampoo, because Lord knows, a bath is in order.

One sniff into the damp, dank living room has my skin crawling. We *both* need a shower, stat. I quickly load up my car before dropping the hatch of the SUV for Porkchop to hop into. Twenty minutes later, I'm lugging all my crap into the spacious breakroom of Huxley Homes. After rinsing off the dog, and taking a nice, long hot shower, I climb into my makeshift bed on the wide couch and stare up at the ceiling.

"What in the hell am I doing here?" I whisper, wondering not for the first time, why I felt this was a viable option.

Despite Logan generally being a bruting asshole, I do love my job and coming to work here every day. How the hell did that turn into me taking over the breakroom and temporarily moving in? In what world did I think this was okay? Shit, I hope I don't lose my job.

Groaning, I breathe through another onslaught of tears and attempt to push back the bout of self-deprecating thoughts that always seem to come whenever my head hits the pillow, but epically fail. How did my life turn out this way?

I'm in my mid-thirties, single as hell, living in a crappy rental with no one for company but my giant dog. I'm not using my college degree and making half the salary I had intended when I signed up for massive amounts of school debt. I live hundreds of miles from my family, have only a few friends, and my dreams of a huge, happy home and big family are dwindling by the day.

Thought after thought, rolls through my mind, shattering my heart piece by piece. I try, I really freaking try to be strong and not let myself fall apart over the way things have turned out, but damn, a girl can only take so much. What else can the world possibly throw at me? How much more damage can my spirit take before it breaks irreparably?

IT'S MY CHOICE
BE PATIENT WITH YOURSELF
Unapologetic MYSELF
love YOURSELF
BE Bold
ALL BODIES ARE GOOD BODIES
beautiful
yes you can
Fearless
be happy
HERE TO STAY
IN CONTROL
LOVE yours
I am enough
YOUR POTENT IS ENDL
FEEL DEEPLY
be kind to yourself
It's my choice
be Brave
I am exactly where I need to be
you are worthy
I am capable
love you
glow
breathe
Perfect
YOU AR enoug

Logan

Seven

"So, big brother. Will you be gracing us with your presence at work today or are you still too busy staring at your pretty new assistant?" Charlie chuckles as he attempts to snag a pancake off my plate. I bat his hand away as a wave of unwarranted anger surges through me.

"Don't call her pretty," I bark, throwing a withering glare in his direction. Charlie stops, his fork halting midair, his brows raised in question. We fall into a silent stare-off, both waiting for the other to back down. He smiles slowly, a mischievous look spreading over his face. My pulse speeds up and my eye begins to twitch with irritation, already knowing I'm going to want to stab him over the words about to leave his mouth.

"Oh?" he murmurs. "Is she ugly?"

"Charles Robert Huxley! Do not call women ugly!" Mom cries as she brandishes her spoon like a weapon at my little brother. Charlie rolls his eyes, earning a smack on the back of his head from Dad. Stephen quietly laughs behind his cup of coffee, eyeing the scene like it's his new favorite show.

"What?" Charlie grunts, rubbing the sore spot as he glowers at me. "It was just a damn question."

"Well, don't ask stupid questions," I reply with a shrug, feigning a nonchalance I don't feel when it comes to Shiloh. In fact, nonchalance is the exact opposite of what I feel when I think of her. My heart gives a squeeze as if to agree.

Mom smiles softly, her eyes twinkling in the way they do when she knows something before it happens. She's not psychic. At least, I'm pretty sure she isn't, but somehow, she always knows shit prematurely. She calls it 'Grandma's Gift' because apparently, her great-grandmother had the same mystical power. I fight a scoff at the thought. If only that *gift* had done its job 10 years ago, things would be a whole hell of a lot different now.

"Don't Logan. Not today," she murmurs. My eyes meet hers and a thick ball of emotion climbs up my throat so rapidly, I'm surprised I don't choke on it. "Anyways," Mom says, thankfully changing the subject. "I'd really like to meet this new assistant of yours. What's her name again?"

Fuck, this isn't the topic I was hoping for.

Charlie grins and opens his mouth, but I jump in, interrupting whatever crass comment he was about to make. "Shiloh!" I shout, far louder than I'd intended, but just the thought of her name on another man's lips makes me all sorts of violent, even if it is my little brother.

Everyone pauses what they're doing to stare at me, varying looks across each of their faces. Charlie looks suspicious, Stephen looks irritated, Dad looks confused, and Mom looks like all her dreams are coming true. Gritting my teeth, I shake my head, ignoring them completely as I finish my eggs.

Every morning for as long as I can remember, we've had family breakfast at our parents' house. We all live relatively close to each other on our family's massive plot of land, so when we moved into our own homes, we easily carried on the tradition. Huxley's have always been early risers and retirement didn't change that for our parents.

Glancing down at my watch, I realize I'm running behind, especially if I want to make it to the office to get a pot of coffee going before Shiloh gets in. I'll also have to remember to turn the heater on, ensuring the building is nice and warm for her to combat the frosty 30-degree temperatures we're having lately.

Charlie was right, I do have to make an appearance at the build site today. I am the foreman, after all. My presence is kind of necessary, but that doesn't mean I can't take care of my girl first.

And she is mine.

It's insane, I'm completely aware, but that doesn't change the fact that it's also true. I tried to fight it at first. Day one, I almost kissed her. Barely knew her name, and I was ready to take her, make her mine. But, like the asshole I am, I walked away.

I didn't show up the next day, or the next, but by Friday I couldn't take it anymore. I had to see her. I couldn't stop it, even if I tried. So, I showed up at an office I hate, pretending I had shit to work on, just so I could be near her. I've gone in every day since.

Over the last few weeks, I've found it increasingly difficult to separate myself from her. Shiloh is like a breath of fresh air, one I haven't truly experienced since before I left for the military. Whenever I'm with her, I forget everything else.

Everything.

The shitty fight I had with my father about not wanting to take over Huxley Homes when I turned 18. The fight that was so bad, so brutal, that I ran away from him, my family, and my obligations. Ran so fast and so far, that I didn't stop until I'd impulsively joined the military as a way out. I forget all about that when I'm with her.

I also forget everything that happened while I was away, fighting in a warzone, losing friends left and right to injury or death. I forget about the fiancé that cheated on me with my best friend, while I was fighting for our country. I forget about the little brother that looked up to me so immensely, that he followed in my footsteps, and joined the military. Only to be killed six months in. A little brother with his entire life before him. A life that was snuffed out in an instant before he'd even had the chance to live.

Liam.

Standing up, I pick up my dishes and take them to the sink. Gaining some much-needed space from my family and thoughts of Liam. I scoff. As if space alone could wipe away the heartache.

"Are you leaving?" Mom asks, coming to join me at the sink. I nod but say nothing as I wash my plate and coffee mug. Her tiny hand reaches up to give my shoulder a squeeze, and I instinctively bend at the knee, giving her access. How 5'3 Dolores Huxley birthed four boys who all grew to be over 6 feet tall, I'll never know. "I miss him too, Lo."

Dropping my head, I allow the weighted emotions to penetrate for just a moment. Just one singular moment, then I can go back to pretending they don't damn near suffocate me daily. My mom leans against my back, wrapping her thin arms around me from behind. They barely reach halfway around my wide frame, making me chuckle. She silences my laugh with a firm, tight squeeze that borders on painful.

After a few minutes, she pulls away and slaps my gut with the back of her hand, effectively ending our emotional moment. "I wasn't kidding. I want to meet Shiloh."

Grunting, I shake my head, side-stepping her in an attempt to avoid this conversation. A wave of possession rises in me swiftly as my eyes meet Charlie's. Hell no. I don't want Shiloh anywhere near my family. She's mine. I've known it from the first time I saw her. Despite the fact that I can barely form more than two words around the woman, I've already claimed her as my own.

Even if she has no idea.

Doesn't matter. She'll find out soon enough.

"Logan Huxley do not ignore me! Shiloh is Huxley Homes' very first employee. It's monumental. I want to meet her, and so does your father. Don't you Theo?"

"Huh?" Dad grunts as he reads through the sports section of the paper.

"See, your father agrees." I open my mouth to protest, waving in my dad's general direction for some backup, but one quick glare from my mother ends my objection. "No. Enough." Her hand slices through the air in a way that's more threatening than it should, given her tiny size. "Bring her to family dinner this Sunday, and do not be late, or else."

"Sunday? That's only four days from now," I growl, running an agitated hand through my hair. How am I supposed to convince Shiloh to go anywhere with me, let alone to meet my whole damn family, when I can hardly speak a coherent sentence around her?

"Or else, Logan!" My mom's hands land on her hips as she sends me a scathing glare, effectively silencing me. And just like that, I feel like a teenager again.

Mom grins knowingly. I ignore the bark of laughter from not only both my brothers, but my father as well, who has apparently finally joined the conversation. Sighing my defeat, I give my mom a curt nod, kiss on the cheek, and practically sprint out of their house before she can make any more demands. "Make sure to watch—" I start to call out, my ass halfway out the door.

"I know, I know. Get out of here."

I do just that.

Jumping into my truck, I high-tail it out of the country and head into town. The Huxleys own one of the largest chunks of land in the county. Sitting at just under 500 acres of mostly untouched forest, our land is full of hidden secrets and beauty. There are a few smaller lakes that connect to the river. A couple of waterfalls and caves. Tons of places to explore, and adventures to be had. It's one of the reasons our grandfather chose the parcel way back when. He dreamed of his kids and grandkids having a real childhood in the wild.

I loved growing up in the country. It was freeing. I have thousands of memories from those days, most of them with my brothers. They're some of the best ones I have. It's why I jumped at the chance to build my home on Huxley soil. I pictured my own kids growing up the way we had. Running through the fields, climbing trees, diving off cliffs, and fishing in the lakes.

For the longest time, the vision was skewed, obscure almost. Like an old memory. You know what happened, who was there, where you were, but the exact scene isn't quite visible anymore. That's what my future looked like to me. Now though, it's changed. Lately, things have started to look and feel more exact, more real.

Instead of just a vague picture, I see it clearly.

Shiloh.

Thoughts of her have me pressing down on the gas, pushing my truck to its limits. She doesn't come into work until 9:00 am, and I have a meeting on the job site for the Taylor project at 9:30. Doesn't give me much time to see her, but at this point, I'm pretty sure even a passing glance would settle my nerves.

I don't understand why I feel the way I do when it comes to Shiloh. I've never felt this way for a woman before and still, I hardly know her. It's not for a lack of trying, but when I open my mouth to do just that nothing comes out. The words die a bitter, acidic death in my gut every damn time. She rattles me. Unsettles and unnerves me. I'm not sure if it's her overwhelming beauty, her killer curves, her perfect smile, or maybe her voice, but *she wrecks me.*

Maybe it's just simply *her.*

I blow through three stop signs, one stop light, and damn near take out the paperboy in my rush to get to the office before her. I somehow turn a thirty-minute drive into ten, but as I pull into what should be a very empty parking lot, I find I'm already too late.

Glancing at the clock, I see it's just after 8:00 am, so technically I'm early, but for some reason, my girl's already here.

My hackles rise, and a sense of panic fills me.

Why? No idea.

Doesn't stop me from basically sprinting into the building in an effort to get to her. *I just need to see her, make sure she's okay*, I tell myself pushing through the door that leads to the staff area. My heart thumps erratically in my chest, and my hand begins to tremble with the need to grab my gun. A gun I don't have. Haven't had it since I came home from the middle east. Still, I crave its reassuring feel.

Calm the fuck down, Logan. She probably just came into work early, and you're going to give the woman a fucking heart attack. Again.

Breathing through my anxiety, I slow my rapid pace, shaking my hands out at my sides in an attempt to get a fucking grip as I move toward my office. Seconds later, I'm at the threshold, and my pounding heart ratchets up a notch, or ten. My stomach clenches painfully with anticipation. I slowly, *calmly*, push the door open, a rare smile spread across my face, but when I enter, I find it empty.

What the hell? Where is she?

My brows furrow in confusion as I spin on my heel, in search of Shiloh. I want to call out, demand that she shows herself, but again, I'm going for cool, calm, and collected. Normal, not obsessed, bordering on insane.

Come on, babydoll. Where are you?

I quickly check the other offices, bathrooms, and stock room, before making a beeline for the break room on the opposite side of the building. I'm just about to enter the dark room when an ominous, otherworldly growl meets my ears. Anger and anxiety swirl around deep in my gut, but I press forward, needing to protect my girl.

I take a step forward, and the growl deepens, sounding something akin to a demon. What the hell is going on? I slowly, *ever so fucking slowly*, slide my hand up the wall, blindly searching for the light switch. My muscles tense, completely prepared to fight off anyone or anything threatening Shiloh. Sweet, perfect, innocent Shiloh. I shake off the distracting thoughts and flick the light on.

I stop dead in my tracks as I take in the sight before me.

At first glance, I'm pretty positive it's a bear.

A fucking massive, black bear, in my breakroom. A giant, demonic, growling, drooling beast on my couch, poised and ready to attack. I stop moving, stilling my body completely, and the beast relaxes, settling its head down on the pile of blankets beneath it.

I relax slightly when the beast does, which gives me a moment to really inspect the creature. As I look past the long fur, the black beady eyes, and the sharp teeth, clarity washes over me. It's a dog. The biggest dog I've ever seen. Laying on—something. No, not something, someone.

Shiloh.

Outrage replaces anger, and genuine concern replaces anxiety, as I glance around the state of what used to be our break room. There are a few duffle bags, a stack of clothes, and a purse piled up on the long wooden table in the center of the room. On the floor, there's a makeshift food and water station for the beast, a few pairs of Shiloh's shoes, and a pile of what appears to be soaking wet clothes and towels.

My eyes move back to a curled-up, sleeping Shiloh, and every single thing I'd previously felt completely disappears. The only thing I feel when I look at her now is adoration. Adoration and protectiveness.

Why is she sleeping here? Why isn't she at home? Did something happen? Did someone hurt her?

A steady stream of questions loops through my brain as I watch her sleep. The dog seems to have relaxed, but its eyes never leave me, tracking me even as I move into the room. I try to keep my movements slow, my posture unthreatening, like I'd approach someone with a weapon or a hostage. My years of training come back to me, and in an instant, I'm that soldier once again.

The hulking dog doesn't move, or growl, *thank God,* as it continues to watch me. After what feels like forever, I reach the beast, opting to introduce myself to him before checking on Shiloh.

"It's okay, Beastie," I whisper, slowly moving my hand for it to inspect. "I'm just here to check on your mama." The dog eyes me speculatively for a moment before sniffing and eventually licking my hand. I coo softly at the creature when it allows me to pet its head. Soon enough, I have it rolling onto its back, begging for more pets. "Ah, so you're a she, huh? Well, girl, you did a good job protecting her, but I've got it from here."

I move to Shiloh's face, leaning over the couch to take her in up close, and my breath stutters at the sight.

During the day, when she's smiling softly to herself, or laughing at a text message, she's beautiful. Effortlessly, so. When she's snapping and telling me off, her hands on her wide hips, her tits thrust forward, and her lush lips curled into a snarl; she's hot as fuck. When she's deep in thought, reading over a contract, or playing with her label maker, her lip tucked between her teeth and the little lines between her brows on display; she's adorable.

But right now, asleep, free from makeup, her hair a mess, spilling across the pillows...

She's unbelievable. I have no words. An angel sent from Heaven.

For me.

I watch her for countless minutes, unable to get enough. I pull out my phone and snap a few pictures of her, deciding I need to keep this moment in case I don't get another like it. I fight the urge to push down the blankets and find out what she wears when she sleeps. In fact, the only reason I don't do just that is the giant dog laying on her feet, judging me as I observe her owner.

Soon enough, I'll have her sleeping next to me every night, and when she does, she'll be naked, and the beast won't be in *our* bed.

"Shiloh," I whisper, already pissed off that I won't be able to stare at her any longer, but I need to wake her up so she can tell me what the fuck is going on. She doesn't stir, still sleeping deeply. Fuck, the things I could do to her body while she slept, completely unaware.

"Shiloh," I say louder, an edge to my voice as my already hard cock throbs. "Wake up, Babydoll." I reach my hand up, pushing her long brown hair from her cheek.

She leans into the touch, nuzzling my hand. My heart squeezes, and it takes everything in me not to claim her here and now. *"Logan,"* she whispers.

My heart stops.

Swallowing down the unexpected lump in my throat, I grasp her face more firmly, my body no longer my own. "I'm here, Shiloh."

A soft smile creeps across her face as she rubs against my hand. My cock begins to leak in my boxers. Fuck, I need her so goddamned badly. I've never needed to fuck, to own, to claim, and possess anyone, the way I do her.

I want, no *need*, to see her perfect golden skin covered completely in my cum. I need her so covered in my scent, in *me*, that no one will dare touch her or take her from me. I need her so fucking full of my seed, that she'll be locked to me for life.

Mine, mine, mine.

"You're not here. This is just another dream," she murmurs, her voice thick with sleep. "A good one."

God fucking damnit. This woman's going to be the death of me.

"Babydoll, I'm here. Wake up, Shiloh." I hate the words, even as they leave my mouth. It's clear she has no idea she's not dreaming, and as much as I want to keep pretending, I want this for real.

Shiloh's smile disappears in an instant as her eyes peel open. The rich chocolate brown of her irises looks almost black in the dim lighting of the break room. If anything, it just makes her features more interesting. Her eyes are like endless, fathomless pools.

"Logan?" she rasps, her voice bordering on shrill. Well, fuck. That's one octave from a shriek. Her head jerks back and her eyes dart around the room rapidly, as if she's trying to remember where she is. "Oh, shit. I can—I can explain. I, uh, I—"

As I take in her panicked expression, I realize that her eyes are red and puffy, like she'd been crying. I hate that. I never want her to cry again. The need to destroy whoever and whatever made her so upset rises up in me swiftly. Her endless eyes gloss over with tears, and I snap, unable to take the look of dread on her face any longer.

"Shiloh!" I bark, and then softer, "calm down, beautiful. Everything is fine. Just tell me what happened."

Swallowing, she glances down, taking the blanket that slipped in her panic, and the breasts that are spilling out of her tiny tank top, before yanking it back up. It takes a tremendous amount of control not to rip the offending material from her body, exposing her to me fully. I don't want her to hide from me, *ever.* Every single inch of her delicious body deserves to be worshiped and devoured.

By me.

"I just, I'm," she stammers, her voice shaky. I stand upright, no longer hovering over her body, even though the distance physically pains me.

"Breathe," I grunt, crossing my arms, so I don't do something stupid like wrap her in my arms. Taking a step back, I lean against the table and cock a brow, waiting for her to speak. "Explain."

Back to the monosyllables, I guess.

"I just fell asleep working late last night, that's all." She shrugs, not meeting my eyes as she toys with the edge of the blanket.

"We left together. Try again."

"Oh, um, yeah, I came back to finish the Taylor contract revisions." Again, she shrugs, but this time she adds in a nod as if to reassure herself that the excuse is a good one.

"And you brought your dog?" I query, jutting my chin in the beastie's direction. The dog's tongue lolls out to the side, and I swear, it looks like she's smirking at me.

"Porkchop doesn't like to be left alone."

"Your dog's name is Porkchop?" I bark out a laugh, causing Shiloh to shoot me a glare.

She reaches her hand out, threading her fingers through its long mane. "What? Doesn't she look like a Porkchop?"

"No," I grunt, shaking my head emphatically. "It looks like Satan and a bear had a baby."

"What?" she cries out, bundling the massive dog in her arms like an infant. "Don't say that. Porky is the sweetest dog in the world. She'd never eat anyone or sentence them to a life of eternal fire and pain." Turning to her dog, she peppers its massive head with kisses; protruding fangs be damned. "Would you girl? You're such a sweetheart, aren't you?" she coos.

The dog shoots a glare in my direction while licking up the side of Shiloh's face, claiming her owner. *Cocky fucker.*

At that moment, I reach a level of angry possession, I didn't know existed. I want to kill a dog for touching *my* woman.

My fists clench so hard, one of my knuckles pops. "Explain, Shiloh. Now!" I growl out my demand, even as my body vibrates with the need to throw her over my shoulder and lock her up in my house. Correction. My bedroom.

"You don't need to yell!" she yells.

"Then tell me why you're asleep in the breakroom before I make you! You're driving me insane, woman." Spearing my fingers through my hair, I begin to pace the room, fighting every single one of my natural instincts when it comes to her.

"Make me? How are you going to *make* me do anything?" she huffs out a laugh and rolls her eyes, muttering something about *asshole-prick-demanding-douche-canoe*. I stop listening after the last insult leaves her plump lips.

"Don't test me, Shiloh," I warn. I'm not exactly sure how I'll make her do shit, but I'm pretty sure I can come up with something. I've never been one for corporal punishment or particularly freaky sex, but when it comes to her, my brain has all sorts of fucked up ideas.

Her eyes widen, and for a second, I think I've gone too far. She's still my employee after all. She has no idea that she's so much more than that.

But then, a different look fills her sweet face. Her tongue darts out, wetting her lips as her eyes become hooded. "How will you make me, Logan?" she asks, her voice thick with need. The raspy sound of it goes straight to my cock, but more than that; the sound of my name on her lips does something to me.

I cross the room in record time, unable to stand the distance for another second. Leaning over her, I plant one hand next to her face, the other on the back of the couch, leaving only inches between our faces. Her breathing becomes a rapid pant causing her breath to waft over my face. Every hot exhale turns me on even more until I'm barely hanging on by a thread.

"Say it again," I growl.

Her brows dip in confusion.

"My name."

Shiloh tilts her head to the side slightly as her eyes consume every inch of my face. Her lips kick up at the corner as she whispers, *"Logan."*

I groan, my forehead dropping to hers. My fingers flex, and my cock *burns* with the need to rut into her tight, hot cunt.

"Do you really want to find out?" I murmur, not giving her a chance to respond before continuing. "Do you want me to tell you that I have so many ideas when it comes to you, and this incredible thick body of yours? Do you want me to tell you that I have so many filthy fucking thoughts about how exactly I could *make* you do something, Shiloh?"

She says nothing as she squeezes her eyes shut.

"I could use my tongue," I rasp. She swallows thickly. Her eyes peel open and dart to my mouth. She licks her lips again, and I lean in closer, only an inch of space between us as we share breath. "Would you like that, Babydoll? Or would you prefer my hands?"

My hand leaves the back of the couch, finding her lush body as if second nature. I trail up the side of her blanket-covered arm before grabbing the material and ripping it off her. I toss it aside and return to her, finding skin now instead of cotton. My eyes never leave hers, even though I want nothing more than to enjoy the sight of her curves. My fingers glide over her silky, smooth flesh, in a teasingly slow caress.

"Is that what you want? Me to use my fingers and tongue to *make* you give me what I want?" This time I pause, my movements and my questions. Shiloh's head nods, and then her eyes widen as if she hadn't meant to respond. I smile, completely understanding the loss of control. I have no control where Shiloh is concerned. None. My body doesn't belong to me any longer. My heart, soul, cock, and brain belong to her now.

My tongue leaves my mouth, and before I know what I'm doing, I'm licking a trail up the side of her neck, her cheek, matching the path the dog took on the opposite side of her face.

Claiming her.

Mine.

I reach her ear, feeling her body tremble beneath me. "Or would you prefer I use my *cock*?" Shiloh lets out a moan that goes straight to my dick, but it's just a small taste of what I'll pull from her body the moment she allows me to. "What a pretty sound, Babydoll. Should I see what other sweet noises you can make?"

"Oh fuck, yes," she whimpers. Her hands reach out as if to grab me, but I move, standing completely and stepping away. It hurts. My body repels the space. Despises it. But I have to. I have to keep my head, even if it fucking kills me.

"Then tell me, Shiloh."

Realization washes over her, and I swear, she looks seconds from releasing a toddler-level tantrum in response.

Me too, Babydoll, me too.

Ten minutes later, I'm ready to commit murder on behalf of my girl. How dare her fucking piece of shit landlord force her to live like that? Fuck no. Not on my watch.

"Get up, get showered, and get ready. You have twenty minutes."

Turning my back, I storm from the breakroom, leaving a wide-eyed and very confused Shiloh shouting behind me.

I have to walk away before I do something that I won't be able to take back. Something insane, like forcing her to give up her shitty rental and move in with me or demand her landlord's information so I can go kill him.

No one fucks over Shiloh Huxley. No one.

IT'S MY CHOICE
BE PATIENT WITH YOURSELF
Unapologetically MYSELF!
love yourself
beautiful
BE Bold
ALL BODIES ARE GOOD BODIES
STAY POSITIVE
be happy
yes you can
Fearless
IN CONTROL
LOVE yourself
HERE TO STAY
I am enough
FEEL DEEPLY
YOUR POTENTIAL IS ENDLESS
be kind to yourself
it's my choice
be Brave
You are pretty
I am exactly where I need to be
you are worthy
I am capable
Love you
glow
breathe
Perfect
YOU ARE enough

Shiloh

Eight

I don't know why I listen to his demands, but I do. Less than fifteen minutes later, I'm dragging a pair of leggings up my thighs as I attempt to avoid Porkchop's judgmental stare.

"What are you looking at?" I grunt, jumping in an attempt to get the tight material over my ass. I have to do the *bend and wiggle* a few times, which is hands down the most unattractive move a human being can make, all the while praying Logan doesn't bust into his office where I'm getting ready.

"It doesn't mean anything," I tell her emphatically, tugging my long sleeve t-shirt over my head. It's fresh from the dryer and clings to my stomach uncomfortably. I pull the material away from my body and tuck my elbow into the front, stretching the cotton to its limits before releasing it.

The shirt glides down my body in a much less restrictive way that allows the length in the back to cover my ass.

I may never look like one of those cute tiny girls on Pinterest, wearing their circle scarves, slouchy sweaters, Lulu's, and Hunters, but my ass sure looks phenomenal in these leggings.

Porkchop tilts her head to the side and stares at me. I know it's impossible, but I swear I hear her scoff at my statement. I wouldn't blame her if she did. We both know I'm a dirty little liar.

Waking up to Logan Huxley all up in my face this morning was the single most confusing experience of my life. Confusing, because while it was embarrassing as hell that I basically marked him like a cat, and whispered his name in my sleep, having him that close to me was incredible. At that moment, I was thankful for my panic as it gave me an excuse to gain some distance before I'd done something stupid.

Like, kiss him.

And I so would have. He's just so *beautiful.* His green eyes and freckles are even more mesmerizing up close. His red curly hair and wild beard are rugged and manly, eliciting visions of him chopping down wood in a forest shirtless, quickly followed by me dropping to my knees to take care of *his* wood, if you know what I mean.

Porkchop makes another chuffing noise as if to say, *everyone knows what you mean, idiot.* I glare at her. She's so rude sometimes.

As I yank my boots over my thick socks, I wonder for the hundredth time what the hell is going on. I feel like I woke up in an alternate universe. I went to bed feeling as though my world was crumbling to bits and woke up with Logan staring down at me, whispering words like *I'm here*, and calling me *Babydoll.* A shiver races up my spine at the memory. I like that name. A lot.

I don't think anything in the world could wash away the memory of what happened next. As if to agree, my still aching, wet pussy throbs. I've been turned on since the day I met Logan Huxley and haven't stopped since. At this point, I'm pretty sure my vagina is trying to kill me. If I lose any more blood flow from my brain that has redirected itself to my clit, I'll need a transfusion.

Would he have really done it? All those things he was threatening? *Make* me tell him by using his tongue, fingers, and.... *shit!*

I cross my legs, squeezing my thighs together in an effort to get some relief. I should have taken care of myself in the shower, but I was too consumed with thoughts and questions to focus. Before I knew it, I'd already been standing under the water for over ten minutes and needed to rush.

I'm definitely regretting that decision now.

"You ready?" Logan grunts, pushing the office door open. Jumping up, I turn, throwing a withering glare in his direction.

"I could have been naked!" I snap, even as a wave of arousal pools low in my belly at the thought. What would he have done? It's obvious he's attracted to me, and wants me on some level, even if it is just sexual. Is that all I want from him?

Logan grants me a rare smile as he prowls into the office. "I think I would have liked to see that," he mumbles, coming to stop in front of me. My neck cranes back, meeting his heated gaze. "There's always later, though."

"Later," I murmur, my voice a little breathless.

He nods, his smile widening. "Later, Babydoll. We have to go, now."

"Go where?" I ask absently, unable to pull my eyes from his. I want to count his freckles. Explore his body and find out if they cover his skin. I want to lick every single one of them. Does he have tattoos? Piercings? Does the red hair cover his chest or his—

"Arms up," he grunts, interrupting my wayward thoughts. Again, I absently and blindly follow his instructions, my mind no longer my own.

My arms raise above my head without questions. Logan produces a sweatshirt from behind his back and tugs it down, over my head and body. It's huge on me, landing just above my knees and extending well past my hands. No guy's sweatshirt has ever been too big for me. I feel tiny in it. Tiny and protected, like a swaddle. I pull the neck of it up, inhaling deeply. It smells like him. Like the forest, right after it's rained.

Fresh. Pine. Earthy. I love it.

Logan sucks his lip between his teeth as he leans back and takes me in. His heated gaze rakes over my body, lighting it on fire with his eyes alone as he goes. I resist the urge to yank on the sleeves awkwardly under his penetrating stare. Instead, I stand up straight, channeling every ounce of womanly bravado I can muster. Faking a confidence I don't feel.

"God fucking damnit. The sight of you in my clothes does things to me." His voice is a thick, growl. If the sound came from anyone else, I'd probably be afraid. But from him, I want to drop to my knees and see if I can make him do it again.

"Like what?" I whisper, my body swaying toward his. I feel drunk...*on him.*

His eyes meet mine again and what I see in them melts me. It consumes me. It completely and utterly *destroys me.*

He steps into me and places a hand around the front of my throat. My eyes widen in response, but instead of fear, I feel nothing but a *hot and achy need.*

"Babydoll, if I had time, I would show you exactly what you do to me. I would prove to you again and again that just the sight of you has me damn near busting at the seams."

I open my mouth to ask what he means, but he punctuates his statement by grinding his extremely hard and thick cock into my hip. Between the layers, I can't feel everything, but what I can feel tells me one very important fact.

Logan Huxley is *hung.*

"Do you understand now, Shiloh?" he grunts, rutting against me harshly. His hips grind into mine, again and again, in a mesmerizing way that has me ready to cum on the spot. He's not even touching my pussy, and I'm ready to combust.

"Please," I whine, pushing back into him. This is madness. Undeniable madness, but I don't care, and I can't stop. I need him more than I've ever needed anything in my life.

Logan bends down, tightening his grip on my throat slightly, using the pressure to tilt my head back. "Please what?" he murmurs.

We're so close now. So close to everything I've wanted since I first met him. So close to everything I desperately need.

"Logan, I need you," I groan, my hands wrapping around his body and grasping his ass cheeks to drag him closer.

Closer, I need closer. I need—I need...

Logan lets out a feral-sounding growl at my plea, and before I know what's happening, I'm being shoved against the wall. His huge, hot body presses into mine, blocking my escape, not that I'd want one. His forearms land on either side of my head as he thrusts his thick thigh between my legs, forcing them to widen and accommodate him.

"Is this what you need, Babydoll? Do you need to use me to take the edge off?" he grunts, rubbing his thigh against my throbbing clit. I squeeze my legs around his, relishing in the pressure he's given me, exactly where I need it so badly. I grind down on him but then, his hands are on my hips, halting me. I let out a sound that's half-groan, half-whine. "Say it, Shiloh. Tell me what you want. I need to hear you say it."

Swallowing, I push past the hesitation. The little voice inside my head telling me not to be greedy. The one saying that I'm asking for too much, that it's not all about me. The one that Cole put there. I ignore that fucker, focusing on the incredible man standing in front of me, offering me exactly what I need.

"I want you to touch me, Logan. Touch me and make me cum."

And then, his lips are on mine.

It's everything I imagined, and so much more. His lips are soft and thick, his beard coarse and scratchy, as he devours my mouth. His kiss is vicious. It's not soft and sweet. It's forceful and borderline painful. Like he's needed this just as badly as I have. Like he's wanted me for weeks and has been holding himself back the entire time.

He's not holding back now, though.

Now, Logan's *taking*.

Taking everything he wants and forcing me to give in to his will. His hands roam my body like an introduction. As if he's meeting every inch of me for the first time and doesn't want to miss a thing. They're greedy as they grope and tug, twist, and squeeze. He's not avoiding my stomach rolls or saggy boobs. He's not glossing over the thick, dimpled curve of my ass or the cellulite covering my thighs.

Logan doesn't pretend those body parts, *my* body, don't exist. He doesn't skip straight to my nipples or pussy. He doesn't stick to the body parts that are muscle or bone instead of fatty flesh like other men do.

He ravages me like a real man should. He devours the feeling of me beneath his palms like he can't get enough. He pulls on the flesh above my ribs, yanking me deeper into his body. It feels like he's trying to consume me. Like he can't possibly get close enough.

It's fucking everything.

I try not to get emotional at the feeling of his hands on me and the way he's worshiping my body. A body so easily dismissed by others, men and women alike. A body that has brought me joy and sorrow. A body that has brought me life and taken it away. A body that my ex ignored and rarely touched, especially as it began to grow and change.

I try not to get emotional, I really do, but against my will, a few tears of complete and utter astonishment and happiness escape my eyes.

Logan's hands slide down the curve of my waist and squeeze my hips as he thrusts his knee against my pussy and begins to *grind me* on *him*. "Take it, Shiloh. Use this perfect, gorgeous body and take your orgasm from me," he rasps, pulling back to speak. "Fuck my thigh and soak my jeans in your juices. I wanna smell like your perfect cunt all day, so everyone knows."

Oh my god, his mouth.

I moan, tipping my head back. It slams into the wall, but I don't care. I do as he demands and ride his leg, taking what I want with a single-minded focus.

"So everyone knows what?" I pant. My hands grip his perfect, round ass again, using it as leverage to fuck myself on his body. Logan groans, rutting his thick cock against my hip. It makes my mouth water.

I want it.

I want it so fucking badly, I can't focus on anything other than thoughts of how it would feel, how it would taste. I want his big, fat cock inside my mouth, my pussy, my ass. I want him to cover me. Fill me. *Breed me.*

God, visions of my wildest, deepest fantasies come to the forefront of my thoughts, adding to the lust coursing through me.

His cock is already so massive. How would it feel with a knot? His big dick would be so deep inside my throbbing pussy as he fucked me, he'd probably bruise my cervix. I moan loudly, grinding harder.

His mouth reaches my neck, and he sucks the flesh there, hard enough to leave a mark. He kisses, sucks, bites, licks—again and again, sending sparks through my body. His breath fans over my ear as he whispers, "I want you to cover me in your cum, so everyone knows who you belong to."

"Logan!" I scream as the most intense orgasm of my life barrels through me just as the last word leaves his mouth. Visions of his knotted cock shoving deep inside me, forcing past the tight barrier of my cunt and stretching me painfully, accelerate my pleasure. He'd lock us together as he shot his thick, hot load deep inside my pussy, coating my walls again and again—

"That's it, Babydoll. Soak me with your scent. *Mark me as yours.*"

If possible, those words make my orgasm even more potent, as one turns into another. I do exactly as he says and soak him with my release. It gushes from my throbbing cunt, coating my leggings and his thigh in an embarrassing amount of liquid.

My legs tremble as I squeeze them together, riding out the aftershocks of my orgasm. Logan drags my earlobe between his teeth, sucking on the flesh as I come down from my high.

"What about you?" I whisper, my husky voice foreign, even to my own ears.

He chuckles, the sound so deep and sexy that my thighs clench again. "The next time I cum, I'll be so deep in your pussy, you'll feel me dripping from you for days."

"Logan," I rasp as a fresh wave of need courses through me.

"Hearing my name on your lips as you squirted all over me was the single best experience of my life," he groans, before adding, "*yet.*"

Slowly, he stands straight, pulling his thigh from between my legs. I'm too embarrassed to look down, already knowing it'll look like I pissed all over him. I can feel the wetness between my legs. My panties are soaked through completely, and my leggings are warm from my release, so I can only imagine the carnage on his jeans.

"Holy shit, that's so fucking sexy." His hot, lust-filled voice pulls my attention to the offending scene without my permission, and my stomach twists at the sight.

Jesus, I've never cum like that before. Ever.

"I can't," he rasps, shaking his head. "I have to taste you. Have to clean you up."

And then, he's on his knees before me. He tears my leggings down so fast I barely have any time to panic that he's about to see...*me.*

He tugs down the material, bunching it around my calves. Looking up, his eyes lock on mine as he grips the hem of my panties, a simple black pair of cotton boy shorts. Slowly, he glides them down my thighs.

"Logan, I—" I open my mouth, ready to explain that my pussy isn't shaved like most women. There's been no point. I'm in such bad a dry spell, I've basically been revirginized.

He interrupts, leaning in and inhaling *deeply.* He lets out a loud groan. "I knew it." He licks a long path up the short curls between my thighs, sucking them clean. I moan, my legs trembling. "Fuck. Can't wait to cover this tiny bush in my cum."

"Oh, shit," I groan, transfixed on the sight of him. This big, strong man is on his knees, devouring my pussy like he's starved. Like I'm the best thing he's ever tasted.

Logan licks, his tongue swiping every inch of flesh he can find. He bends one of my knees and cocks it to the side, giving him better access. His thumbs peel me apart, opening me up for his mouth and fingers to worship.

He doesn't try to make me cum again, just does exactly like he says and cleans up the mess we made. But when he flicks his tongue over my clit, I detonate anyway.

"Fuck, Logan," I whimper, gripping his hair and holding him against my cunt. "Oh my god, you feel so good."

"You taste incredible," he grunts, licking me languidly as I come down from my second, maybe third, orgasm. I've honestly lost count at this point. He pulls away, wiping his soaking beard across the sleeve of his flannel. My eyes widen. He says nothing, just smirks as he pulls my bottoms up as though nothing happened. Standing, he kisses me again, thrusting his tongue into my mouth so I can taste myself on him.

God, he's incredible. I want him more than I've ever wanted anyone in my life. I almost allow myself to drag him back into me for round two, but then, he's stepping away from me and shaking his head.

"Don't look at me like that," he grumbles.

"Like what?" I ask innocently.

"Like you want me to fuck you against the wall." He reaches down and adjusts the unbelievably obvious hard-on. He gives his cock a firm squeeze as he stares at the wet patch on his pants, his tongue darting out to lick his lips. "Fucking Hell, Shiloh."

"What?" I murmur, just as enthralled by the sight as he is. Is it weird that I want to lick my cum from his thigh?

Logan growls, releasing his cock and grabbing my hand instead. "We have to go. *Now.*"

I barely have a chance to form a thought before I'm dragged through the Huxley Homes building, toward the front door. I open my mouth to object, my eyes darting around in search of my dog. Logan, once again, beats me to it, though.

"Porkchop! Truck!" he shouts, and sure enough, seconds later, *my* dog is bounding after us. Logan plucks my purse from the reception desk and passes it to me as he pushes through the front door.

When did that get there?

Yep. Definitely, woke up in an alternate reality. What is my life, and why am I allowing all of this?

He opens the door to his big, white truck that sits at a ridiculous height from the ground. Logan wordlessly lifts me up and deposits me in the passenger seat, as though I weigh nothing. My mouth gapes open in shock.

That's new.

"Why are you looking at me like that?" he grunts, his movements pausing.

Swallowing thickly, I murmur, "No one's ever been able to lift me up like that before."

Logan stares at me for a minute, a look of anger drowning out his previous contentment. His hand reaches up, and his thumb swipes across my cheek in a soft caress. "That's not your fault, Babydoll. You were just with weak men before me."

Bending over, he buckles me in, kisses my cheek like it's a normal occurrence, and closes my door, leaving me speechless. My eyes dart all over the place in confusion. They land on the backseat. All the things I'd brought with me last night, pillows and duffle bags included, are stacked in a pile. My confusion deepens.

In the rearview mirror, I see him drop the hatch, bark the word *load*, and again, my dog responds like Logan's her new master. He slams the hatch shut, and hops in the driver's seat. All the while, I stare in shock, unable to speak.

Logan flicks the radio on, turning it to a popular country station, and reaches over, wrapping his big hand around mine.

"Tell me where you live," he demands. My eyes drop down to our joined hands as he gives mine a squeeze. My heart echoes the movement, and emotions well up in my eyes. I blink them back, completely confused and shocked by this strange turn of events. I genuinely have no clue what's happening here, but my gut, my heart, and soul *really* fucking like it.

"Why?" I choke out, unsure what I'm referring to. Logan's eyes dart to mine, once, then twice, before he focuses back on the road.

"You know why." Again, I'm not sure what either of us is talking about. Does he mean my address? Or why this morning has gone down the way it has? I want to ask. I want to demand answers, but every question dies in my mouth as Logan's thumb begins to rub the back of my hand in the single sweetest gesture I've ever received.

"Blossom Street. Number 232," I murmur, a smile spreading across my face as I continue to watch his thumb make little swishes *back and forth, back and forth.*

Logan lifts our joined hands and kisses where he'd just been rubbing. His lips press in and hold firm as his eyes meet mine. "Thank you," he says, his lips ghosting over my skin as he speaks.

Those words and the look in his gaze tell me everything I wanted to know but was too afraid to ask.

We weren't talking about my address at all.

Be patient
with
yourself

Unapologetically
MYSELF

Be Bold

ALL BODIES
ARE
GOOD BODIES

love yourself

beautiful

yes you can

Fearless

IN CONTROL

LOVE yourself

HERE

I am enough

DEEPLY

your potential

be kind to yourself

Brave

It's a choice

exactly where I need to be

you are worthy

YOU ARE enough

I am capable

love you

breathe

Perfect

be happy

Shiloh

Nine

"Holy shit," I screech, pushing past Logan and into the fucking *lake* that was once my living room. The small hole in the wall where the water had come from is now a gaping chasm of destruction. Instead of only my living room being wrecked, it's now everything. "I don't understand! He was supposed to turn it off!"

My booted feet splash through the inches of water as I make my way toward my kitchen, ignoring Logan's shouts for me to come back. I can't. I have to see how bad it is.

"Goddamnit, woman!" he barks, catching up with me in just a few short strides. "Stop before you hurt yourself."

I whirl on him, anger and frustration pulsing through me. "Hurt myself? It's water Logan, not a gunfight." He winces at my words and grits his teeth, his jaw flexing with the movement. Curiosity replaces some of my irritation, but I ignore it for now.

"No, and you're damn lucky you'll never have to experience one, but that doesn't change the fact that there could be electrical wires in the water."

Shit. I hadn't thought of that. I hadn't thought of anything besides checking on my house and the only possessions I have left, post-divorce. Glancing down, I take in my sopping feet, the water now having soaked through my boots completely, when something dawns on me.

For the first time since I ran inside, I truly pay attention, taking in my surroundings. Inches of water cover the entirety of my living room, kitchen, dining room, and hall. I haven't checked the bedrooms, but I can assume it's spread like the plague and consumed every inch of my tiny house. The worst of the damage is the living room across from the busted wall. My couch is wrecked, my coffee table can't be salvaged, and my armchair is now two different colors.

However, the one thing that sticks out above all else, *is the smell.* It's sour, rancid, and strong.

Oh hell no.

I scream as I launch myself at Logan, throwing my arms around his neck and climbing him like a spider monkey. Later, I'll question why I'd thought this would be a good idea, or maybe why I assumed he'd be able to catch me. He doesn't disappoint, though, as he wraps his muscular arms beneath my thighs, cradling me to his chest like a small child.

"Is it poo water?" I ask, swallowing back bile. My toes curl in my soggy socks, bringing on the realization that I'm covered in an unknown substance. I gag, tucking my face into Logan's neck. Inhaling deeply, I take in his pine and rain scent, allowing it to calm me.

"Is my house covered in shit water, Logan?" My lips coast over his skin with every word. His body involuntarily shivers beneath me. I smile faintly, loving the way I affect him so easily.

Logan chuckles as he turns away from my kitchen and toward the front door. "No, Babydoll. I highly doubt it's *poo water.*" I swear I hear him roll his eyes. He opens the front door, and the cold wind blows through, sending another wave of sour water smell my direction. I gag again, afraid vomit might actually come up soon if I have to stay in this place.

"Then why does it smell like that?" I cry, burrowing deeper into his neck.

*Again...*later I'll question why I feel so comfortable with Logan Huxley, trusting him implicitly to take care of not only my house, but me. I'll question why I allow him to carry me outside, his strong arms wrapped tightly beneath my thighs. I might even wonder why I feel so dang comfortable that I never want to move, despite the fact that I barely know him.

Later. I'll overthink things later.

I'm vaguely aware of us reaching his truck. He shifts his hold on me, sending me slightly off balance. Somehow, he opens the passenger door, never dropping or releasing me, until I'm settled back in my seat. Reluctantly, I peel myself from his warm, comforting body. Logan stands, stepping back slightly, and with that tiny amount of distance a wave of embarrassment floods me so rapidly, I get light-headed.

"Shit, I'm sorry," I murmur, my head dropping to my chest. I can't look at him. How fucking embarrassing. I threw myself in the man's arms. He *had* to carry me. It was that, or drop my big ass in the gross water. Oh my—

Fingers under my chin force my face up to meet his. Logans' bright green eyes stare deeply into mine, a serious, almost annoyed, look on his face. I don't blame him. I'd be annoyed if my employee jumped me, too.

Oh my god! I'm his employee! He's my boss! What are we doing?

"Stop it, Shiloh." My brows furrow in confusion. I open my mouth to question him, but he interrupts me. "Stop whatever stupid fucking thoughts are rolling around in your head. You look embarrassed and you shouldn't. If I didn't have to go back in your house to check shit out, I'd have held you all damn day."

He's just being nice.

I roll my eyes in an effort to minimize the way his words make me feel. It's ridiculous. The warmth coursing through my body over just those simple words is insane and irrational. It's not like he confessed his undying love, but to me, he may as well have.

"I'm too heavy," I scoff.

His lip quirks. "You're not. Try again."

Lies.

"Your arms would get tired," I point out with a shrug.

He smiles. "Babydoll, I'd hold you till my arms gave out."

Stop. Please don't say things you don't mean.

"That wouldn't take very long."

"Then I'll sit down and keep holding you. Wanna keep arguing?" He chuckles like this is some sort of joke. Like he isn't shifting my world on its fucking axis.

Still, I try again. Pushing him away, reminding myself that pretty words don't mean a thing. "Those are just words, Logan. Nice ones, I'll give you that. But it's not real."

Logan steps forward, his hands landing on my thighs. He squeezes the flesh. My immediate response would be to cringe from the inability to hide my imperfections. "Shiloh. Listen and listen good, because I'm about to get *real* with you. Every fucking inch of your body is beautiful." I shake my head, tugging my lip between my teeth. "Yes, it is. You're thick in all the right places—"

"I'm thick in *every* place, Logan," I growl, gesturing to my body as if it isn't obvious.

"Shut up," he barks. My head jerks back in shock, even as my mouth snaps shut. "I'm still talking, Babydoll, and I don't like to be interrupted. As I was saying. You're thick in all the right places. These thighs?" He squeezes them again, his fingers just below the apex. The place I'm already throbbing for him. "I look forward to the day when I can have them wrapped around my head while I eat your sweet cunt. I want my tongue buried so deeply in between your *thick* thighs, that I fuckin' suffocate."

My heart rate picks up, beating painfully hard in my chest.

He doesn't look like he's lying.

"Your tits and ass fit in my hands like they were made for me, Shiloh. We fit together. Every inch of you fits with every fucking inch of me. You see that, don't you? You get it?"

I reluctantly nod, the corner of my lip tipping up. Fear of the unknown claws at my gut, but I ignore it, focusing solely on his words.

Oh, God, they're everything.

"These arms?" His hands travel up my body, grasping my fleshy biceps. His thumbs swipe back and forth. The heat from his skin burns me, even through all the layers. "The feeling of them wrapped around my neck a few minutes ago was one of the best things I've ever felt in my life. You feel warm and comforting." He takes another step forward until we're face to face. "I want to fall asleep with these *thick* arms wrapped around me every fucking night."

The walls around my heart crack, splintering the barrier that's protected me for so long.

This can't be real.

"Do you wanna know the craziest part? The part about your body that I love the most? The thought that's circled around in my head every damn day since I first saw you?"

Love?

Crack.

He swallows thickly, his adam's apple bobbing with the movement. His eyes bore into mine, penetrating in a way that makes me feel both exposed and seen, all at once. I nod again, my heart now in my throat. My eyes burn and

I have to blink rapidly to see straight. Logan's hands reach up, wiping away the wetness spilling across my cheeks.

"Yes," I whisper. "Tell me."

"Do you really wanna know, Shiloh? It's too much. It'll scare you away." He squeezes his eyes closed, and the fingers still on my cheeks tremble. My arms move without thought, mirroring his position. I wrap my much smaller hands around his face, smoothing my thumbs over his dry cheeks. His coarse beard tickles under my palms, but I love the feeling.

His eyes open, and he leans in, resting his forehead on mine. Our hands never move, and this is the single most intimate moment I've ever experienced.

"The part of your perfect, beautiful, *thick* body that I love the most, is this." One of his hands leaves my face, and slides down the front of my throat, caressing softly over my breasts and my ribs. Down, down—I think he's aiming for my pussy, and I barely contain a scoff, but then, he shocks me as he stops on my...

On my stomach.

I try to pull away, memories of the way Cole refused to touch it. The fattiest, most unflattering part of my body. Rolls and excess flesh that is covered in stretch marks. A testament to all my body's been through over the years. The growth, the loss—

Logan halts my movements. "This. This is what I fantasize about. This belly, rounded as you carry my baby. *Our baby*. I want to pump you so full of my cum, you'll be knocked up before I even pull out. I want you dripping with my seed, Shiloh. Is that *real enough* for you?"

My heart drops. Completely and utterly *drops*. Falls from my chest, through my stomach, the stomach his hand is lovingly caressing, and onto the ground. It stops. Everything stops. My breath wooshes out of my body, my heart no longer beating as time stands still.

What?

His hand tightens on my cheek, his forehead presses harder into mine, like he's trying to hold on.

"I told you it was crazy." His voice is a gravelly rasp, thick with emotion. "It's fucking insane. I know. We hardly know each other. I'm your boss. There are a hundred reasons why this is all sorts of stupid and unrealistic, but it doesn't matter. It doesn't change a damn thing. I want you. I want you so fucking badly that it keeps me up at night. I want every part of you. Body, mind, heart, and soul. I want your present, your future, your belly big with our kids. *I want it all."*

Tears are now steadily streaming down my face, and it takes everything in me to hold in my sobs. There is no second guessing it now. Logan's serious. He means every single word coming out of his perfect mouth. I want to believe him. I want to believe that he seriously might feel even an ounce of everything he just said.

That he might feel for me, what I feel for him.

I want the picture he painted. I want every single second of it. Him, us, babies. A family. Holy shit, a family. But I can't—I can't and he doesn't know.

The cracks forming around my heart begin to rapidly tape themselves back together, repairing the damage he created. He'd torn that damn wall down so effortlessly, so quickly, and now I have to work to put it back up. Erect the fortress once more, because after I tell him that his dreams, *our future*, isn't a possibility, he'll leave.

Just like Cole.

"Logan," I whisper. I open my mouth, almost choking on the words, but am interrupted by a loud *bang*. I duck as Logan wraps his body around mine, pressing me deeper into the cab of the truck.

"Fuck!" he shouts, clinging to me tightly. "Shit, shit, shit," he mutters, his arms banded so tightly around me, I feel like I might snap in half. The sound of an old truck sputtering and then driving away penetrates through the tension.

"It's okay," I murmur, trying to free my hands to push him away. He holds me tighter and it's then I notice that his body is shaking, *hard.* "Logan," I call his name, again and again, but he doesn't respond or let go. I realize that for him, that sound must have been triggering. I don't know why or what his story is, but suddenly, I need to know. I need to know everything about him. "Logan," I say softer, soothingly. "Baby, everything's fine. It was just a truck backfiring."

Still, nothing.

So, I let him hold me. I rock our bodies back and forth the best I can in his death grip. I hum quietly under my breath, a Portuguese song my mom used to sing to us when we were little. His body relaxes slightly, but he doesn't release me. Instead, he burrows his face in my neck.

My father has PTSD from the war, and I've been around plenty of times for his flashbacks and panic attacks. I'm not sure what Logan's been through, but I'm pretty sure that's what's happening here.

The feeling of this hulking man, wrapped around me and seeking comfort, shifts something in me. It feels right. *He feels right.* Down to the marrow of my bones, Logan Huxley in my arms feels perfectly, unbelievably right. I want him. I want this. All I can do is hope and pray that when I tell him my secret, he'll still want me, too.

I don't know how long we stay like that, but then Porkchop's there, nudging her body against his legs as she whines. She probes and prods, trying to coax him away from me, or maybe, she's trying to comfort him. I'm not sure. She's always been good at knowing when I'm upset and plopping her body on mine, like a weighted blanket.

Something in her actions must finally get through to him, because only a short minute later, Logan's releasing me. Slowly, he pulls back, his eyes somewhat frantic as he searches my body, and then my face. I'm not completely positive, but I think he's checking me for injury. I smile at him reassuringly, letting him do his inspection. I have so many questions, but I bite my tongue, knowing it's most definitely not the time for an inquisition.

"We're okay," I say instead. "We're all good."

He nods and steps away, saying nothing. Bending down, he pats my dog's head, letting her nuzzle his hand for a moment before pulling back. "I need to go figure things out. I'll be back." Then he turns and walks into my house, like the last twenty minutes never even happened.

IT'S MY CHOICE

BE PATIENT WITH YOURSELF

Unapologetically MYSELF

LOVE YOURSELF.

BE Bold

ALL BODIES are GOOD BODIES

beautiful

Yes you can

Fearless

HERE TO STAY

IN CONTROL

LOVE yours

be happy

I am enough

FEEL DEEPLY

YOUR POTENTIAL IS ENDL

be kind to yourself

It's my choice

I am exactly where I need to be

be Brave

you are worthy

YOU AR enoug

I am capable

Love you

glow

breathe

Perfect

Shiloh

TEN

I'm not sure how much time passes while I wait for Logan to come back out, but I get lost in my head, thinking about everything he'd done and said. Everything that's happened since waking up this morning. I'm finding it extremely difficult to wrap my brain around all of it. How did we go from arguing on day one, to a silent yet comfortable existence for the last few weeks, to *this?* It seriously makes no sense.

This gives zero to sixty, a whole new meaning.

At some point, the sound of the front door closing pulls me from my wayward and confusing thoughts. Turning, I find Logan storming down my walkway, his arms full of crap. No, not just crap. *My* crap. Throwing the door open, I jump out and barrel towards him.

"What are you doing with all my stuff?" I snap, counting the number of bags tossed over his broad shoulders. There are six. No, *seven.* Four overnight bags and three totes. Every single one of them is stuffed to the brim. Logan says nothing as he pushes past me and opens the back door of the truck, tossing everything inside. "Logan!" I cry out, my hands flying in the air.

Stupid, pig-headed, good for nothing—

"You're staying with me. Get in." His barked command is emphasized by the sound of the door slamming shut. As if his point was made and he expects it to be a done deal, he circles the truck and climbs into the driver's seat.

Nerves race through my body, culminating in the pit of my stomach and making me feel ill, but I push past the feeling. I shoot a glare in his direction and cross my arms over my chest. My feet stay rooted to the spot as I refuse his demand. Looking up, I see my dog staring at me from the bed of the truck. Her head cocks as though she knows there's about to be a showdown.

"I'm not staying with you." *I can't. I'll fall even more for you. I won't be able to come back from it.*

Logan lets out a growl that goes straight to my clit. "Get in the fucking truck, Shiloh."

"No!" I stomp my foot, shooting daggers at the smug jerk.

"Yes!" he snaps back, climbing from the truck. He leans against the hood, his face a mask of irritation.

"I don't want to." *I want to more than anything, but then you'll find out that we have no future.*

"You can't stay here." Logan throws an angry hand at my house as though the structure personally offended him.

"I'll stay somewhere else." *I have nowhere to go.*

Sighing, he spears his fingers through his wild curly locks, and squeezes his eyes shut as he mutters something. It sounds a whole lot like *Lord, give me the patience to not strangle her,* but the words get lost in the wind, so really, he could have said anything.

"Come home with me," he says, his voice gentling as he adds, "Please let me take care of you, Shiloh."

Well, that sounds kind of nice.

My eyes flit to the back where all my bags are as my resolve waivers. "What did you even pack?" I mumble, feeling myself about to give in.

Logan grins, shrugging his shoulders. "Girl crap."

Girl crap? I roll my eyes. No doubt he packed fifty pairs of panties, no bras, or pants. He probably didn't even pack my socks. Shit...that means he went through my stuff.

If he did, then he saw—

Spinning on my heel, I charge back into my house, once again ignoring his protests. "If it's safe enough for your giant ass, it's safe enough for mine!" I shout over my shoulder before taking one last deep breath of fresh air. I make a beeline for my bedroom, preparing myself for the carnage.

Surprisingly, it's not terrible. There's barely any water on the hardwood. The main area seems to have received the brunt of the damage. However, that's not what has my attention. No, what does is the mess left behind by Logan.

Every drawer I own is open and *empty*. Every. Single. One.

Fuck, fuck, fuckity, fuck.

Running to my bedside table, I find the bottom drawer cracked open, which, believe it or not, stands out more than any of the rest. It's the only one that hasn't been pilfered. Or so it would appear. Slowly I open the drawer, finding it still chuck full of its contents. My forehead drops onto the end table as I release a heavy sigh of relief.

"Oh, don't worry, I saw it." My head darts up, finding Logan leaning against my door frame, an unreadable expression on his handsome face. "That's quite the interesting collection you have there." He juts his chin to where I'm kneeling as if I needed the clarification.

Humiliation washes through me. Shit. I can't believe he found my stash.

I have—tastes. Very, specific, interesting tastes. Kinks, if you will.

The knotty kind.

"So, what are they?" he murmurs, his voice much closer now. I jump, slamming the drawer closed.

"Shit, Logan. You're insanely quiet for such a big guy."

He grins, dropping his ass on my bed and settling in. "What are they, Shiloh?"

Gritting my teeth so hard they grind together, I ignore his question and deflect like a pro. "How bad is the damage?"

Logan's smile drops. He runs a hand through his hair, anger and frustration morphing from his previously happy expression. "Fuck. It's pretty bad, Babydoll. The pipes are old and rusted. They should have been replaced a long fuckin' time ago. You rent, right?"

I nod, my gut churning.

He sighs. "Yeah, thought so. This area's all pretty much rentals these days." Logan stands, his eyes roaming around my bedroom, taking in every tiny detail. "Your landlord's gonna have a massive bill ahead of him and a shit ton of work." He shakes his head, looking down at me again. "I could bore you with all the details, but honestly, I need to talk to him. He shouldn't have let anyone move in here."

"You don't need to do that, Logan" I protest. I grip the edge of the bed to stand, but then he's there, lifting me to my feet. His hands stay wrapped around my ribcage as he looks down at me.

"I know," he smiles, his voice taking on a hint of teasing. "I don't *have* to do anything, but I want to. You may not have agreed to what I said outside, but that doesn't change the facts."

"What facts?" I murmur breathily.

"*That you're mine.*"

He kisses me then, silencing the argument sitting on my tongue. It's hot and demanding, sending shivers across my skin. My thighs clench together as arousal courses through me. Logan bites my lip, tugging it between his teeth. I moan into his mouth, already needing more. God, was it only a few hours ago I came all over his thigh? My panties are still damp from cumming, and they're getting even wetter by the second.

The kiss is over way too quickly, leaving me heated and needy. "Don't argue with me, Babydoll. Please. Just let me take care of this for you. Let me handle your landlord, your house, and bring you home so I can make sure you're okay."

"I'm fine," I whisper. "I—"

"I said don't argue," he grunts, seconds before his massive palm is landing on my ass. The slap is hard, and the sting of pain makes me cry out, but then, he's rubbing the small hurt away and squeezing the flesh like he can't get enough. "Questions?"

I swallow, fighting down the urge to ask for another spanking. Instead, I say, "How long will I be staying with you?"

Grinning, he leans down to my ear and whispers, "Forever, if I have it my way."

I groan, pushing him away.

Lies, lies, lies.

Deflect.

"Fine," I nod, stepping back toward my nightstand. "If I'm staying that long, I'll need supplies." Turning away from him, I bend down, giving him a nice view of the ass he supposedly loves so much as I yank out open my sex-toy drawer and dump its contents onto my bed. "Hand me that bag please," I gesture to the backpack sitting on the floor of my opened closet.

"Fuck no!" he barks, shocking me. His hands cut through the air as he shakes his head rapidly. "No, absolutely not."

"Excuse me?" I stutter.

He ignores me as his eyes scan the various knotted dildos, monster cocks, plugs, and vibrators. Leaning forward, he inspects everything, touching and sifting through them like he's never seen such a thing before. In reality, he probably hasn't. Finally, he steps back and crosses his arms. "*No.*"

"What the hell do you mean, *no?*" I scoff. "You can't tell me what to do, Logan." I turn around and begin to pile them up, picking out my favorites as I go.

The tentacle is nice. Definitely not the thickest, but it hits my g-spot every time.

Add.

My knotted werewolf is my favorite, so obviously, he's coming.

Add.

The Egg-Layer 3000 comes with an ovipositor and a set of alien eggs.

Add, add, definitely add.

Oh! My vibrating knotted Monster with the cum tube! Hell yes.

"Wanna make a bet?" Logan growls, halting my packing. "You're not taking those, those—*things*!"

Lord, help me. The audacity of this man. What does he think this is? The 50's? He can't tell me what I can and cannot put in my body. If I want to impale myself on a nine-inch, double-knotted unicorn cock, then I'll damn well do it. Who the hell is he to kink shame me?

"They're called dildos, for shit's sake! It's not like I'm trying to bring an anaconda into your house!" I shout, planting my fists on my hips as I glower up at the prick.

His hand flies out, and he points an accusing finger at my Dragon Dong. "There's one right there!"

My eyes widen at the alarmed look on his face. I don't think he's grossed out by them. Nor do I think he's judging me. If anything, he seems maybe...*jealous?*

Oh my god.

My face burns with the effort to hold in my laugh until finally, I can't take it any longer. I double over, peals of laughter falling from my lips. I laugh so hard; tears coat my cheeks as I begin to wheeze and cough.

"What is so fucking funny?" he snaps.

Breathing rapidly, I force myself to calm down as I wipe my cheeks. "You're jealous of a bunch of dildos?" I rasp, meeting his gaze.

Logan's light skin is red with anger, making his brown freckles pop. His green eyes are thin slits, and his jaw is ticking uncontrollably. "Fuck yes, I am. No one, and I mean *no one*, gets inside your cunt but me."

My laughter dies a quick, brutal death.

"If you need to get off, you come to me. If you need something pounding deep in your pussy, splitting you in half until you're crying for more? Come to me. If you want something shoved up your perfect asshole making you feel fuller than you've ever felt before? *Use me.*" Logan steps forward and bends, wrapping his arms beneath my thighs. He lifts me, and suddenly, I'm upside down and over his shoulder.

"Logan!" I scream, bracing my fists on his back for support. His hand lands on my ass cheek, once, twice, three times.

"Babydoll, you need to get with the fucking program. If you think being mine means you get to fuck yourself with rubber cocks, you're wrong." I breathe heavily, trying to get a hold of my bearings as he barrels out of my house, once again.

"I never said I was yours," I say weakly, the words like gravel on my tongue.

"Still can't decide? Maybe, I didn't outline the benefits package very well then," he laughs, slamming my front door behind us. "If you're mine, that makes me *yours*. You own me, Babydoll. *All of me.*"

My heart races at his declaration.

I want that.

I hear a gasp and look up, finding my neighbor, Mrs. Peters, standing on her front lawn in her nightgown, staring at us with a shocked look as though we're making a porno in my driveway.

She's such a nosy bitch. I can't stand her.

I smile and wave before slapping Logan's ass. He grunts, and I cackle, delighting in Mrs. Peter's appalled expression.

"And if you didn't know," Logan continues, oblivious to what's happening behind him. "My cock is fantastic. Thick and veiny. Long too with a slight curve. It'll hit your g-spot in ways that fucking *thing* can't." Mrs. Peters screeches as she crosses herself. "My cock is all yours. To suck, to fuck, to ride. Anything you want."

He drops me, letting me slide down his body, grinning as he grinds said cock into me. He's hard. Again, or maybe still. My mouth dries, and my pussy throbs.

Holy shit, he's going to kill me with his cock, isn't he?

Bending down, he murmurs, "Now get in the fucking truck, Shiloh."

I'm so drunk on everything that is Logan Huxley, that this time, I do.

IT'S MY CHOICE
BE PATIENT WITH YOURSELF
Unapologetic MYSELF
ALL BODIES ARE GOOD BODIES
be happy
Love yourself
beautiful
Fearless
yes you can
IN CONTROL
LOVE yours
HERE TO STAY
I am enough
FEEL DEEPLY
YOUR POTENT IS ENDL
be kind to yourself
It's my choice
I am exactly where I need to be
be Brave
you are worthy
I am capable
YOU ARE enough
glow
Love you
breathe
Perfect

Shiloh

ELEVEN

A little while later, we're turning down a long driveway deep in the heart of the country. The land in this direction is undeveloped, for the most part. From what I've seen, it's all pine trees and nature.

"Are we near the river?" I ask, glancing in his direction. He smiles and nods, his fingers drumming on the steering wheel. His other hand is wrapped possessively around the back of my neck, massaging the tense muscles absently. I like it. Probably too much, if I'm being honest.

Emotion clogs my throat, and I quickly look away. My eyes take in the miles and miles of endless land, stretching around us, as we drive down the long dirt road that I assume leads to his property.

"This is beautiful," I murmur, watching the slightly snowy terrain pass. "It's like a movie." It's early November, and for the most part, we won't get much snow around this area for another month or so, but this last week gave us a small taste of it.

"It is, huh?" he says, a hint of awe in his voice. "This is my family's property. We own over 500 acres."

"Holy shit!" I cry, my head snapping in his direction. "What do you do with all of it?"

Logan barks out a laugh. "Do with it? The land, you mean?" I nod. His hand flicks off the steering wheel, gesturing to the open, vast wilderness before us. "This." He shrugs, gripping the wheel once more. It doesn't escape me that he used the hand not touching me to point with, never breaking our contact.

"By *this*, do you mean nothing?" I grin, feeling lighter than I have for years. Logan brings that out in me, I've noticed. A side of myself I haven't seen in a long time. Not since before Cole.

Before...everything happened.

Logan smiles widely and a small dimple pokes out from beneath his beard. "Yeah, Babydoll. Nothing. My grandpa bought this land so we could experience nature exactly as it is. We mill the trees when they get out of control and use the lumber for build sites. We propagate new trees, making sure to keep the forest full, but safe. Other than that, we leave it as is."

"Well, if there's nothing out here, then where are you taking me?" I ask, tugging my lower lip between my teeth.

Logan's eyes slide from the road and drop to my mouth. He groans, a long, low sound, full of sex. "Stop that," he murmurs.

I release my lip with a pop. "Why?"

"Because it makes me wanna put other things in your mouth."

God-fucking-damnit. My panties will never dry at this rate.

Logan snickers, his eyes crinkling around the edges as he notices my shifting thighs. "And to answer your question, I brought you here because it's where I live. Where my whole family lives."

"You're bringing to meet your family?" I screech, my fists clenching on my lap.

His snicker turns to a full belly laugh, his head tipping back with the movement. "No, Babydoll. Not today." I open my mouth to tell him *not ever*, but stop short, knowing it's a lie. Knowing that deep down in my gut, and my heart, I want nothing more than to meet his family.

Fuck, I know it's stupid and irrational, but I want nothing more than to *be* Logan's family.

Damnit. I'm screwed. So, fucking screwed.

"My parents live a few miles South of my property in our childhood home. My brothers live to the West. I have my own house. We built all of them together years ago when Huxley Homes first took off."

Looking up, I avoid his knowing gaze and glance back out the window. "So, where is this house of you—"

My words dry up in my mouth as the single most incredibly stunning home I have ever seen comes into view. "Oh my god," I breathe, unable to pull my eyes away from the sight.

It's huge. Massive, yet homey. It's beautiful without being ostentatious.

His house is two, maybe three stories, but with four pitches at different heights, it's hard to tell. I can only describe the exterior as a modern, luxury log cabin. The front is adorned with massive windows, allowing unobstructed views of the property. The façade combines dark wood siding, slate grey stone, and black trim. Huge pillars are supporting a deep, covered, wrap-around porch.

The right side of the house has a huge deck with matching beams. There's a sliding glass door, connecting the deck to the house on one end. The other has stairs leading down to the biggest manicured front yard I've ever seen.

God, that yard is made for kids.

"This is where you live?" I gasp. In response, Logan presses a button, opening the double-wide garage door tucked to the left and hidden from view. The space is so big, it could easily fit four large vehicles. A few snowmobiles and four-wheelers are pulled up along the side, next to a good size fishing boat. It only confirms what I'd already suspected. Logan's definitely outdoorsy.

Turning off the truck, he leans back, an unreadable expression on his face as he watches me. "What do you think?"

His words are flat, unlike the previous levity of our conversation. If I had to guess, I'd say he's nervous. Of what? Was he worried I wouldn't like his house?

Smiling, I reach out, grasping his hand in a move that feels far more natural than it should. "Logan, it's perfect."

His face instantly softens as he releases a heavy exhale. "Really? I wasn't sure if you'd think—" he breaks off and palms the back of his neck with an awkward shrug. "I thought you'd think it was too—I don't know, rustic."

My body leans forward subconsciously with the need to kiss his adorable face. I resist, second-guessing myself, But Logan's there, closing the distance and pressing his lips to mine. His fingers thread through my hair as he cups my head, using his hold on me to move me where he wants. It's brief, over all too quickly, despite my best efforts to keep us locked together.

Logan pulls away, chuckling when my lips chase his. "As much as I'd like to sit here and make out with you, I wanna show you around."

Smiling, I nod my agreement and turn to hop out, excited for a tour. My hand has just reached the handle when Logan barks, "Don't you dare."

I swivel, turning a confused look in his direction, but he's already jumping out and jogging around the truck. My jaw hits the ground when Logan opens my door, wordlessly leans over, unbuckling me, and lifts me from my seat before settling me safely on the ground.

"You know I can get out of the truck by myself, right?" I ask, a little dazed by his actions. Logan ignores me and moves to release the hatch. Porkchop jumps out and takes off, moving faster than I've ever seen her before.

"Porkchop!" I cry out, moving to take off after her. Not that I'd be able to catch her. Logan wraps his arm around my waist, hauling me backward. His chest presses into me, and I can feel his laughter along my back.

"She's fine, I promise. Let her explore. Worst case scenario, a hunter mistakes her for a bear."

I yank myself away and whirl on him. "Are you fucking serious?" I cry, anger and panic filling me in an instant. Logan chuckles again and shakes his head as he opens the back door and begins to pile all my crap into his arms.

"I'm just kidding, Shiloh. No one hunts these lands. Everyone knows it's restricted and private property. I promise you, she's fine." He slams the door shut with a kick and juts his chin toward a door that I can only assume leads to the house. "Come on. I have to head into work for a little bit, and I want to feed you first."

"Feed me?" I ask, my voice full of indignation. "I'm not your pet, Logan." He leads me toward the house, batting my hands away when I try to lighten his load.

Glancing back, he smirks, a devious look on his face. "No, you're definitely not," he pauses, the silence weighted, and I already know I'm going to want to punch him over his next words. "If you were, you'd be so much better behaved."

I growl, and the sound makes him fall into a fit of laughter. The sound is raspy like he doesn't do it often, but to me, it's the most beautiful thing I've ever heard. "I liked you better when you didn't talk."

"Liar."

He's not wrong.

We enter through a laundry room/mudroom that's simple and clean. The floors are tiled with black slate, the walls are grey, and there are built-in dark wood cabinets and shelves for storage. Logan kicks his boots off, sliding them into a cubby along the floor before stepping through a second door. I slip out of my boots quickly, not wanting to get left behind.

"Keep up, Babydoll," he calls, a hint of humor lacing his tone. I roll my eyes, but jog a few steps to catch up.

We enter a kitchen that's more incredible than I could have ever imagined. The ceilings are vaulted to a peak, adorned with thick dark beams adding both style and support. The cabinets are the same dark wood, which under a brighter light, I can tell is stained pine. The walls are all white, allowing the rich woods to make a statement and provide warmth. The floors are natural wood, in various shades, that tie the colors of everything together.

There's a huge island in the center, that instantly brings on thoughts of family breakfasts, and late nights sharing ice cream. The counters are tan and brown granite, fitting with the rustic vibe. The living room and semi-formal dining area are all one big space. Natural light cascades in through the floor-to-ceiling windows, which I can now see are not just at the front of the house, but at the back as well, giving a 360 view of the scenery.

"Each of us customized our homes the way we wanted. Mine is sort of based on my parents' house. Everything is open and connected so—" he breaks off, nervously glancing back at me.

"So, your family can be together," I say softly, nodding my head as I look around. It's rustic without feeling like a hunter's cabin. He has a leather couch, faux fur rugs, and dark rich accent colors, but there aren't any antlers or taxidermy heads on the walls. A fact that I appreciate greatly.

"Exactly," he murmurs, clearing his throat. "There are two bedrooms and a full bathroom over there, but both are empty. For now." He gestures to a hallway behind the stairs, opposite a massive stone fireplace. The chimney reaches the vaulted ceiling, disappearing into the beams, making it the focal point of the entire space.

All I can think is how beautiful this room would look decorated for Christmas. A thought that I try to keep to myself but can't. "Holy shit, Logan. This place would be awesome for the holidays. You could fit the biggest Christmas tree in here."

Logan points to an open space next to the fireplace and smiles. "What do you think about putting it right there?'

My eyes dart between him and the space, my belly clenching with nerves and excitement. "It would be perfect," I whisper.

Visions of early Christmas mornings with cocoa and carols, the kids in their pajamas opening presents while Logan and I cuddle in front of the fire, dance through my mind. It's so potent and visceral, my eyes begin to sting.

I shake it off, pointing to the stairs. "What's up there?"

Logan smiles softly as he leads me up to the second floor, which opens directly to a huge loft. The biggest TV I've ever seen sits above a smaller stone fireplace and across from a comfy-looking, deep, wrap-around couch. It's large enough that ten people could sit on it at once, with room to spare, and I immediately want to dive in.

"The rest of the bedrooms are on this floor." He continues down a long hallway, pointing out doors as we go. "There are three bathrooms up here. One's a half bath, and the others are Jack and Jills, connecting two bedrooms. There's nothing in any of them yet, but I do have a guest room at the end of the hall."

"And where is your room?" I ask absently as my eyes dart inside the few rooms with open doors. He wasn't lying. They're all empty. Why would he have so many empty rooms? Logan stops walking abruptly, and I slam into his back. He turns slowly, looking down at me.

"On the other end of this floor," he says, his voice a low rasp. "Why?"

Clearing my throat, I shift from foot to foot. "I thought you were giving me a tour. Are you not showing me your room?"

Logan shakes his head, and my stomach drops. "I'm not taking you to the master bedroom unless you're going to be sleeping in my bed."

"What?" I murmur.

He steps into me, aligning our bodies as best he can with his arms full of my stuff. "If you step one foot in my bedroom, I'll have you sprawled out across my bed, naked and beneath me, before you even know what's happening, and I won't let you leave again. You'll be mine." Leaning down, so our faces are only inches apart, he growls, "Still wanna check out my bedroom, Babydoll?"

Swallowing, I stare at him, not knowing what to say. Everything inside of me screams *yes, yes, yes,* but indecision has me pausing. He's serious about all of this. His possession of me lights me on fire, burns me up in the best way imaginable, but something inside me holds me back.

He doesn't know you can't give him what he wants. He doesn't know you're broken.

My inner voice penetrates through the dreams, the pictures he's painting, and reality comes crashing down. "Guestroom, please."

Logan winces, and guilt claws at my insides. I have to tell him.

I *will* tell him.

Tonight.

IT'S MY CHOICE
Be patient with yourself
Unapologetic MYSELF
Love yourself.
Be Bold
ALL BODIES are GOOD BODIES
be happy
beautiful
yes you can
Fearless
HERE TO STAY
IN CONTROL
I am enough
FEEL DEEPLY
potent is enol
young
YOUR
be kind to yourself
Brave
It's my choice
I am exactly where I need to be
you are worthy
I am capable
YOU AR enoug
Love you
glow
breathe
Perfect

Logan

Twelve

"**B**abydoll, I'm home," I call out, stepping through the garage door. I drop my keys and wallet on the island and listen for Shiloh but hear nothing. "What do you think, Tank? Wanna meet your new mama?" He gives a little chuff that I'd like to think means *hell yes*, making me grin.

Bending down, I set him on the hardwood, making sure his harness is on straight, and give him a little pat to get going. He hightails it across the slick surface as fast as his tiny little legs can handle. Shaking my head, I dart past him and head upstairs, eager to get back to my girl. It's been too many hours since I left her, and I'm aching to have her back in my arms.

Earlier, when we'd gone to see the damage at her place, I'd shot a text to Charlie, letting him know I had an emergency and that he'd need to cover for me with the Taylors. As much as he prefers working with his hands, he's a smart guy and can handle stepping in to handle business when needed. Still, I'm the foreman and had to be the one to do the inspection and sign off on the paperwork, so I had to go in. The whole damn thing ended up taking way longer than I'd intended.

I left Shiloh, fed and lounging on the upstairs couch in front of a fire, giving her free reign of the house and a promise that I'd be back soon. My stomach twists. I feel like such a fucking prick. I left her alone, in a new place with no car, for most of the day. Increasing my pace, I take the stairs three at a time, hoping she's okay.

Reaching the top step, I come to an abrupt halt when I find her passed out and curled up under a thick wool blanket my mom crocheted when I was a kid. My heart squeezes at the sight.

Stepping closer, I lean over, much like this morning, and take her in. She's so damn beautiful when she sleeps. Her face is peaceful and relaxed. A small smile tips the corner of her full lips up, and the overwhelming need to kiss her fills me instantly. Her lip twitches, and the sight hardens my cock.

Goddamn.

Will it always be like this? Will just the sight of her, asleep and wrapped in *my* stuff, in *my* house, always make me feel this way? Because right now, I feel like the luckiest man in the fucking universe. I feel like every single dream I've ever had for my future is lying just inches before me, sprawled out and ready for the taking.

Her golden tan skin and long dark brown hair look angelic under the dim light from the fire, and my mind starts to conjure up visions of what our kids will look like. Will our daughter have green eyes like me or chocolate brown like her mama? Will our son have brown hair or red? Mine's definitely a strong gene. Just look at my entire family.

Fuck. It doesn't even matter who they look like. They'll be perfect, just like my Shiloh.

I've always wanted kids and a big family. Growing up the oldest of three wasn't always easy, but it was awesome. I loved it and knew even from a young age that I wanted the same thing someday. There was a time when I imagined that life with my high school girlfriend, turned fiancé, Sadie.

We'd dated all of Junior and Senior year, broke up for a short time when I enlisted, then got back together one Christmas when I was home visiting. I'd proposed, idiotically and drunkenly, the following Thanksgiving. She'd happily agreed, gushing and crying about how excited she was.

We were good for a while. She supported me emotionally while I was away. Stuck it out during the long months when I couldn't get back to see her. Called me every chance she got, going on and on about wedding plans and our future.

I thought I'd finally found it. The mother of my kids, my wife, my forever. I was a fool. A stupid, young, naive fool. We didn't even make it a year into our engagement before she started cheating on me. A buddy of mine from back home sent photos of her fucking my best friend at a Halloween party while I was stationed in Iraq. I ended things over an email with her and a fistfight with my best friend.

I re-upped my contract with the military after that and did another tour. That was the tour that changed everything. Liam enlisted that year, saying he'd wanted to follow in my footsteps. He'd said that if I was happy enough to sign on for another four years, then it was worth a shot for him. Little did he know it was the exact opposite. While I found a purpose in the army, I hated every minute of it. I wasn't there because of duty or honor; I was there because I didn't know where else to go.

Finishing out my final years after he'd been killed was hell. Coming home was even worse. My family tried to pull me out of my angry depression, but I was buried so deep in it that I almost gave up altogether. They forced me to get back into the family business, building houses, using my hands and creativity.

We began construction on our homes that year, and honestly, it saved my life. Being in nature, on our family property, with Stephen, Charlie, and our dad, bonded us in ways I'd never expected. We healed from Liam's death. Enough to function, at least, and grew closer. A year later, we each had our own custom homes, built with our own hands. I was given a second chance at the future I'd always wanted, and though I genuinely thought I'd never get it, I held out hope.

Looking at Shiloh now, I know I held out for the right reasons. It was her. All along, she was the one I was waiting for.

"Logan," she whispers, her eyes cracking open momentarily before she closes them again, blinking heavily. "You're back."

A wide smile spreads across my face, and my heartbeat picks up. My hands reach down, cupping her round cheeks as I drop my forehead to hers. She smells so fucking good. Like vanilla and cupcakes. It reminds me of home.

"I'll always come back to you, Babydoll. You hungry?" My words are a husky whisper against her. I want to cover her face in sweet kisses just as badly as I want to fuck her into this couch. I do neither, but I also don't move away.

I realized when I left earlier that I've basically bulldozed my way into her life. I forced her to get in my truck, to come home with me. Fuck, I practically locked her in my house like some kind of kidnapping situation. I don't want to force her into this life with me or take away her choices, but I've found that I can't help it when it comes to her.

I can't stop. She's mine, and I'll be fucked if she thinks she can leave me. That doesn't mean I shouldn't give her space or at least the illusion of it...until she comes around, that is.

She smiles and shakes her head, keeping her eyes squeezed closed. "Sleepy," she murmurs. My smile widens, and another thought dawns on me. I've smiled more since Shiloh walked into my life than I have in the last 15 years.

"Okay," I murmur, and this time, I do kiss her. She kisses me back, but it's weak and soft like she can barely move her mouth. My girls exhausted. Fuck, I should have known. She must have barely slept with the shit going down at her place last night. "Let's get you to bed."

I slide my hands beneath her body and pick her up, blanket and all. She tenses but then melts into me, curving her body into my chest. My cock hardens to the point of pain, and the thick material of my work jeans rubs against it as I walk, but I don't care. The feeling of her in my arms is everything.

Reaching the hall, I hesitate. I want her in my bed, *our* bed, more than anything. I want to fall asleep with her in my arms every fucking night for the rest of my life. I want to wake up every morning and lazily make love to her when we're still half-asleep, enjoying each other's bodies slowly. I want to be next to her for every fucking moment until I die, worshipping her, enjoying her, *loving her.*

But I meant what I said earlier. It has to be her choice. She has to know what getting in my bed means. When she steps through that door, she needs to know that I'm never letting her go again.

Gritting my teeth, I turn to the right and make my way to the spare bedroom. *It's just for now,* I tell myself. *Just give her time.* Easier said than done. I kick the door open softly, finding it exactly how I'd left it earlier, her bags on the ground and pillows in a pile on the armchair. She must not have moved at all this afternoon.

Leaning down, I gently settle her on the bed, smiling when she refuses to release her hold on my shirt. Reluctantly, I peel her tiny fingers away and hand her a pillow to cuddle instead. I want nothing more than to curl up next to her, but I noticed Porkchop still wasn't back when I got home, and I need to head out to find her before it gets too dark.

It takes a great amount of effort to leave Shiloh alone in a bed that's not mine, but I do it. A pit forms in my stomach, clenching and clawing at my guts as I close the door behind me. It feels wrong.

So fucking wrong.

It's just for now, I remind myself again. I'll keep saying it as many times as I need to until it sinks in. Let's just hope it doesn't take too long for her to decide.

It takes me over an hour to find the big beastie, and I almost piss myself laughing when I finally do. Out of all the places I assumed Shiloh's dog would be, never in a million years would I guess the dog would be curled up in a ball in my ten-pound chihuahua's doghouse in the backyard.

What's even more shocking is that Tank, my long-haired, handicapped rescue, is curled up with her, right in the center of their makeshift bed.

"Well, Tank. Looks like you got a new sister, too," I chuckle, snapping a photo of the two of them for Shiloh to see when she wakes up. Porkchop ignores me, settling her massive paw protectively over Tank's hindlegs, wheels, and all. "He's a little wobbly sometimes, but he's not broken.

Just be careful with the little guy," I say sternly. In response, the huge dog uses her paw to pull Tank closer.

Smiling, I leave them to it, happy that the new siblings are getting along so well. I'll admit, when I first saw Shiloh's bear-sized dog in the breakroom, I was worried about introducing her to Tank. I rescued him from a Veterans adoption facility when I moved into this place. The animals are all rescued from war zones worldwide and sent to Vets who have been through similar experiences.

Tank was injured by an IED and lost his ability to use his back legs. His long tan hair was singed off permanently in some areas, but his skin healed well. The non-profit worked wonders on his body, but his mind still struggles. He has a lot of anxiety, which is why he spends his days with my mom when I'm at work. Though the war may have damaged his body, his spirits never once suffered. He's a fighter and survivor. We understand each other.

After making a quick dinner of chicken, steamed broccoli, and mashed potatoes, I set everything in the oven to keep warm for when she wakes up. I try to keep myself busy, giving her space instead of laying on the bed and watching her sleep the way I want to. I last ten minutes before I find myself upstairs, hovering outside her door.

"Just leave her the fuck alone," I growl, forcing myself to turn around seconds before barging into her room. The upstairs loft is as far as I can physically distance myself, and I decide it's good enough as I drop down onto the couch. The cushion bounces with my weight, and something hard lands on the floor. Bending down, I pick up a small, thin electronic device.

Squinting, I turn the item over in my hands, inspecting it. I'm not a backwoods hillbilly; I know about technology. I even use a tablet on job sites. But this thing is way too small to be an iPad and too big to be a phone. Finding a tiny button on the bottom, I press it, waking the screen. Words cover the display, and it takes me a second of reading to realize it's a book, which means this thing's an e-reader. My mom got one for Christmas last year. I'm pretty sure she called it a Kindle.

I've never used one, and even though the display is black and white, the touch screen is quick and responsive. I flick through the pages, moving backward so as not to lose her place. I scan the words briefly, wanting to know what kinds of books my girl enjoys reading. I want to know everything about her. *Everything*.

My eyes widen when I land on a certain passage that's highlighted with a little note attached to it. The words are graphic and borderline vulgar, but even I have to admit, they're hot as fuck.

What is this? Porn? Goddamn, Babygirl.

The chapter is written from the main female characters' perspective. She's describing, in great detail I might add, the way her lover's body looks as he undresses for her. Of course, he's ripped, built like a Greek God, tall, and covered in tattoos. I scoff, rolling my eyes. Would it kill someone to write about a manly dude with a hairy chest and beer belly every once in a while? Where's the dad-bod representation?

As I go on, I find that the guy, Westley, has black hair and a jaw made of stone. His eyes are blue, and in all honestly, he's kind of a fucking asshole. I ignore all that, focusing on the story itself and the insanely detailed sex scene. I'd be lying if I said my cock wasn't hard three sentences in.

The way the author describes Westley eating out his girl's cunt, fucking her with his fingers and tongue, devouring her like she's his favorite meal, is hot as hell. By the time I've read two paragraphs, I'm pulling my dripping dick out.

Thank God this thing is so small. I can hold it with one hand and jack off with the other. It's almost like they made it with this kinda thing in mind.

My fist slides up and down my cock slowly, using my precum as lube, while I read through the scene. She bends down, ready to take his dick in her mouth, and mine twitches in response. *Fuck yeah.* My heart thumps in my chest as excitement and need pool low in my gut. I come across another highlighted passage, and I smirk, wanting to know what my girl liked so much she had to save it for later.

My eyes drift across the words, taking them in as I stroke my cock.

"I don't want to fuck your mouth, Kitten. I want your cunt," Westley growls, his breath fanning over my face with every word. "Do you want that? My cock and my knot, so deep in you I split your pussy in half?" I moan, nodding vehemently. God, yes, I want that so bad. "Say it, Kitten.

Tell me you want my knot. Tell me you want me to fill your pussy with my seed. Tell me you want me to breed you."

I still. My hand falls from my throbbing cock as I read the passage again.

And again.

And again.

My brows furrow. What the fuck is a knot? I get the seed and breeding part. Both the words and the idea make another wave of precum spurt from my dick, but my brain keeps pausing on the knot part. Do I have one? Is that another word for cock?

I skim through the chapter, seeking out the word in hopes of an explanation. A few pages later, I find it.

"Take it, baby. Take my cock, all of it," Wes grunts, thrusting harder into my aching pussy. Oh my god, he feels amazing. His mouth drops down to my neck, and he bites the flesh below my ear. A shiver wracks my body as anticipation fills me.

"You want me to claim you? Mate you? Are you ready for it, baby? Me and you, forever." I nod, moaning loudly at the thought. I want it so bad. "I'm gonna keep breeding you again and again." His thrusts pick up, and his huge dick pistons into me so deeply I can feel him against my cervix.

"Keep your belly big and round with my babies. Keep you filled with my cum every fucking day for the rest of your life. You want that?"

"Yes!" I scream, my orgasm crashing into me like a tidal wave, brought on by the impact of his words. I want his ba-

bies so bad it hurts. I want him to breed me, mate me, more than anything...except— "I want your knot, Wes, please!"

"Shit," he shouts, shoving his cock deep, forcing his thick knot past my sopping entrance. It hurts, but it's the best thing I've ever felt. "Shit, Jade, your pussy's strangling me. Let me in. Take my knot. I need to fill you right the fuck now."

I relax, letting him in. His knot enters me with a pop, locking us together seconds before he's filling me with his hot seed.

"Take my cum, baby. All of it. I'm gonna knock you up, Jade. Fill you with so much fuckin' cum, you'll be pregnant by the time we're done." Then, his teeth are sinking into my neck. The sharp burst of pain is quickly washed out by the overwhelming euphoria of our bond snapping into place.

He's mine. Mine for life. Mine forever. Mate.

Without even touching my cock, I explode. I cum so hard, and so long it pools all over my shirt and dick. I barely stifle my groan of pleasure as my head drops onto the back of the couch. My heart's racing, and I'm breathing heavily with the force of my orgasm. What the hell was that? Erotica? Fuck, that was like some mystical voodoo shit.

God, I think it's safe to say I have a breeding kink.

I breathe deeply, forcing my heart rate back to normal. Ripping my shirt off, I clean up the mess and tuck my cock back into my pants. I'm pissed off at myself for cumming without Shiloh, and a wave of self-hatred washes over me, dampening my post-orgasmic bliss. *Shit.*

My eyes drop back down to the Kindle, and curiosity replaces some of my irritation. There were a lot of highlighted quotes in the chapter, and I'd only read like ten pages. All of them were about that knot thing, which I can only surmise is a special doodad at the bottom of the guy's cock that helps knock the woman up. Though it seemed like the chick really liked it, so maybe it's more of a *his and her pleasure* type deal.

Is it a sex toy? An upgrade? Like a Cock 2.0, or is it an expansion pack?

Picking the Kindle back up, I glance at the hallway, making sure Shiloh's still tucked in her room. Finding the door closed, I look back down at the open book. Indecision flits through me for all of five seconds before I'm clicking the back arrow, taking me to her library.

It's just research, I tell myself; *it's for Shiloh.*

Four hours later, I've found every single one of her highlighted passages in her saved books, and I've come to a very interesting conclusion.

Shiloh Huxley has an unbelievably intense breeding, knotting, and stuffing kink. Yes, that last ones a thing.

My girl *fucking loves* cum. Love's reading about cunts being stuffed so full of it that it's dripping down their thighs for hours. Loves the idea of their pussy's being so full of seed that there's no way they aren't getting knocked up. Shiloh highlighted *hundreds* of quotes about being bred and knotted, which I now have a pretty good understanding of.

My girl likes when men talk filthy, and by that, I mean straight-up *nasty*. I even found myself adding some of the quotes to the notes section of my phone because they were so fucking hot. I wanted to make sure I remembered to say them to my girl when I stuff her full of my own cock and cum.

Soon. My already aching and throbbing cock pulses in agreement. I've been hard this entire time. I honestly don't understand how women read shit like this with pants on. God, do they read it in public? I would die. Straight up, die. I'd be fucking my fist in a public bathroom like a pervert if I tried to read these books out in the wild. I'd be walking around with a nine-inch boner pressing against my zipper all day.

The whole time I was reading, thought after thought of me filling Shiloh with my cum circled around my brain. Before, it was like a craving. A desperate, twisted idea that I've had from the first time I saw her. A way to keep her locked to me for life. Me and me, alone. *Mine.*

But now? Now it's like a visceral need. I feel like I'll die if I don't get my cock and cum in her pussy soon. I need her so fucking full of my seed that there won't be any doubt or question who she belongs to.

Groaning, I close out of the book I'd been reading and pull up the one Shiloh left off on, so she doesn't know what I've been up to. I drop the device on the coffee table and pick up my phone to check the time. Fuck, it's after midnight. Shiloh's still asleep, and it's safe to say she won't be eating dinner. I move to get up and clean the kitchen when a thought crosses my mind.

If Shiloh likes the idea of breeding so much, does that mean she wants a baby? Is she aching for a family as badly as I am? And what about this whole knotting thing? Almost every book she had contained dudes with knotty cocks in them. Is that something she needs? Something my cock's not capable of?

A burning fire fills me instantly at the thought of her finding someone else who can do what I can't. *No. Not happening.* Shaking my head, I open the search engine on my phone and look up *knots.* The search comes up with millions of knitting and craft results which makes no sense, so I try again.

Knot Sex

Hundreds of book recommendations pop up, and not for the first time tonight, I consider buying my own Kindle. Exiting the search, I ignore the thought, putting it off until later as I continue my hunt. Search after search comes up empty. Thinking about the types of books with knots in them, I remember most of them had these things called shifters in them. A lot of them were wolves.

Knotted wolf dick.

Holy fucking hell.

I may or may not lose twenty minutes of my life looking at fanfic art of wolves with big, weird-looking cocks railing hot women.

My head is a very confusing place right now, but my dick seems to be solidly on board.

Groaning, I try one last time, hoping this last one works. If it does, it means I still have a shot.

Knot Sex Toy.

Bing-fucking-O.

Hell yes. An hour and hundreds of dollars later, I'm filled with renewed excitement. In 1-3 business days, I'm going to make my woman's knotty fantasies come true.

IT'S MY CHOICE
Be patient with yourself
Unapologetic MYSELF
Love yourself
Be Bold
ALL BODIES ARE GOOD BODIES
beautiful
Yes you can
Fearless
be happy
HERE TO STAY
IN CONTROL
LOVE yours
I am enough
FEEL DEEPLY
your potential is endl
be kind to yourself
It's my choice
I am exactly where I need to be
I am capable
beautiful
breathe
Perfect

Shiloh

Thirteen

"Good morning, Babydoll." Smiling, Logan sets a full stack of pancakes on the kitchen island next to a steaming cup of coffee. I stumble over my feet, my brows furrowed as I take in the scene before me. Logan, the big, hairy, muscled lumbersnack, is shirtless and making me breakfast.

He's shirtless.

Logan is shirtless and not wearing a shirt.

I think my brain is misfiring.

No. I think it's broken. My eyes are caught on his chest. On the miles of light skin covered in freckles and a dusting of red hair that trails over his perfectly sculpted six pack, leading down...down...

Down.

My eyes home in on the very obvious bulge protruding from his light gray sweats. My mouth dries so suddenly that my tongue actually gets stuck to the roof of my mouth. My eyes are wide as saucers, and my pussy lets out a flutter of acknowledgment, waking up from her slumber.

"Sleep well?" he asks, his voice laced with amusement as he notices me staring. I nod but still can't speak.

This morning, I woke up more refreshed than I have in a long time. I rolled out of bed, stumbled into a beautiful en suite that I hadn't even looked at before passing out yesterday, and took the longest shower of my life. My muscles are relaxed, my hair smells like my delicious vanilla sugar shampoo, but my stomach is empty. A fact that it loudly makes known immediately following his question.

"Sit," he grunts, pulling out a tall barstool.

"I slept like the dead," I respond, finally finding my voice as I close the distance between us. Stopping in front of him, I do my best not to gawk at his half-naked body as I continue. "I'm so sorry I slept the day away. I didn't realize I was so tired."

Logan ignores my apology as he effortlessly bends down and hefts me onto the stool. I let out a squeak of protest, my arms windmilling for balance. "Don't apologize. You needed it. I'm glad you slept. Just sorry it wasn't in my bed."

A blush fills my cheeks, leaving them burning under the weight of his words. At one point last night I had woken up. Thoughts of Logan filled my dreams all night long and one, in particular, had me shooting up in bed, searching for him. I'd almost gone to his room. It took almost an hour of restlessness and second-guessing before I fell back to sleep. Though I did sleep well, something inside of me instinctively knew I'd sleep so much better next to him.

As if on cue, his words from yesterday replay in my mind for the thousandth time.

If you step foot in my room, you better be prepared to stay forever.

My stomach clenches, and it's not from hunger. Fuck, I'm in so damn deep with this man.

"Eat, Shiloh." He pushes the plate closer to me as he speaks before returning to the other side of the island. My eyes watch his back, never losing sight of him, even as I dig into my food. There are a few visible scars on his back, and one large one across his arm, beneath a tattoo of a symbol I recognize as belonging to the United States Army. Next to it is a beginning and end date, with the words, *Rest in Peace, Brother.*

He lost someone.

"You were in the military." Things from the last few days click into place, and suddenly, it all makes sense. His panic attack yesterday. The PTSD response. His comment about being in a gunfight. His overall cagey, rough behavior. Though, that could just be him. "Did you lose someone?" I cringe as soon as the words leave my mouth, knowing not everyone likes to talk about their time in the military, especially those they lost. I know my father hates it.

Logan tenses, his hands gripping the edge of the sink as he pauses in his quiet, methodical dishwashing. His head drops, and he releases a heavy, weighted sigh.

Shit, shit, shit.

I hop down from the stool, leaving my half-eaten plate abandoned as I follow my instincts, which are screaming that he needs me. My mind and heart begin to race, worried I've brought up something too painful for him, or worse, triggered another attack. Stepping into his periphery, I make sure to stay in his line of sight, and as much as it kills me, I keep my hands to myself. *For now.*

"Fuck, Logan, I'm so sorry. I shouldn't have brought it up, especially not like that. That was careless of me." My fists tense at my sides, squeezing so hard my nails bite into my skin. Logan shakes his head, showing the first sign of awareness in minutes.

Slowly, he turns toward me. His face is guarded, his brows pinched together tightly. His bright green eyes look darker now, almost completely taken over by the pupils. He looks so.... *broken.* I can't take it.

"Oh, baby," I breathe, my eyes burning with emotion. I take a step forward, closing the distance between us, and wrap my arms around his waist, squeezing him tightly. Logan doesn't move, but his heaving breaths slow the longer I hold him. "Come back to me," I whisper.

Seconds later, his body shudders against mine. His arms instantly band around me, one gripping my low back, the other palming my head. He presses our bodies tightly together and leans in, inhaling deeply. "Cupcakes," he grunts. I swallow down a choked laugh, but it still comes out in a small giggle. "Beautiful. *My Shiloh.*"

I don't know why I utter what I do next, but right now, in this perfect house built for a family, wrapped in this broken, incredible man's embrace....

It feels right.

"Yours," I agree.

Logan stills, his muscles tensing. His heart picks up its heavy pounding beat beneath my cheek once more, and for a second, I worry that I'm losing him again. He pushes me away, peeling my body from his, and my stomach bottoms out. What did I do?

But then, Logan's hands are on my face, his eyes wide as he stares down at me. "Say it again," he demands, his voice rougher than I've ever heard him sound before. It takes me a moment for his words to click, but when they do, I smile.

My heart races, and this time, it's in excitement. I'm not nervous about what this could mean. I'm not worried about the future. I'm just...happy.

"*I'm yours.*"

Then, his lips are on mine. Logan palms my cheeks softly, even as his mouth dominates mine. He controls our kiss completely, and I let him. I go weak, allowing him to give and take, opening when he wants, giving him access when he demands. He pushes my body backward, and I stumble, grasping his hips for balance. He presses me into the island, locking me in place, his mouth never leaving mine.

Logan's mouth is electric. It's live wires and lighting bolts in the middle of a hot summer storm. Electricity crackles between us, burning me alive. My nerve endings tingle beneath my skin, from head to toe, even as my brain short circuits. My stomach is full of butterflies, fluttering around with massive wings, scraping against my ribcage. Or, maybe that's my heart, trying to escape my chest.

He thrusts his leg between my thighs, and I gasp into his mouth. My pussy clenches in anger and frustration at being so completely empty when all it wants is his big, thick cock. His hand's palm at my breasts, tweaking my hard nipples through my dress and bra. I resent them, the clothes. I resent every single layer between us, even as he lifts his knee, connecting it with my drenched core, only separated by a thin pair of wet panties and his sweats.

Logan's mouth becomes firmer on mine. More demanding and insistent. His teeth crash into mine as our kiss shifts from hungry to *starving*. I tug his lip into my mouth, yanking it between my teeth. My nails drag down his chest, landing on the edge of his sweats. My mouth waters.

He grinds his hips into mine, working his thigh between my legs. I know what he's doing. He's trying for a repeat of yesterday, and as much as I'd love nothing more than to squirt all over him again, that's not what I want right now.

I break the kiss as I place my palms flat on his abs. My hands clench around the hard muscle, taking the opportunity to enjoy the feel of them. *Later. I'll explore him later.* Right now, there is something else I need to do that's far more important.

His brows furrow as I separate our bodies. We're both panting. His pupils are blown wide, my hands are trembling. My pussy is dripping indecently down my thigh. But I don't care.

"What's wrong?" he breathes, his eyes darting over my body instantly, like he's checking for injury. It's sweet, really it is. "Are you okay?"

My head shakes slowly in response, my fingers curling on his stomach. "No, Logan. I'm not okay," I murmur. His eyes widen, and he begins to step back, releasing his hold on me. Before he can get too far, I drop to my knees before him. "*I'm starving.*"

Logan chokes. Literally chokes.

I take advantage of his distraction and grip the waist of his pants. My eyes focus on the massive protruding cock that's barely contained by the thin cotton. Holy shit, I love gray sweatpants.

Channeling all the Omega sex goddess energy I can muster, I rip them down, freeing him, only to discover he's going commando. His cock bobs free and smacks me right in the face. I almost follow him into a fit of choking at the sight.

Oh, I'll be choking soon enough…

"Jesus, Logan!" I whisper-shout, my wide eyes enjoying the human marvel before me. This man is literally a masterpiece. It's like all of my favorite smut books got together to create the perfect man for me, produced Logan Huxley, and deposited him right in my lap. The only thing that would make this better would be a bow wrapped around his anaconda-sized cock so I could unwrap him like the gift he is. "You're massive."

Logan barks out a laugh, having finally composed himself. His hands settle on the sides of my face, pulling my attention from his cock. "Thank you, Babydoll, that's very sweet of you to say. Now shut up and open your fucking mouth so I can feed you my cock."

My brain misfires.

I blink. Then blink again.

My mouth drops open, my eyes never leaving his. Logan lets out a feral-sounding growl as he thrusts forward, wasting no time at all. Tears instantly spring in my eyes as he hits the back of my throat. I gag, despite my best efforts not to. He starts to pull away. My hands shoot out, gripping the back of his thighs as I pull him forward, telling him without words that I'm fine.

"Shit, Babydoll. You want me to fuck your throat, don't you?" He groans, threading his fingers through my hair. I nod, licking the underside of his shaft. Logan wraps my long hair around his fists, using them like handles to control the pace. I love it. I love it a stupid, ridiculous amount. "That's it. You're taking me so well. Such a good girl for Daddy."

Daddy? Hell fucking yes, please.

I moan loudly around his cock—more turned on by his filthy mouth than I've ever been in my life. None of the men I'd been with before Logan were any good at dirty talk. If anything, their words always made me cringe and feel uncomfortable. But with Logan? Every single word out of his mouth, uttered in his deep, growly voice, is like a direct line to my clit.

One hand reaches to grip the base of his cock, working the few inches I can't possibly fit in my mouth. The other drops between my thighs and beneath my dress. I spread my thick legs further apart and slide my hand into my soaking wet panties, finding my hard clit in seconds.

"You need to cum, don't you?" he grunts, tightening his hold on my hair. I nod, my eyes pleading. Logan smirks, and the look is so unlike him, so unhinged and dominant, that I find myself entranced, waiting on edge for his commands. "Spread your perfect thighs wide so Daddy can see his pussy while he fucks your mouth."

I immediately obey, my body trembling with need. I've never been so turned on in my life. I rip my hand from my panties and yank my dress up, giving him the best view possible. I know he can't see much. My wide hips, heavy belly, and thick thighs hide most of the view, but when Logan's eyes go hooded with hungry appreciation, I know it was the right move.

"Play with your cunt, Shiloh," he growls, picking up his pace as he fucks me in short, deep thrusts. "Fuck yourself hard. I wanna see you gush all over our kitchen floor."

Ours.

Again, I obey. I relax my throat as I slide two fingers into my sopping wet pussy. My thumb finds my clit, and I curve my fingers upward, finding that elusive spot that has me trembling in seconds. Logan groans loudly as his cocks slips an inch into my throat. Then two. I swallow around him, breathing through the panic the best I can as I focus on the way we feel together.

"That's it. You're Daddy's perfect girl, aren't you, Baby-doll? My perfect little cum slut?" I moan so loud the vibrations around his cock make him shudder. "I'm gunna fill you so full of my cum, you'll be addicted. Every time you're hungry, you'll crave your Daddy's cum, Shiloh. You'll be on your knees, begging for it, won't you?"

I nod again, screaming *yes, please,* which comes out garbled around his dick. My fingers pick up the pace, and my throbbing pussy clenches and clenches with my impending orgasm. Logan's cock throbs and swells in my mouth. My jaw aches and I'm drooling all over the place, but still, I don't dare stop. I'm so close. We both are. I need this. Need him.

Need his cum.

Need it. Need it. Need it.

"Cum, Daddy," I cry out, hoping he understood my words. Logan grunts, shoving deep into my mouth, his hands palming my head in a possessive, loving way that's far too sweet for the moment but somehow has me barreling over the edge.

"I'm cumming, Babydoll. Swallow every drop, like the good cum dumpster you are." My eyes widen, and I choke. Not on his cum, but on his words. *Jesus.*

The first spurt of his cum down my throat sends me into an intense orgasm. My thighs tremble, and I part them further as I feel the first gush of hot liquid trickling from me. We cum together, our eyes locked, our bodies completely in sync, and the moment transcends into something else entirely.

We become one.

Suddenly, it's not just me, and it's not just him. It's us. It's Logan and Shiloh. Its possibilities and futures. It's a connection. A connection so deep, so perfect that it all becomes so simple and obvious. There's no point denying or questioning it any longer.

He was made for me, and I was made for him.

Everything else will just come with time.

A little while later, we're stepping onto the front deck and into the cool November air. I tug my jacket tighter across my chest and, once again, regret my choice to mostly pack dresses to wear to work. Luckily, my leggings are thick, and my knee-high boots are fur lined. After our sextivities, we'd gotten cleaned up and prepared for our day in a comfortable, happy silence.

"What are we doing out here? Aren't we going to be late?" I ask, as he tugs me forward by our joined hands. Logan looks over his shoulder, tossing me a wink and an adorable, dimpled grin. My car's still parked at the office, so for the time being we have to carpool. I pretended to complain when he'd told me, but internally, I was dancing with glee.

"I want to show you something," he grunts, tipping his chin at the coolest, custom-built dog house I've ever seen. My stomach drops to the floor as panic fills me.

Releasing Logan's hand, I screech. "Shit! Where is Pork-chop? Oh my god, I completely forgot she ran off yester-day!" In an instant, my eyes are filling with anxious tears as they scan his vast property. I'm seconds from diving off the deck to go hunt for my dog when Logan stops me with a fierce hug from behind.

"Look up, Shiloh," he murmurs, his hot breath fanning over my cheek. "She's fine. She's been here the whole time."

My rapid heartbeats slow slightly, as I look in the direc-tion he'd pointed. The doghouse. My brows furrow. It's tiny. Certainly, she can't fit inside. But then, as if to prove my unspoken thought wrong, my massive dog pokes her fluffy head out, her big, pink tongue lolling to the side in what I assume is a grin.

Holy shit, she's really okay. My heart slows, even more, regaining its natural cadence. "I'm a terrible mother," I whisper. Logan huffs a laugh, nuzzling his bearded face against mine.

"You're a wonderful dog mama, and you'll be an even better human mama." The organ in my chest clenches. With the cardio it's getting lately, I'm genuinely concerned for my health.

Tipping my head back onto his chest, my eyes take in the bright blue, cloudless sky above us. My hands begin to shake in my pockets, and it's got nothing to do with the cold.

"Logan," I murmur, my voice unsteady. He stills, sensing my emotional shift. How he can recognize my subtle cues so early into *this*, is beyond me. I'd be lying if I said I didn't love it, though. "Logan, I have to tell you something."

His body tenses for a brief moment, but he quickly relaxes, resting his chin on the top of my head. The arms banded around my middle give a reassuring squeeze. "Anything," he says softly. "*Everything.*"

Crack. Another fissure in my crumbling wall.

Shit. This is insane. Completely and utterly insane. How can my heart be breaking over a man I've just met? Breaking over the knowledge that he won't want me anymore as soon as I tell him my secret. The thought causes my knees to buckle. As though he senses me growing weak and dizzy with fear and nerves, Logan's arms tighten even more. He tugs me into his body, pressing us together so deeply, I'm not sure where I end, and he begins.

"Tell me, Babydoll. Whatever it is, we'll get through it together. I take care of what's mine, and that's you now, Shiloh."

Crack.

"Logan, I—" a loud bark, followed by another much smaller one, breaks the tense silence and has me jolting in his arms. My eyes fly toward the doghouse seconds before something light runs over my booted foot. My gaze snaps down, and I let out an embarrassingly loud screech of excitement. I drop to my knees. The fall softened by Logan's hold on me. "Oh my god! Who are you?"

Tiny black eyes peer up at me in shock. Whether from my scream or my sudden presence, I'm not sure. My eyes rake over the tiny dog's body, zeroing in on its midsection where a harness supports a wheeled contraption over its damaged hind legs. Its skin is mottled with scars and patchy light brown hair, yet, it's one of the cutest animals I've ever seen.

Logan chuckles as he bends down next to me, scooping the tiny god up. "This is Tank. He's been through some shit." I huff and roll my eyes at his explanation because *duh*. He passes the dog to me, and I gently bundle him in my arms. "Come on, we gotta drop the kids off at my mom's before we head in."

A tendril of anxiety wraps itself around my throat, but it's quickly washed out by overwhelming joy.

The kids.

He says it so simply. The way the words roll off his tongue, as though second nature, does something to me. Logan is so sure, so steadfast, in his belief that we're inevitable. No, not even. In his mind, we're already together. He speaks of babies and futures like he and I are a foregone conclusion.

It scares me, but not nearly as much as it fills me with a giddy type of euphoria. All thoughts cease as my body moves on instinct, following Logan down the short flight of stairs from the deck. I follow him blindly, fully trusting him to lead me in the right direction. It's a wild feeling. My implicit trust in a near stranger.

The thing is; Logan doesn't feel like a stranger. He feels like *forever.*

"Porkchop!" he calls out, wrapping his thick arm around my shoulders as we make our way toward the garage, where his truck idles, warm and ready. Logan glances up at the sky, then down at my dog. He jerks a quick nod, having come to some sort of decision. Opening the back door, he points in a silent command.

My heart squeezes. He cares enough about my dog's comfort to allow her in his nice truck, dirty paws and all. *He's perfect.*

Moving to the front, he helps me in, my arms still holding Tank safely. He buckles me in and presses his mouth to my forehead in a lingering, sweet kiss.

Crack.

A few minutes later, we're pulling up in front of an equally beautiful home, similar in style to Logans. My heart thumps, picking up its pace as he jumps out. I move to unbuckle my seatbelt, unsure of what to do, but pause, my hand hovering in midair. Am I ready to meet his family? Shit. Are we moving too fast? We know nothing about each other. We can't—

"Don't worry, Babydoll. You aren't meeting them." My head snaps up, glancing at him over my shoulder. Porkchop hops out, following Logan like he's her new bestie. He opens my door, taking Tank from my arms. My stomach does a flip, and this time, it's in disappointment. "I want you to meet my whole family, Shiloh, and you will."

He closes my door and jogs away. The door opens and an older, red-haired woman, peaks out. She tries to push him aside, and the sight makes me chuckle. She's tiny compared to Logan. They go back and forth, clearly in a heated discussion. Finally, she looks down at the two dogs and smiles. She waves in my direction, a wide smile on her aging face. Unsure what to do and feeling mildly uncomfortable, I smile back and wave. She disappears, the dogs trailing behind her, then closes the door.

"We're coming for a family dinner on Sunday," Logan grunts, climbing into his seat. My head swings to the side, finding him already looking at me. He swallows thickly, his brows dipping as he mutters, "that okay?"

My face splits into a huge smile that quickly morphs into a laugh. "Are you really asking me that?"

Cranking the wheel, he spins the truck around, pointing us toward the main highway that will take us to town. His eyes narrow further as he looks from me to the road, then back at me. "What do you mean?"

"Well, normally, you kind of just tell me what we're doing. You don't usually ask for permission."

Logan shakes his head, his lips tipping up in a sexy smirk that goes straight to my pussy. God, I really need him to fuck me soon. "Fine. We're going to family dinner Sunday whether you like it or not. Better?"

Grinning, I nod and wrap my hand around his, initiating contact for the second time. It's becoming increasingly difficult not to be touching him at all times. I'm afraid I'm becoming just as obsessed as he is.

We sit in comfortable silence for a while as we weave through the wilderness. Massive pine trees cover the land, a light layer of snow coating their branches. My mind is calm and content for the first time since I don't know when. I'm not thinking about my health issues or my future.

I'm not worried about who my man could be fucking on the side since I'm not getting any. I'm not worried about my weight or how I look to anyone else. I'm not even thinking about the tragic state of my house anymore.

All I can do is focus on *him.* I see *him,* feel *him,* smell *him.* It's all Logan.

When did that happen, and how did it happen so quickly?

I don't worry about how my body looks or doesn't look when I'm with him. It's clear as day that Logan loves how my body looks. I haven't thought about my rental, because in the grand scheme of things, it's all just *stuff.* Stuff I don't need, stuff left over from a shit show of a marriage. It's a house, but it's not mine, and it never felt like home.

Logan's house does, though.

Correction. Logan feels like home.

"I had a good childhood," Logan murmurs, his voice gravelly, pulling me from my happy thoughts. I look up, finding his eyes locked on the road before us, his face unreadable. He squeezes my hand, threading our fingers together and settling them on his lap. "I'm the oldest of four boys, and growing up, I loved having a big family. Our parents were always around, and our grandparents lived on our property. We were happy, close as hell. Spent a lot of time together, especially out in the woods."

He pauses, a smile tipping up the corners of his lips. I lean in, listening with bated breath as he tells me his life story. I eat up every single word, eager for more.

"My parents are in love. Have been since day one, and they've never hidden that. They're affectionate, openly. They have a love that I thought didn't exist in real life, but they showed us what it could be like, you know?" He glances toward me, his eyes raking over my body, heating immediately at what he sees. Tugging my lip between my teeth as a blush spread over my cheeks, I nod. "I always wanted that. A big family. A wife to love, to cherish, and worship. I wanted all of it. Still do."

His hand squeezes mine, punctuating his words. Butterflies break out in my gut, flapping their huge wings wildly. His eyes leave mine, and his jaw ticks as he focuses on the road again.

"You said four?" I cut in, his previous words trickling through the spell he has me under. "I've met Stephen, and he'd mentioned your youngest brother, Charlie, but no one else."

Logan shakes his head once, his hand flexing on mine. "No, he wouldn't mention him. Our youngest brother, the baby of the family, Liam, died when he was 18." My heart sinks. I open my mouth...to say what? No idea. But the sadness and devastation etched across his face demands I say something, to do something, anything, to help. Logan shakes his head. My mouth snaps shut as he trudges on.

He tells me all about his past, his childhood, and what led to Liam's death. He tells me about Sadie and the fight with his dad. About Liam looking up to him and following in his footsteps. He tells me about how he almost lost his battle with depression, riddled with PTSD and flashbacks when he returned from the military. And all the while, I listen and I cry.

I cry for the man he could have been, the man he was. I cry for the brother he, and his family lost way too soon. I cry for the heartbreak in his eyes, the deep, soul-wrenching pain he so clearly feels. I cry when his voice breaks. I cry harder when tears drip down his cheeks.

Logan doesn't look at me once. He doesn't stop speaking until he does, his eyes remaining on the road the entire time. He doesn't offer platitudes or hopeful sentiments. He just simply tells his story. He empties the contents of his mind, his heart, and his soul right there in the cab of the pickup. What he does do, though, is hold my hand. He holds it as though I'm his lifeline, the only thing connecting him to this world.

And I hold him back, wishing I could do more.

With every word, every devastating and brutally honest admission, I feel more for him. I feel so many big emotions for this incredible man, that by the time he stops talking, one thing is plainly and obviously clear.

I am falling head over heels in love with Logan Huxley, and there is not a damn thing I can do to stop it.

BE PATIENT WITH YOURSELF

Unapologetic MYSELF

BE Bold

ALL BODIES are GOOD BODIES

be happy

YOURSELF

beautiful

yes you can

fearless

HERE TO STAY

IN CONTROL

LOVE yourself

I am enough

FEEL DEEPLY

YOUR POTENTIAL is endl

be kind to yourself

Brave

It's my choice

I am exactly where I need to be

you are worthy

love you

I am capable

YOU ARE enough

breathe

Perfect

Fourteen

"Are you sure the dogs will be fine with your parents overnight?" I ask as I jump from the lifted truck. Logan releases a barked curse, ignoring my question.

Before he can accost me, I tug the waistband of my jeans up, doing a little wiggle and making sure everything's tucked away. I'm smoothing down my lacy sweater by the time he reaches me, none the wiser to the issues high-waisted jeans cause women with fupas.

My outfit's far more form-fitting and revealing than anything I'd ever worn around Cole. I almost second-guessed the whole thing, but when Logan had seen me step out of my room this evening, his reaction calmed my nerves.

Okay, correction. His reaction made me want to jump his bones.

"Don't do that," he growls, wrapping his large, calloused hand around mine.

Smirking, I roll my eyes. "Do what? Help myself out of the truck for once? Behave like a grown ass, independent woman?" I scoff. "I've been independent my entire life, Logan. Hell, I was basically taking care of myself, even when I was married."

Logan comes to an abrupt halt.

Shit.

Panic fills me in an instant. I hadn't meant to say that. Slowly, he pivots, turning to face me. "Excuse me?" he murmurs, his voice barely audible over the loud music coming from the bar behind him.

I don't respond—*can't.* I can't even bring myself to look at him. Tugging my hand, I try to pull away, needing the distance, and needing the space.

Needing to protect myself from the impending rejection.

Logan tightens his grip, refusing to let me go. He steps forward, closing the distance between us. I don't allow it, retreating as he advances. He walks me backward, step by step until there's nowhere left to go. My back hits the truck and anxiety claws at my throat. His meaty palms land on either side of my head, bracing himself against the cold metal as he bends down, bringing us face to face.

"Look at me," he grunts. I ignore him, staring dutifully at my boots. I'm wearing my black leather pair tonight, the ones with a stiletto heel. They're my favorites. They make my legs look a mile long, and my round ass look nice and plump. "Look at me, Shiloh." His fingers grip my chin tightly, tipping my head back. Reluctantly, I meet his eyes. Though it's difficult to see them in the dark, I can tell they're narrowed as he stares down at me. "Wanna run that by me again?"

"Not really," I mutter, swallowing thickly around the lump in my throat.

He growls. Legit *growls* and I almost pass out from the sound. *Shit,* he's gone all feral like some sort of bear shifter from one of my smutty books. My pussy throbs. Thoughts of all the filthy, knotty things those bears always do to their mates fill my head.

We stand in silence, our eyes locked together in a battle of wills. Finally, he breaks the tense stare down with words that shock me to my core. "Are you married, Shiloh?" His voice is guttural like he tore the words from his very soul.

My eyes widen as anger and indignation rapidly consume me. "What?" I all but shriek. "You-you—" I break off. My words and emotions are a mess. I run my fingers through my long, silky hair, creating tangles at the ends where they brush across my breasts. "How could you even think that, Logan? You think I'm what—here with you, cheating on my husband?"

He grunts out a sound that could honestly mean any number of things. Eyeing me, he takes in every inch of my face, my body, and my behavior. He's analyzing me, trying to figure out if I'm being honest. Finally, he sighs, his body deflating some. "Tell me," he murmurs, settling his hands on my hips. "*Please, Babydoll.*"

It's the *please* that breaks me. Breaks my will, and my resistance. As difficult as it is to talk about everything that happened with Cole, I owe it to Logan. He's been nothing but wonderful to me, especially for the last few days.

He bared his soul for me this morning and all day at work, telling me tidbits of information about his life and his family. What it was like growing up in the country. I reciprocated, regaling stories about growing up in a low-income part of town in a mixed-race family. I told him all about my parents and how much they struggled financially. How much it affected our family and ultimately caused them to split when I was a teen.

I told him about my dad and his battle with PTSD. I told him how my entire family needed so much distance from one another that we all split, moving to different states the moment we were old enough. I told him that I love my sister Camila, but I kind of can't stand her. I told him that even if my family and childhood were shit, I still can't wait to have one of my own someday.

He learned my favorite food and ice cream. Where I went to college and my major. My birthday, my favorite holiday. The fact that I prefer rose gold over all other metals...an odd question he'd randomly asked. He learned that I'm allergic to peaches but love the smell of them anyways.

Today, Logan learned all there is to know about me and then some. I told him everything.

Except...*this*.

I couldn't bring myself to do it. We'd had such an incredible morning that turned into an even better day. He held my hand, rubbed my neck, and played with my hair. Always needing to have his hands on me in one way or another. He kissed me stupid while we waited for the coffeepot to brew, and again when he returned from running errands. He explained the situation with my house as he fed me a home-cooked lunch, leftovers from the meal I'd missed last night.

It was bliss. Utter perfection.

I didn't want to ruin it the way I am now as I tell him the sordid details of my relationship with Cole. The beginning, middle and tragic end.

I tell him about my PCOS and my miscarriage. I tell him how Cole lied and manipulated me into staying with him, despite the fact that he never wanted what I did. The way he body-shamed me, both verbally and physically. The way his actions and words made me feel. The heartache over my inability to conceive and the loss of my child, but the absence of heartache when I left my husband.

With every broken word and devastating reality that I give him, my soul lightens. I cry, and Logan holds me. I purge everything, right there in the middle of a busy parking lot, out front of one of the only bars Blue River has. I give Logan the burden of my past, letting go of the ugly pieces once and for all.

And he...takes them.

He holds me, wiping away my tears. He rocks my body, swaying us as I work through my catharsis. He doesn't get mad or resentful. He doesn't say hurtful things or push me away. He just holds me and listens.

When I've finally finished, snot is running from my nose, matching the steady tears streaming from my eyes. Logan peels my face from his chest and, once again, sends a wave of devastating cracks through the wall wrapped around my heart as he lowers his mouth to mine and fuses our lips together. He kisses me like his life depends on it. Like he needs me to fuel his every breath.

When he finally releases me, I'm breathing hard and leaning on him fully, allowing him to hold me up. Something in my heart shifts once more. Knowing that if I give him the chance, Logan will *always* keep me standing.

One of his hands grips my head, tilting my face side to side as he uses the sleeve of his flannel to dry my face gently. When he's done, he palms my cheeks and tilts my head back. "Are you okay?" he murmurs. I nod, then shake my head before shrugging helplessly. I have no idea how I feel right now. Logan smiles softly. "Do you wanna go home?"

"Home?" I breathe, hope soaring in my chest.

Leaning forward, he presses his mouth to my forehead in a whisper of a kiss. His lips brush against my skin as he mumbles, "Yeah, Babydoll. Home, with me."

My eyes close without thought as I wrap my arms around his waist and breathe in his pine and rain smell. It's freezing outside, but here, in Logan's arms, I feel warmer than ever before. It's a different kind of warmth, though. One that penetrates through my skin, passes through my bones and organs and settles deep in my soul.

"I thought you'd have more to say," I murmur, my words muffled by his heavy coat. Logan huffs out a humorless laugh and exhales heavily.

"Oh, I've got a fuck ton to say, but I don't think now's the time for any of it." My body tenses with his words, but he quickly continues. "I'm not mad at you, Shiloh. None of what happened was your fault, and this changes nothing. Do you hear me? *Nothing.*"

"But what about kids, Logan?" I ask, pulling away with a sniffle. I have to know. Have to make it clear to him. "There's a chance that I—"

"No, there's not," he growls, gripping my chin, this time much harder. "You *can* and *will* be a mama, Babydoll. One way or another, you will be. If we have to adopt, then we do. If you want to foster a hundred kids who need a family, we will. If you wanna spend the rest of our lives trying to make a baby that's a little of you and a little of me, then we'll do that. And if it never happens, then I'll enjoy the honor of stuffing you full of my cum every chance I get, till I die."

My breath wooshes out of me, and a moan escapes with it. "You have to stop saying things like that to me."

He cocks a brow. "Why?"

"Because if you don't, I'll be begging you for babies and a ring by next week," I chuckle, trying to dismiss the honesty of my words as a joke. But inside...inside I'm fucking *dying*.

Logan doesn't laugh. He doesn't even smile. No, he does the opposite. Before I know what's happening, his hand is wrapped around my throat, not hard enough to cut off my air, but enough to show me who's in control right now. He presses me against the truck and bends, bringing us face to face.

"You better decide right this fucking second if we're going into that bar or not, Babydoll, because the second I get you home, I'll be balls deep in your perfect pussy. And I guarantee that when I do, I'll be fucking a baby into you."

"Logan," I groan, my pussy throbbing in time with his words. "*Please.*"

"Please, what, Shiloh? Be very fucking clear. Are we going in or not? Either way, it's my cock you'll be riding tonight. My cock that's gonna put baby after baby in your belly. *Mine.*"

Oh my god, oh my god, oh my god!

"*Yours,*" I nod, my head spinning with the need his words have created in me. Holy hell. He better be serious because not only has my pussy fully jumped on board with that plan, but my heart has as well. We stare at each other, the tension and desire so thick between us, I'm practically choking on it. "I—"

"Shiloh! Logan! Hurry the hell up!" Stephen barks, shocking us both back to reality. Logan's head snaps toward the bar, finding Stephen, Dom, and a man I don't know staring back at us, amused looks on their faces. "We've been waiting for half an hour."

Logan grunts, glaring at his brother as he slowly releases my neck. I lean in, chasing the sensation, making him chuckle. Looking back down at me, his lips quirk as he tilts his chin at the men, leaving the decision up to me.

Smiling at the man who has barreled into my life and changed everything I thought I knew about love and possibilities; I reach down and wrap my hand around his.

"Come on, Daddy," I purr with a smirk, tugging him along.

His resounding groan goes straight to my clit.

"We're getting another round," Dom declares, grabbing my hand and yanking me from my seat. Logan cocks a brow at us, his eyes dropping to where our hands are connected. His face scrunches up adorably in irritation.

Rolling my eyes, I press a sloppy kiss to his cheek, making sure to leave a nice imprint of my lipstick behind. His hand darts out to slap my ass, but I dance out of his reach with a giggle. His possessive ways are a bit much, but secretly, I love it. The entire time we've been here, he's had me practically sitting in his lap, a claiming hand around the back of my neck. I like it...probably too much.

Safe to say, it's been the longest two hours of my life.

I hope he meant what he said about fucking me tonight.

"We'll be back, boys," I announce, wiggling my fingers over my shoulder as Dom and I sashay away. We laugh, stumbling over our feet as we make our way to the bar.

Scooters is a staple in Blue River, or so I've been told. It's really cute, in an older, rustic country bar kind of way. Most of the crowd is here for drunken line-dancing with the live band, which I've found hilariously entertaining to watch.

Being originally from a large city, then moving to Denver before coming this direction, my experience with country living is limited. Though I've lived in Blue River for a couple of years, I haven't gone out to explore much. The school Cole and I worked at was in a larger, more modern town up the road, and he preferred to spend most of our free time there. I assume he still does.

Leaning against the bar next to Dom, I shake off thoughts of my shitty ex and order another beer for myself and Logan. Dom does the same for him and Stephen before grabbing another water for Roman who doesn't drink alcohol.

"Sooo..." Dom drawls, bumping my hip with his. Turning a megawatt smile in my direction, he waggles his eyebrows. "Tell me, tell me, tell me! I'm dying to know what's going on between you two!"

Groaning, I rub the space between my brows, feigning irritation as my heart gives a squeeze at just the thought of him. "There's nothing to tell," I lie. "We're just—" I break off, loathing the word *friends* even existing on my tongue.

Swallowing down the lie, I glance at Logan over my shoulder, finding him laughing loudly at something Roman had said. His head is tipped back, his cheeks are pink and his dimples peeking from beneath his beard.

He's beautiful.

I know that's weird to say about a guy, but it's true. He's beautiful and handsome. He's sweet, funny, caring, and considerate. He's everything I never knew existed in another human being, especially someone who would want to be with me.

"That's bullshit, Shiloh!" Dom barks. My eyes snap back and widen when I realize I've just said all of that out loud.

"Shit, I didn't mean to say all that," I say quickly, my cheeks burning with embarrassment. "Maybe I'm drunker than I thought." Which is odd since I've only had two beers and a ton of carbs to keep me sober.

Dom's thick black brows knit together. He shakes his head once. "No, girl, I don't think that was the alcohol talking. That was something else entirely."

"Oh yeah?" I smirk, "And what would that be? The cheese sticks?"

He scoffs, tipping his beer back for a long drink. He sets it down and licks the salt from his lips, considering me for a long moment, his head tipped to the side. "That was love, *Babydoll.*" He cackles when I smack his gut playfully.

"Don't use that word," I murmur, my mind distracted by his previous statement. I do love Logan. I'm in love with him. The thought isn't a shocking one; I'd already suspected it. But—"Isn't it too soon?"

Dom drops down onto a barstool, putting us at eye level. He takes another drink, thinking out his answer, which I appreciate, though it makes my stomach clench with nerves. Finally, after what feels like forever, he smiles softly, a knowing glint in his dark eyes.

"Forget about when you met and how many days it's been since you started spending time with him. Forget about the societal norms programmed in your head, and what people might think of your situation. Put it all out of your mind." He pauses, waiting for some sort of confirmation I've done as he's demanded. I nod with a shrug. "Good. Are you happy, Shiloh? Like really, genuinely happy with him?"

"Yes," I breathe, not even having to think about my answer. "So fucking happy, Dom."

His face breaks out in a massive smile, giving him a boyish look. "There you have it. Fuck everyone else, Shiloh. Fuck what society says, or what your ex might think. Fuck the negative thoughts telling you that this is too fast, or too soon. Follow your heart. You deserve to be happy and if jumping into bliss with fine-as-hell Logan Huxley makes you happy, then do it."

My heart races in my chest as determination settles over me. He's right. Elation fills me so rapidly; I get woozy on my feet. The need to see him, and inhale his rainy nature scent, feeling his strong, warm body, beneath my hands becomes almost unbearable.

I want him, and I want him now.

Picking up our beers, I spin in my shiny stiletto boots, ready to find my man. The drinks nearly slip from my hands as I run smack dab into my past.

"*Shiloh?*"

Fuck.

My heart stutters to a stop. The damp beer bottles slip again, and I have to squeeze my fists to keep them from careening to the floor.

"Wow, you look different," Cole murmurs, his eyes gliding down my body, taking in my skintight jeans and sweater. They linger on my heels, his brows furrowing in confusion before slowly returning to my face. "You sure never looked like this when we were together."

My heart starts back up again, racing painfully in my chest like it's trying to make up for lost time. I don't give Cole the same inspection, not really giving a shit what he's wearing or how he looks. All I want to know is why he's *here.*

I ask him just as much. "Why are you in Blue River?" After we divorced, he'd sold the house and moved closer to the school, or so my lawyer had said. I honestly never expected him to be here. "You hate this town."

He cringes, bringing the hand not holding his drink, *whiskey, no doubt*, up to palm the back of his neck. "Things change."

My brows lift. Wow, they must have changed a lot if he's willingly spending a Friday night in a county-western bar instead of a chic club in the city. "Okay, well, I'd say it was nice to see you, but..." I trail off, my skin starting to itch with the need to put distance between us.

His eyes trail over my body once more, this time homing in on the exposed swells of my breasts. "Don't you think you're showing off a bit too much skin?" he grunts, his words laced with disdain. "That's not really the kind of outfit you should be wearing."

"Oh?" A deep voice grunts from behind me. "And what exactly do you mean by that?" I sigh, my shoulders relaxing instantly. *Logan*. A small smile tips the corners of my lips as he settles his hands over my stomach possessively. "I'd suggest you stop looking at my woman's tits before you lose the ability to see."

Cole's head jolts like he's been struck. His slicked-back blonde hair barely moves despite the force of it. "What?"

"You heard me. Now answer the fucking question," Logan barks, pulling me into his body. My head tilts back, resting on his muscular chest. In heels, I come up just below his jaw, which I find I enjoy immensely. Especially when he turns his head and presses a kiss to my throat. "Why shouldn't she dress like this? I'm sure you had a point somewhere under all that gel."

Cole's mouth gapes open and closed, and despite my best efforts, a loud laugh escapes me. My ex's eyes narrow as rage and embarrassment fill his preppy boy face. His angular jaw ticks uncontrollably. Taking a step forward, he sneers at me, clearly not considering his own lifespan with a decision like that.

Cole apparently woke up and chose stupid today, because my man wakes up and chooses to protect me *every day*.

"Look at her," Cole snaps, gesturing at me with his whiskey glass. "Women who look like *that* shouldn't wear shit that shows their bodies off. It's embarrassing."

Pain spears through my gut so intensely that I'd assume there was a knife protruding from my body. I barely have time to let Cole's hurtful words sink in before Logan's there, washing them away with his kindness and posses-sion.

I don't know what I expected from him, but it's not what I get, that's for sure. He barks out a loud, deep laugh. A real one. One that goes on and on, his body shaking mine with the force. When he finally settles down, he bends, grinning into my neck.

"You lying, jealous prick," he grunts, shooting a glare at Cole as he plucks the beers from my hands and passes them to someone out of view. "You're perfect," he whispers the words, just for me. Love swells inside of me, replacing the hurt Cole had created.

Logan's hands palm my belly in a way that's anything but innocent as he says loudly, "You're right. She shouldn't wear clothes, should she?" His hands slide up my stomach to grip my ribs. "She should be naked."

Cole's lip curls, but his eyes follow Logan's movements as they trail up my body.

"This body is meant to be explored," he says, his hands continuing their upward path. "Worshiped." He cups my breasts, palming them in his huge hands. "*Devoured*." Logan licks a long trail up the side of my neck, and I barely stifle a moan. My eyes drift shut as I lose myself in him.

I want to be angry and embarrassed at his clear show of ownership over my body, especially in front of Cole, but I'm not. In fact, that's the opposite of what I feel as Logan fondles my tits, squeezing them together, grinding his hard cock into my ass.

"Shiloh's body is perfection. Every incredible, delicious inch of her." His hands leave my breasts, and slide back down my body, leaving my flesh burning in his wake. I tense for a split second, already knowing what he's about to do. My eyes fly open, and find Cole with a murderous expression on his face as he watches Logan's hand slip between my thighs. He cups my pussy, and this time, I do moan. "But *this*? This right here is fucking *Heaven*, and I have to thank you for not worshipping it the way she deserves because now, I get to be her God."

Cole snaps.

He squeezes the glass in his fist and sends it flying across the room. Seconds later, I hear it shattering somewhere behind me. Logan reacts instantly, dropping his possessive show and shoving me behind him. One hand reaches behind to grip my hand, keeping me in his reach, even when he can't see me.

"I suggest you fuck off before you make an even bigger fool of yourself. Leave Blue River and leave my *wife* the fuck alone." My heart thuds at his words. Stepping forward, he fists Cole's collar with the hand not holding me, and yanks him forward. "Do not contact her. Do not talk about her. Don't even think about her. Keep her name out of your mouth. Got me?"

"Wife?" Cole shouts, his face turning a nice shade of red as he tries to push Logan away. It doesn't work, and it's kind of a funny sight to see if I'm being honest. He's so much smaller than my man. Looking past Logan, Cole's eyes settle on me. His previous sneer is nowhere to be seen. In its place, confusion and maybe even hurt. *Too fucking bad.* "Shiloh? What's he talking about?"

"You're literally trying to die, aren't you?" Dom drawls, coming up to stand next to Cole. His arms cross over his chest as he glowers at my ex. "Personally, I think Logan here should put you in a body bag. You deserve it for how you treated her."

Cole's brows pinch together. "How I treated her? The fuck? I didn't do shit. It's not my fault she's defective."

Crack.

Splinter.

Shatter...

Went my ex-husband's face.

Logan releases Cole's limp body, dropping him onto the floor like a sack of shit. He spins, charging toward me like a man on a mission. His face is pinched with barely contained rage, but his eyes are full of nothing but *love.*

He hefts me into his arms, and in a move I never thought possible for someone my size, my legs wrap around his waist as I grip his shoulders. Logan smashes his lips to mine in an all-consuming kiss, that's honestly not really suitable for public. He rips his mouth from mine as Stephen tucks something in Logan's back pocket which I assume are his keys. His brother grins at me and pats Logan on the shoulder with a chuckle.

Logan storms through the bar, stepping over my past and charging toward my future.

IT'S MY
CHOICE

BE PATIENT
WITH
YOURSELF

unapologetically
myself

BE
Bold

ALL BODIES
ARE
GOOD BODIES

be happy

beautiful

love yourself

you can

fearless

HERE
TO STAY

IN CONTROL

LOVE
yourself

YOUR
POTENTIAL
IS ENDLESS

I am enough

FEEL
DEEPLY

be kind
to yourself

IT'S my choice

you
are
worthy

I am exactly
where I need to be

I am
capable

love you

beautiful

breathe

Perfect

YOU ARE
enough

Shiloh

Fifteen

"You're not defective," I growl, my lips moving against hers as I shove her perfect, thick body against the side of my truck. "You're not defective." I keep saying the words, again and again, wanting to make sure she really hears them. Needing her to know what that fucker said isn't true.

Fuck that piece of shit. I should go back inside and end him. The few punches I got in weren't enough. I need him to bleed. Need him to feel every ounce of the pain he made my girl feel. I knew the second I saw him leering at her that she was uncomfortable. It didn't take a genius to figure out who he was by the panicked expression on her face.

I wanted to kill him. Still do. Especially after everything she told me tonight.

Fuck, I think I'm still processing. Not the part about her struggling to get pregnant, but everything else.

Other than the fact that it breaks my heart *for her.* Her illness doesn't change how I feel about her. Not one fucking bit. If she gets sick or isn't feeling well, I'll take care of her. If she gains weight, I'll devour her new inches. Shiloh's body is a wonderland, and I'll worship every dip and curve until the day I die. If it takes years of trying for my seed to take, giving us a baby, then so be it. We'll have fun practicing. If she changes her mind and doesn't want kids, I'll get snipped so I can keep stuffing her full of my cum.

Point is, it doesn't fucking matter. We'll figure it out. *Together.* That's what a marriage is. A partnership. A team. I'm here, and I'm not leaving. My girl will never have to go through a damn thing alone, again.

"I know, baby," she whispers, her voice a husky rasp that goes straight to my cock.

She should be a phone sex operator.

No. Not happening. Her voice is mine and mine alone.

I groan. "I love when you call me that, but I prefer Daddy."

Shiloh giggles, but the sound is cut off when I tug the flesh of her neck into my mouth and bite down. "Take me home," she groans.

"Ask nicely," I murmur, sucking and licking the small hurt. She huffs, and I grin against her skin before biting again. This time harder, as I grind my throbbing, leaking cock against her cunt. I can feel the wet heat of her needy pussy seeping through her tight jeans, and it just about snaps my control.

Shiloh tips her head back, meeting my eyes. She's so turned on; she looks high as a fucking kite. "Please take me home and fuck my pussy...*Daddy.*"

Snap.

I'm moving before I'm even aware, throwing her door open and tossing her in. "Buckle up!" I bark, slamming the door. I adjust my aching cock as I round the truck, moving on autopilot. My head is spinning with thoughts of filling her tight cunt. Fucking her again and again until there's no question who she belongs to.

Mine.

We're halfway down the highway before I come to, that singular word reverberating through my hazy mind on repeat, coupled with visions of my cum dripping from every inch of Shiloh's body.

Claim her, fill her, breed her.

The feeling of her hand on my cock squeezing firmly makes me jolt in my seat. Glancing down, I find Shiloh bent over, fumbling with my jeans as she desperately tries to free my dick. Fuck, I can't believe I checked out like that. She unzips me and lets out a whine of frustration when she sees I'm wearing boxers. She tugs and pulls, clawing at the material like a needy kitten. All the while, I watch, barely keeping track of the road, too entranced by the sight of my girl beside my cock.

"Please," she whimpers, looking up at me with so much desire that a spurt of precum shoots from my cock.

I growl, gripping the steering wheel with one hand and palming her cheek with the other. "Do you need a cock in your throat, Babydoll?"

Shiloh nods, her head bobbing up and down vehemently. She tugs her fat bottom lip between her teeth, and the sight breaks my patience. I wanted to wait. Wanted to have her splayed out before me, on our bed, naked and crying out for my cum—but *fuck*.

Lifting my hips, I grunt, "Take my cock out." Hell, when did I become such a demanding bastard? I've never been like this before her. Never.

It's her. She does shit to my head... and my cock, apparently.

Her face lights up like all her birthdays have come at once. She practically rips my jeans and boxers down my thighs, just enough to have my pulsing cock in her hands. Then her mouth. Shiloh wastes no time deepthroating me, sucking me deep inside her hot mouth.

"Fuck!" I growl, wrapping my hand around her long hair, fisting it like the leash it is. "That's it, just like that." Her tiny hand wraps around the base of my dick, pumping what she can't fit in her mouth as she sucks and licks me. "You're so good to Daddy."

Jesus. Where did this Daddy kink come from?

Shiloh moans around my dick, swallowing me down until I'm practically balls deep in her throat. She sucks hard, licking the bottom of my shaft. Her poor mouth can barely wrap around my size, and her teeth repeatedly scrape my sensitive flesh, but I don't care. She could bite my cock off for all I care, and I'd beg for more.

"Earn my cum, Babydoll," I groan, thrusting my hips up hard enough that my balls slap her chin. My eyes flick back and forth between the dark, empty country road, and my girl in my lap. Making sure to keep her safe even when I'm being an idiot. I shouldn't put such precious cargo at risk like this, but I can't stop.

Shiloh pauses and pops off my dick, looking up at me with wide eyes. She shakes her head slowly, her chocolate eyes filled with tears from sucking me so hard. One drips down her cheek, and I wipe it away with my thumb.

"What's wrong?" I murmur, my heavy breaths filling the car. "Did I hurt you?"

She shakes her head again, her eyes dropping to my throbbing cock that's now turned an angry shade of red. *Ginger problems*. I quickly look back up at the road. The full moon shines brightly, lighting up the road and casting a warm, white glow over the trees.

"I don't want to swallow your cum," she murmurs, her voice sounding nervous. My brows pinch. "I—I want—"

She breaks off, but I need to hear her words. If she says what I think she's about to say, I'll die. Straight up, keel over. "Say it," I grunt, my fist collaring her throat roughly. *That's new.*

"I want you to do what you said earlier," she pants. "I want you to cum inside me." *God-fucking-damn it. Just hold out, Logan. You'll be home in your bed in five fucking minutes.* "I want you to breed me, Daddy."

Nope. Absolutely not. Can't do it.

The car jerks to the side as I pull over. The tires bump along over the thick brush and gravel. Shiloh sits up quickly, her eyes raking over the road as if she's checking for trouble. "What's wr—"

"Get out!" I snap, tugging my jeans up to cover my ass. I leave my aching cock out, unable to shove the hard-as-steel appendage back in my pants. Her head swivels in my direction, her mouth gaping open in shock or confusion. Probably both. "Out!"

My door flies open, and I practically throw myself from the truck, slamming the door behind me. I can't wait. Need her. Need her now. I round the hood, finding her slowly sliding from her seat. She looks terrified.

Can't have that. Ever.

"Need you, Babydoll. Can't wait." I snarl. Fuck, I sound like a caveman.

I charge forward, picking her up. My hands gripping her round, juicy ass. God, it's like a Georgia peach. Ripe and ready for the taking. Not tonight, though. Tonight, I need her cunt so full of me and my cum that she won't be able to walk for a week without feeling me inside her.

"Logan!" she cries, her hands grappling with my shoulders. I yank the hatch of my truck down and drop her on it. I say nothing as I rip my heavy coat off and bundle it up, creating a makeshift pillow.

I may be about to destroy her like a beast, but she's still my princess.

I lay the thick material down behind her and gently press her back until she's lying flat. Then, I'm tearing her pants down her thick hips and thighs. I need another taste. I could live off her sweet nectar. I've been dying for more since the other day.

"Shit," she cries as her bare ass hits the cold metal. I should stop. Should wait. Should take my time with her, worship her in front of the fireplace like she deserves. I should, and I will…later.

"Let me have you, Shiloh," I groan, parting her thighs the best I can with her tight jeans keeping her legs trapped together. I don't want her to be cold. Otherwise, I'd have her naked. "I need to taste you."

"You wh—oh God!" her words break off as I descend on her, eating her like the starving creature I am.

My thumbs open her up, giving me access to her dripping cunt. She's so wet; it's leaking down her thighs. My tongue lashes out, cleaning up every bit of her honey, not wanting to waste a single drop. I shove a finger inside her sopping entrance, curving to find her g-spot as I latch onto her clit, sucking it hard. Her ass arches off the truck bed. She spears her fingers through my messy hair as an orgasm barrels through her in record time.

"Logan!" she screams. My hand slaps the outside of her thigh in a warning. The flesh jiggles beneath my palm, and my cock throbs in response. How it hasn't fallen off from the cold is beyond me, but I guess it's holding out, knowing it'll be wrapped in her hot cunt soon. "Daddy," she moans, correcting her mistake.

Fuck. Yes.

I thrust in a second finger, fucking her pussy roughly, and prolonging her pleasure. Releasing her clit, I scissor my fingers back and forth before pushing in a third. It's a tight fit.

"Take it," I growl. She squeals, pressing her thighs together like she's trying to escape me. She won't. She's stuck with me for life. Again, she tries to push me away. "I have to stretch your tight cunt, Babydoll. You want my cock, don't you? I'm too big. I'll hurt you," I coo, twisting my hand to make sure she's good and ready for me.

I'm not one to brag, especially about dick size, because frankly, I could care less, but her pussy is small, and I'm a big man.

Shiloh reaches her hand down and surprises me when she tugs my fingers out. Sitting up, she shakes her head. "No, don't. I like it."

"Like what?" I grunt, confusion pressing in on my lust haze as I try to piece together her meaning.

Shiloh scoots forward, pushing me back as she slides from the truck. Her hand drops down, squeezing my hard cock, jerking me roughly. My body jolts, and my dick twitches. "I like the stretch. I want you to split me in half."

Like a tidal wave, memories of her books, and her highlighted quotes, come flooding back in. The knot, the pain-filled pleasure. She wants to struggle to take my thick cock and fuck if I don't wanna feel her stretching around me.

Shiloh smiles coyly as she turns around and bends over the hatch, presenting herself to me. They did that shit in the books too. She's *presenting* for her alpha, and suddenly, I feel like a primal beast ready to rut into his mate.

Goddamn, I can see why shifter porn is so popular. I get it now.

The golden skin of her juicy ass glows under the moonlight, looking like every wet dream I've ever had, come true. Shiloh looks over her shoulder and whispers, *"Breed me, Daddy."*

I must blackout. There's no other way to explain the seconds I miss between those words and my cock being balls deep in her soaking cunt. Shiloh screams...*loud.* Her fingers claw at the harsh cold metal beneath her, and I go still.

"Fuck, baby, are you okay?" I ask, my hand rubbing soothing circles across her back, even as my cock throbs with the need to move. Shiloh whimpers, her pussy walls clenching around my shaft. I groan.

Without my permission, my hips press in, flattening against her bouncing ass cheeks. There's nowhere else for me to go. She's somehow taken all nine of my thick inches, and still, she clenches like she's trying to suck me in deeper. "More," she moans. "*Move.*"

She's going to kill me. There's no way around it. I'm going die here and now, balls deep in my woman. I pull back until just the head of my dick is inside her. Gripping her hips, I lift, tipping her, so she doesn't get hurt against the metal.

Then—*I fuck her.*

My thrusts are relentless. Again and again, I pull out almost completely, then slam home again. I fuck her hard and deep. I fuck her fast, pounding into her wet, hot pussy like I'm trying to imprint myself on her flesh. Maybe I am.

"You feel so fucking good, baby," I grunt, loving how she flutters with my words. "So perfect." *Thrust.* "So wet." *Slap.* "So, fucking tight." *Thrust.* "Mine."

Thrust. Thrust. Thrust.

"Oh shit," she cries, long nails scrapping along the metal, adding to the brutal soundtrack of our primal fucking.

The sound of the crickets filling the night air is drowned out by the wet, sloppy noises her cunt is making as she sucks my cock into her body. My balls slap against her clit with every brutal thrust. Her nails against the metal screech. The shocks on my truck thump and squeak. My breathing is a harsh pant. But nothing beats the sound of her.

My Shiloh.

Her pleasure-filled moans are everything.

"You want me to breed you, Shiloh? You want me to fill you so full of my seed; you'll be dripping for days?" Bending my knees, I shift my angle and shove in deep. When I grind my hips against her flesh, she moans. Her walls tighten around my dick, letting me know I'm hitting the right spot.

She tilts her head to the side and presses up onto her elbows. Her dark eyes are barely visible. Regret fills me momentarily. I should have waited. Should have done this right. Should have worshipped her, looked her in the eyes while I made love to her the way she deserves.

But then, she's pushing back, fucking herself on my cock. "I want it so bad," she groans. Shifting again, she places her palms flat on the truck bed, giving her better leverage. Holding her hips tightly, I stay still, letting her use me. "I want you to fill me up, Logan. I want your cum."

"Goddamn, Babydoll," I grunt, my eyes rolling to the back of my head as she picks up pace. I shove my hand between her thighs, finding the little bud I know will set her off in no time. With two fingers, I rub back and forth the way she likes, picking up the pace when she screams. "That's it. Use me to fuck yourself. Take what you need."

Her cunt's so wet; she's leaking down my balls with every sloppy-sounding thrust. My eyes rake down her body, finding the only flesh visible. Her ass. It calls to me, like a beacon. It's so fucking perfect. Fat and round, the perfect amount of flesh to take a brutal pounding without hurting her. I could drill this woman into the floor. Dig my fingertips into her flesh. I could toss her against the wall, fuck her within an inch of her life. She'd be able to take it all.

My hand arcs back, landing a hard *slap* on her juicy cheek. I watch as it jiggles and almost jizz on the spot. I ignore the sensation, slapping her peach again and again.

Shiloh screams.

"Daddy!" she cries out. Her cunt clenching so hard, I see stars as she detonates around me. Her pussy gushes, releasing wet, hot liquid down both of our thighs. The feeling of her gripping me like a vice as she squirts is too much, and I lose my battle with holding out.

"Fuck, Shiloh! Your pussy's strangling me," I grunt. Banding my hand around her chest, I lift her up, needing her closer. Her hands wrap around my forearm, holding me just as hard. "Gonna fill you up," I grunt into her ear, my words more beast than man. "Fuck my babies into your belly right the fuck now."

Her head tips back, lips finding mine blindly in the dark. Our mouths crash together as I cum deep inside my woman's cunt, filling her womb with my seed. The hot gush sets her off again, prolonging both our orgasms. Our tongues tangle with each other. Our bodies as close as humanly possible.

In the middle of the night, on the side of an empty country road, I fall.

I fall so hard, so deep, so much....I'll never come back from it. Never not love her.

She's my life now. My world. My future.

Pulling away, I rest my forehead on hers as we catch our breath. My cock is still hard, deep inside her, as emotions fill me to the brim. I've never felt this way before. Never needed someone the way I need her. Never wanted to spend every second of my day with another person the way I want to with Shiloh. It may be fast. It may be sudden. But right here, holding her like this, I know none of that matters. Just her.

"You called me your wife," she whispers, her voice thick with emotion.

"You just now realizing that?" I chuckle, panting hard against her. My arms tighten around her body, clinging to her the way I'm clinging to this moment. *Never gonna let her go. Never.*

She huffs out a breath. "You called me your *wife*, Logan."

"You didn't deny it." I cock a brow, daring her to argue. I hadn't meant to say what I did, but I'd been so fucking mad, so on the edge, it just came out. Not that I didn't mean it. I've been referring to her as Shiloh Huxley since the day I met her.

She pauses, her eyes boring into mine, my cock still deep inside her. We stay like, silently staring at each other for I don't know how long. Finally, she whispers, "No, I didn't."

And just like that, I know she feels it too.

I love her.

My lips connect with hers once more, this time in a slow, sensual kiss. I kiss her the way I should have before. The way I should have the first time I kissed her. I kiss Shiloh the way my future wife, the mother of my children, deserves to be kissed, with my whole fucking heart.

Shiloh shivers, and I pull away, realizing how cold it is. "Come on, let's get you home."

"Home," she sighs quietly.

I pull out, already loathing not having my cock inside her. She whimpers, clearly not happy about the loss either. A gush of our combined releases spills out with my dick, and the feeling does something to me. I've already realized I'm a possessive bastard with her, but the knowledge that my cum is inside her makes me feral.

"Are you on birth control?" I grunt, my fingers scooping my cum up and pushing it back inside her.

Shiloh moans, her pussy fluttering around my digits as I slowly finger fuck her, making sure all of my seed is exactly where it belongs. She glances over her shoulder, her lip between her teeth, and shakes her head. A heavy breath wooshes from my lungs.

Pulling my fingers free, I raise them to her mouth, painting her lips with our flavor. Her tongue darts out, wrapping around my fingers. She sucks them into her mouth, dutifully cleaning them.

"How do we taste?" I grunt, my eyes tracking the way her tongue works around me like she's imagining it's my cock.

She releases me with a pop and smirks. "Perfect." Her smile fades as she pulls her panties and jeans up. I follow suit, tucking my cock away. Leaning over, I grab my coat and bundle it around her shaking shoulders. "Logan, we need to talk."

My heart squeezes in my chest painfully. I nod. If she wants to talk, we'll talk. "At home."

IT'S MY CHOICE

BE PATIENT WITH YOURSELF

Unapologetic MYSELF

Love YOURSELF

BE Bold

ALL BODIES ARE GOOD BODIES

be happy

beautiful

yes you can

Fearless

IN CONTROL

LOVE yourse

HERE TO STAY

I am enough

FEEL DEEPLY

YOUR POTENT IS ENDL

be kind to yourself

IT's my CHOICE

I am exactly where I need to be

be Brave

you are worthy

YOU AR enoug

I am capable

Love you

Beau

breathe

Perfect

Shiloh

SIXTEEN

It's official.

I'm freaking out.

Correction. I'm freaking out because I'm *not* freaking out. Shouldn't this be weird? Shouldn't this all feel like too much, too soon? This should feel crazy. It probably is crazy, actually. To anyone else, to any normal, sane person—this would be absolute, mind-bogglingly-absurd.

But to me?

To me, it's perfect. It's kismet. He's everything I've ever wanted in a man and so much more. He's everything I ever imagined for my future, and it's not just because he so clearly wants to get me pregnant—*something we definitely need to talk about,* but because he wants to build the same kind of life I want.

Logan wraps his hand around mine, silently pulling me from my spiral or lack thereof. He leads me upstairs, and when we reach the loft, he turns left instead of right. My heart pounds in my chest. My hand twitches in his, almost like it's trying to sweat but can't in his presence. Thank God, too, because that would be embarrassing as hell.

We reach the threshold of his room. The room he said I couldn't enter unless I was sure. Unless I knew what I wanted. He'd said once I entered his bedroom; I wouldn't be leaving.

I'd—*I'd be his....*

Logan stops. He doesn't turn to face me. He doesn't speak. He just stops.

We stand there, on the precipice of our futures. It feels as if time stands still while he waits for me to make my decision. Am I in or am I out?

His hand flexes on mine. He's nervous. Our combined palms are sweaty now. I squeeze my free hand into a fist. My fingers trail across my palm. It's dry. My heart slams to a stop. He's not nervous—he's *terrified.*

Logan thinks I won't choose him. Silly boy. He should have realized it was never a choice at all. It's been him from the moment our eyes met.

This is stupid. I know what I want, and hesitating isn't lessening that want...it's only making it more intense, more visceral. We've got things to discuss, conversations need to be had, but it doesn't matter. Nothing matters but Logan and me.

I take a step forward. Then another. Then another. Three steps. That's all it takes to solidify my future. I pull his hand as we cross the barrier together.

Together. That's how it should always be.

No sooner have I stepped through the doorway, than am I in his arms. He picks me up like I weigh nothing. One arm beneath my thighs, one under my back. My arms wrap around his neck as I meet his eyes. The green is bright and shiny, even under the dim light. It takes me a second to realize they've glossed over with unshed tears. My stomach gives a squeeze as gratitude and *love* for this man fills me.

His forehead drops to mine. "You know what this means right?" his voice is a low growl that sounds more animal than man.

That I love you.

That I want to spend my life with you.

That your mine and I'm yours.

"Of course," I choke out. "That I'm hoping your bed's more comfortable than the guest bed."

Logan somehow slaps my ass without dropping me. I squeal, a huge smile on my face. My cheeks are going to fall off at this point.

"Say it" he grunts, his feet powering through the room. He charges toward what I can only assume is the en suite, but he's yet to turn on the lights, and my eyes are too busy staring into his to care.

"I don't know what you're talking about," I joke, though my voice comes out a breathless pant. "Why don't you say it first."

"Don't fuck with me, Shiloh," he growls as he comes to a stop. He releases my legs, letting me slide down his body as

I stand. Our bodies are flush, our faces only inches apart. "Does this mean what I think it does?"

Be brave, Shiloh. What's the worst that could happen?

Insecurities careen into me so hard and fast that I'm surprised when I find I'm still standing. My eyes burn, and this time I don't keep the emotion in. I don't hide from him like I have in the past. I don't diminish my emotions for someone else's comfort. I don't pretend I'm fine so as not to be a burden.

Logan sighs as his thumbs brush my tears away. "Fine," he grunts. "I'll go first."

A giggle bursts from my mouth. Of course, even now, he has to be a grumpy prick. His lip tips up at the corner. I can just barely make out the movement beneath his beard. His almost-smile drops. His face takes on a serious look that I've only ever seen when he's mad. His heartbeat pounds against his chest so hard I can feel it beneath mine.

"I called you my wife." My smile drops as the world freezes around us. "I don't care if it's too fast. I don't care if we barely know each other. I don't give a fuck about any of it. I've said it before, and I'll keep saying it 'til it sinks in. *You. Are. Mine.*"

"Logan," I murmur, shaking my head. With narrowed eyes, he glares down at me, his expression unreadable.

What am I doing? Why am I resisting this? He's perfect.

Unable to meet his stare, I look down, my eyes raking over my body. "You don't know me. I might not be able to get pregnant. What Cole said was—"

"It was bullshit," he barks, taking a step back. I'm not sure if he's looking at me or if he's angry. I don't want to find out, either. "It was bullshit. Fuck him. What he said wasn't true, and you know it."

"You don't know me, Lo—" I start, but again, he interrupts me. This time, his fingers grip my chin in a move I'm coming to enjoy far too much.

"I do. I know you," he insists, tightening his hold when I look away. "You love cherry ice cream and hate seafood. You're allergic to peaches. You have a 200-pound dog named Porkchop that you love like a real kid, even though the fucker sheds and drools on everything. Your favorite movie is *Young Frankenstein,* which I find weird as hell, but whatever. You want babies. Lots and lots of babies. *I know you.*"

"Those are just facts I told you about myself. That doesn't mean you know me," I protest, shaking my head the best I can, which is hardly at all.

Logan nods, surprising me. "You're right." His agreeing with me so easily should make me feel better, knowing I'm right, but it doesn't. He's silent for so long that I worry he's rethinking everything he's just said.

Logan turns, pivoting our bodies. He walks me backward until my ass hits the vanity. He lifts me up and drops me on the counter. I fight a cringe, feeling the dampness from our roadside activities clinging to my panties. He plants his hands on my thighs and squeezes.

"You color-code your pens, but not in a way that makes sense." My brows furrow, and my mouth opens to explain.

He shakes his head once, silencing me. "Yellow, blue, orange, purple, pink, red, green, black, silver. It took me a while to figure it out, but then you told me your favorite holidays." I gasp. Does he really pay that close of attention to me? "Easter, Halloween, Valentine's Day, Christmas, and New Year's."

His hands flex as I remain silent, not knowing what to say. I feel more seen than I ever have before and slightly embarrassed that he noticed my odd behavior.

"It's weird and quirky, but it's you," he says quietly. "And I find it completely adorable."

"I like the things I look at to feel festive," I whisper, my shoulders shrugging so hard, I smack my ears. Sue me. I like the holidays and colorful shit. I was a kindergarten teacher for years. It comes with the territory.

Logan nods. "I know. I also know that you like your coffee with two and quarter packets of raw sugar, a three-quarter packet of Splenda, and two teaspoons of almond milk. You love to wear dresses, even when it's freezing, but you don't like ones with patterns. You love to watch the sunset and hate waking up early. You don't smile until at least 10:30 in the morning when you've had a whole pot of coffee."

I smile at that. His hands glide up my body, eliciting a trail of shivers in their wake before landing on my neck. He tilts my head back, the warmth from his palms burning through my skin.

"I know a lot of things about you, Babydoll, but I want to know *everything.* I can't do that if you don't give me a shot."

Swallowing thickly, I give him my deepest fear. The one bigger than being afraid I can't get pregnant and make our dreams come true. The one that plagues my nightmares. The one that haunts me even in the day.

The scars Cole created. The way he stopped touching me when my body changed. The way he sneered. The comments he made. The hurt. The insecurities.

"You've never even seen me naked, Logan. My body—" I gesture to myself as if it's all the explanation needed.

He growls. The sound is deep and angry, and it goes straight to my sore, stretched-out pussy. *God, that was so fucking hot.* I haven't even really allowed myself to reflect on everything we did, but damn, I won't be walking right for a while.

Stop it, Shiloh. It's not the time for that.

Tucking his chin to his chest, Logan shakes his head. "Fuck that guy. I should go back and kill him," he mutters. "Fine. You wanna talk about your body, Shiloh?" he glances up at me through thick, red lashes. "I told you that I love your body. Have I not made that clear by the way I can't stop looking at you? Touching you? By the way I repeatedly tell you that I find you so unbelievably perfect that I want to fill you with my cum and live out my days with my cock stuffed deep in your cunt?"

"Jesus, Logan," I whisper-shout, my wide eyes dilating with every filthy word.

He lifts a shoulder, completely unbothered. "What? I meant it then, I mean it now, and I'll still mean it after I see every inch of you. In fact—" He pauses, releasing a heaving breath. "I choose you, *Shiloh Huxley*. I choose you as my friend, my partner, my wife. You are the mother of my children, my future. I choose you now, and I'll choose you, again and again, every day for the rest of our lives."

Shiloh Huxley.

His hands grip my face. He stares down at me, hiding nothing. Letting me see every vulnerable, broken piece of him. The fractures and heartache. The anxiety, panic, and trauma. I see it all and what I see has my walls damn near crumbling completely. He's beautiful.

"I choose you now before I've seen your body, and I'll choose you again, after."

My wife.

A tear drips down his face. The hands on my cheeks tremble. He squeezes his eyes shut and inhales sharply. Even now, he's preparing for rejection. My walls tumble, crashing down into shards, breaking irreparably.

The mother of my children.

"I choose you."

My words seem to shatter his composure. He exhales a breath that shakes his entire body. Another tear falls down his perfect face. A face that has seen wars and heartache. Unimaginable amounts of loss. A face that spends days outside, earning an honest living as he supports those he loves so fiercely. He's a *good man,* and he's *mine.*

Be brave.

"I choose you, Logan Huxley," I whisper, forcing myself to be strong, to not let the *what ifs* stop me from taking what I want. "I choose you as my friend, my partner, my husband. You are the father of my children, my future. I choose you now, and I'll choose you, again and again, every day for the rest of our lives." I shakily repeat his words, quietly sobbing as I speak.

His body shudders as his face drops to my neck. He buries himself there, and I instantly feel the wetness he's trying to hide. *My big, strong protector...is crying.* My arms band around his body, holding him just as tightly as he's holding me.

There, in the bathroom, we collide. Two broken hearts, not repaired, but healing. Two broken hearts that found each other in an ugly, damaging world, against all odds.

"I love you," he breathes, his lips moving against my neck.

Three words.

Three tiny words that separately are insignificant. But together...life-changing

8 letters and every single defense I built up around my heart in a last-ditch effort to protect myself disappear *completely.*

"I love you, Logan." He sighs a breath of relief, and like the calm after a storm, everything inside me settles. I made the right choice.

His mouth opens against my neck as he begins to kiss and suck along my flesh. His hands slide down, gripping the hem of my sweater. He lifts the material slowly, and I have a moment of dread that he's going to see my stomach for the first time in such an unflattering position. Before I have time to self-sabotage our moment, he's yanking my shirt over my head and tossing it on the floor.

Stepping back, his heated gaze glides down my body so intensely that it feels as though he's touching me. "Fuck, Babydoll," he murmurs, his voice filled with awe. He zeros in on my bra. It's simple and black. There's no lace or padding to push the girls up. Logan doesn't seem to mind a bit as he adjusts his cock while staring at my boobs. "Need to see all of you."

His mouth descends on mine as he reaches around my back and attempts to unclasp my bra. He tugs and twists but fails epically. I laugh against his mouth. Then laugh harder when he grunts in irritation. My laughter dies a quick death when he goes all Lumber-Hulk and rips the thin material clean off my body.

"Holy shit," I moan, "that was so fucking hot."

Logan barks out a laugh, adding the shredded fabric to the ever-growing pile on the floor. "Something one of those shifters in your books would do, huh?" My brows lift so high; I'm pretty sure they've disappeared into my hair. He grins. "What? I like to read, too."

"Oh yeah?" I murmur, completely unconvinced but also wildly impressed. This man read my books. "Why did you read my Kindle, Logan?" I'd thought he may have when I noticed my books were all out of order but hadn't thought to bring it up.

He palms my breasts, silencing my questions. My head drops back, thudding against the mirror. He squeezes the flesh, testing their weight before taking one of my nipples into his mouth. I yank his hair, pulling him closer, and gasp when he bites down. He laves the small hurt, and my clit throbs in response.

"Perfect tits, Shiloh. Look how well you fit in my hands," he groans as he switches to the other side, giving both breasts equal attention. He sucks and licks, exploring every inch of them in a way no one ever has before him.

With one last kiss to each of my nipples, he stands. "I told you I want to know everything about you," he says, answering my earlier question. "And that includes what you think about in that pretty head of yours."

His fingers wrap around the waistband of my jeans, and together, we slide them down my legs. He grunts when he notices my thick socks pulled up to my knees. Dropping to the floor, he slides them down my legs in a move that's far more sexual than it should be. His eyes flick up to mine, his gaze molten.

I get lost. In his stare. His touch. His hot breath fanning against my cold flesh. I get lost in *him*. I get so lost I don't even realize I'm naked until Logan's standing before me, still completely dressed, devouring my body.

My thighs are flattened out and squished against the counter. My stomach has more rolls than a dinner pack. My boobs are sagging in two different directions. The stretch marks covering my skin are clear as day beneath the bright bathroom light. My legs haven't been shaved in a few days. The neatly trimmed curls on my pussy are peaking out between my legs. He can clearly see the dimply flesh of my ass in the mirror, which I'm sure is beyond unattractive.

I'm on display for him. Fully and completely. Hiding absolutely nothing. Normally, I would be petrified. Humiliated even—as I wait for his rejection.

Yet, the way Logan Huxley is eating me up like I'm the best meal he's ever seen has me feeling like a *motherfucking goddess.*

He slowly drags his eyes up my body in the most sensual perusal I've ever been on the receiving end of. His gaze locks on mine as he whispers, "I choose you."

I choose you now before I've seen your body, and I'll choose you again, after.

I practically fly off of the counter, barely catching myself as I crash into him. We're a mess of teeth and tongues. I *claw* his clothes from his body, ripping off layer after layer, my lips hardly leaving his. He mauls me with just as much vigor. His hands explore every inch of my exposed skin, kneading, scraping, and tugging as he learns my body, committing it to memory.

And then...he's naked.

Logan's body is a work of art. His light skin is covered in freckles and coarse, red hair. His chest is thick and muscular, matching his arms and thighs. His body is a testament to how hard he works day in and day out. His round ass has adorable dimples on each cheek. More scars, similar to the ones on his back and biceps, are on his legs.

My fingers trail over them as I inspect his body the way he did mine. "Shrapnel," he whispers, letting me take my fill. My stomach clenches. I can only imagine what he's been through.

I circle him, the pads of my fingers gliding over his skin. He shivers. I reach his front, taking in the miles of abs, his cut Adonis belt, and the very large, very thick cock, pointing right at me. I almost drop to my knees then and there, but first...

Looking up, I smile, my unprotected heart squeezing in my chest. "*I choose you*," I pause, swallowing. "I love you."

Logan groans, a low, deep sound in the back of his throat. "Goddamnit. I wanted to take my time with you." My eyes narrow in confusion, not expecting him to respond that way.

He turns, stepping into the walk-in shower. He turns it on, and steam instantly fills the stall. Turning back, he closes the distance between us in record time. Bending, he picks me up, tucking my legs behind his back, and carries me to the shower.

"I wanted to bathe you. Take care of you. Worship you." He steps in, letting the glass door slam behind us. "But then, you had to go and say you love me again."

He presses me against the shower wall, the cold tiles only adding to the sensations coursing through my body. "This should have happened earlier, but I got carried away. Consider this our official discussion. I want you with my ring on your finger and my babies in your belly. You're not on birth control, and I'm not using condoms. I'm clean. You?"

I roll my eyes, "A bit late for that." He grunts, thrusting his hard cock against my achingly wet core. I moan, my head dropping to his shoulder. "I'm clean. I'm not on birth control, but that doesn't mean—"

"It means you'll be pregnant with my kid by Christmas. Fuck, if I have it my way, you'll be knocked up by Thanksgiving." He drops his face, burying it between my boobs and inhaling deeply. "*Cupcakes,*" he murmurs, sending a shiver down my spine.

I groan, but a quiet laugh still rumbles through my chest. "That's in less than three weeks, Logan."

His hand slaps my ass as he mumbles against my skin. "I'm adding something to the agenda of this official meeting." I scoff, shifting to give him more access as he latches onto my flesh and sucks.

"How can you be joking at a time like this?" He thrusts against me again. I moan, grinding down on his cock as it slides between my soaking pussy lips. His mouth lifts from my breast with a pop.

"I'm not joking. This is serious. When we're naked, call me Daddy." I open my mouth to protest. Why? No idea. Personally, I love it. Maybe I just like being difficult. Logan silences me by shifting his hips, pressing the throbbing head of his cock at my opening. Every word in my brain quiets, except—

"Fuck me, Daddy."

He groans deeply, his eyes moving down my body to watch where we're connected. He presses in another inch, pausing in a way that's nothing but torture for both of us.

He steps back adjusting my legs on his hips, pressing my back harder into the shower wall to let it support some of my weight. My hands grip his shoulders, wishing I could see what he sees.

"Shit, Babydoll. Your cunt's sucking my cock in. I can't slow it down."

"Don't," I gasp. "Don't be gentle." He slams home before I even finish my sentence.

Logan fucks me hard and fast. His body pounds against my thighs with every punishing snap of his hips. Leaning in, he smashes our lips together, connecting every inch of our bodies. He kisses me like he fucks me. Like he's trying to brand my soul with his.

"Mine" he murmurs, his lips moving against mine as he slows his pace. My pussy pulses around his thick cock, stretching to accommodate his massive size.

"Yours" I nod.

"Mine to *fuck*," he pulls out completely. I whimper at the loss, my head slamming against the wall.

"Yours" I agree, my voice a breathless rasp.

"Mine to *breed*." He thrusts in again, harder, deeper. Pulling back out, his eyes meet mine.

Swallowing a sudden lump of emotion, I nod again. "*Yes, please.*"

"Mine to *marry.*" This time, he slams into me so roughly I can feel bruises welling on my thighs. His hips roll, making his dick hit me in just the right place. My nails scrape down his chest as I moan out my pleasure. "Say it, Shiloh," he barks, his voice rougher than ever before.

I don't even think before I speak. Too lost to the feelings running through my body, my veins. It's pleasure and joy and elation. It's intoxicating bliss.

It's him. It's Logan.

"Yes" I scream, meeting him thrust for thrust as we chase our orgasms.

"Mine to fucking *love*." I detonate, cumming so hard and so fast I get lightheaded. If not for his arms wrapped beneath my thighs, I'd fall to my knees in ecstasy. "Fuck yes, Shiloh. Squeeze my cock. Milk my cum from me."

"Fuck, *Daddy*!" I cry out as stars and black dots dance behind my eyes, blurring everything around me until all I see is *him*.

He bites down on the swell of my breast, pushing me into a second orgasm. "Gonna breed this tiny, tight pussy, baby." He shoves deep, his pace faltering as hot spurts of cum coat my walls. Logan growls out his release, both of us crashing into the abyss of undeniable pleasure.

We hold each other tightly. Our heavy breaths filling the shower and getting lost in the hot spray. He slowly releases me, helping me to my shaking feet. I droop against him, leaning heavily on his chest. My weak arms slack at my sides. Logan chuckles deeply, his body rumbling with the sound.

"Let me take care of you, Mrs. Huxley," he murmurs, a slight lilt to his voice.

I groan. "I'd roll my eyes if I could, but I can't even open them right now."

Logan barks out a laugh, moving our bodies beneath the water. "Oh, you didn't know? That was an official ceremony. We're married now." He wets my hair, tilting my head back to saturate the long strands.

"Har har har. You're a funny guy," I mumble, half-dead from all the orgasms. "You'd have to be ordained for that to count."

Logan huffs out a sound of displeasure. Bending down to my ear, he whispers, "*I am*." My eyes fly open meeting his. He shrugs. "I got ordained when I was in the military. Married a buddy of mine overseas."

My heart thuds in my body and my knees go weak. Logan notes the panic on my face and breaks out into a fit of laughter that I honestly cannot wrap my post-orgasmic head around.

"I'm just kidding, Babydoll. Well, not about the ordained part, but I can't officiate my own wedding." I grunt, fighting the urge to punch him in the gut. No...you know what? I do just that. He barely even flinches. "You hit like a pissed off kitten."

"This kitten has claws, mister," I growl.

He slaps my ass. "We're still naked."

"Oh, after that, you'll be lucky if I ever call you the D word again." It's a half-hearted, barely there threat and we both know it. I like calling him *the D word*, way too much.

Logan snickers as he massages shampoo through my hair. "You'll be calling me Daddy soon enough." A pang of longing hits me hard, and I tense. He continues to rub my head, though I know he felt it. "All joking and sex-talk aside; it will happen when it happens, Shiloh. Or it won't. We'll figure it out together."

Together? God, that sounds amazing.

We fall into silence, his words eating away at the previous damage done to my heart. He conditions my hair next before scrubbing my entire body, focusing on his favorite areas for far longer than necessary. I try to return the favor, but he bats my hand away and washes his body quickly. He just about blows my mind when he sweetly shaves my body, allowing me to lean limply against him the whole time.

When we're done, he wraps a towel around me and quickly uses another to dry my hair. He knots one around his waist and leads me to the bedroom, flicking a light on as we enter.

I get my first look at the room he didn't want me to see until I was sure I'd be staying, and my breath wooshes from my body at the sight. For one, it's *huge*. Like larger than any bedroom has a right to be. For two, it's *beautiful.*

"Holy shit," I gasp, spinning in a circle. My eyes dart from top to bottom, corner to corner, as I take it all in.

It's got a vaulted ceiling, with beams like the living room, as well as a matching fireplace with stone detailing. The walls are natural pine shiplap, giving it a warm, rustic feel. The floors are the same wood as the rest of the house, but beneath the massive California king bed sits a huge, plush rug.

There's a couch in front of the fireplace. A tv is attached to the stone above the mantle. Round, iron chandeliers are suspended from the beams; one above the couch, another above the bed. There's a door on either side of the bathroom that I can only assume are two matching walk-in closets.

Everything is simple and warmly decorated, though it could definitely use a woman's touch. The best part, however, is the floor-to-ceiling windows that surround the fireplace, and the opposite wall, looking out at hundreds of acres of wilderness.

Logan comes up behind me, wrapping his arms around my middle. His chin rests on my head, and I lean back relaxing into his body. "Do you like it?"

"Logan, I love it," I breathe. "It's so perfect."

"Good, I'm glad." Releasing me, he wraps his hand around mine and tugs me toward the closed doors next to the bathroom. "I want to show you something."

He opens the one on the right, and sure enough, a massive walk-in closet that's filled less than a quarter full lights up before me.

"Wow," I chuckle. "You really need to go shopping to fill this thing." He grunts, shaking his head.

"If you want me to fill it with clothes for you, I will."

Peeking up at him, I grin. "I don't need you to shop for me. I can do it myself, and I don't want to take over your closet. I'm sure there's another." There I go, talking like this is my house. Like I live here already.

Logan shrugs. "It's our closet, Shiloh. Fill it up. Throw my stuff on the floor or in the dresser. Doesn't matter to me."

My brows lift. I glance behind him, looking at the second door. His eyes follow my gaze. He smiles again, this one a bit more guarded than the rest. He flicks the closet light off, closing the door behind him as he pulls me toward door number two.

Turning to me, his eyes dart between mine, a nervous expression filling his handsome face. "Move in with me." My mouth drops open. I say nothing. "Move in with me," he repeats.

My mouth closes, then opens again, bobbing like a fish out of water. "What?" I murmur. "Are you serious?"

"Do I look like I'm playing? At any point in these past few days have I fucked around like that?" I shake my head. He hasn't. He's one of the most honest, serious people I've ever met. He doesn't fuck around, not when it comes to me.

"Logan, what about my place?"

He shrugs. "It's destroyed. I didn't want to tell you before, but it's fucked."

"What?" I screech. "*Holy shit!*"

"I went to see your landlord yesterday. He's probably going to need to tear the place down and start over." His words are so nonchalant, that I honestly can't tell if he's kidding, or not. "It's old, Shiloh. It needs a hell of a lota work, and he's too much of a cheap bastard to do it. I offered, but he said no."

I stare at him, shock and irritation replacing some of my previous bliss. "Why didn't you tell me?"

"I didn't think it mattered."

I step away, unsure what to say to his crazy ass right now. I want to scream and shout, stomp my foot and throw a tantrum. But what would be the point? If we're really doing this...if we're really jumping into this relationship, the way we both so clearly want to—why wouldn't I want to move it?

"It's the principle of the thing," I growl. "You should have told me about my house instead of banking on us moving in together. We've only known—"

"Don't you dare!" he snaps. Raking a hand through his hair, he growls, "Don't start that shit again, Shiloh. Who the fuck cares how long it's been. You love me, I love you. That's it. Find a different argument."

"How about—this is—it's—" I stumble over my words, my hands flying in the air in exasperation. I've got nothin'. We both know it. Logan storms over, closing the distance between us, and slams his lips to mine. Shutting me up with a harsh kiss.

Ripping his mouth from mine, he growls, "Stop talking woman, and move in with me."

"Fine!" I shout, grabbing his cheeks in my palms and yanking his bearded face back down for another kiss.

I tug his lip between my teeth and bite down, showing him my anger in the only way I can. He licks my lips like an animal. It's primal and very shifter-y of him, and I whine like a wanton omega. He huffs out a smug as fuck sound as he trails kisses down the front of my throat.

"We have to stop," he murmurs, not stopping. "I have to show you something." With a groan, he pulls himself away, seeming to struggle immensely. "Maybe this will make you feel better since you seem so pissed off about agreeing to live with me." He rolls his eyes, but his lips tip up, giving away his sarcasm.

He wraps his body around mine from behind, covering my eyes with one hand and guiding us toward the other door. I hear it click open. Light shines between the cracks of his fingers as he walks us deeper into the mystery space.

"I love you, Shiloh," he whispers. "I can't wait for our future."

My heart swells with his words. If he keeps this up, I'll be dead from all the cardiac acrobatics he's causing before we even move in together. He removes his hand, and I blink, adjusting to the light. Confused, I tilt my head.

"It's an empty room?" I ask, my eyes sweeping around the small replica of the master bedroom. The only difference is the lack of a fireplace, and this room has white shiplap instead of natural pine.

Large windows are covering one full wall. The view is similar to the master, but my eyes catch on something reflecting the moon in the distance. "Is that the Colorado River?"

Logan nods, his beard brushing against my cheek with the movement. "I built this house with my dreams in mind. A big family, a wife, holidays, and Sunday breakfasts. Lazy mornings in bed with the kids. Late nights with my wife in my arms. For the longest time, the vision was hazy and vague. I could see the dream, but there were no faces." His mouth trails down my neck. He squeezes me as tears coast down my cheeks for the hundredth time since meeting him. *Happy tears. Every single time.*

"It's a nursery," I choke out.

He nods. "It's you. It was always you."

IT'S MY CHOICE

Be patient WITH YOURSELF

Unapologetic MYSELF

stay positive

BE Bold

ALL BODIES ARE GOOD BODIES

be happy

YOURSELF

Yes you can

Fearless

IN CONTROL

LOVE yourself

HERE TO STAY

I am enough

FEEL DEEPLY

YOUR POTENTIAL IS ENDLESS

be kind yourself

IT'S MY CHOICE

be brave

I am exactly where I need to be

you are worthy

I am capable

YOU ARE enough

Love you

breathe

Perfect

Shiloh

Seventeen

"Come on, Babydoll. We're gonna be late!" I shout, tucking my wallet into my back pocket. Shiloh groans so loud, I can hear her from the kitchen. "Get your ass downstairs."

She ignores me, but I hear a door slam in response. I pause, waiting for her footsteps. When I hear nothing, I chuckle, knowing she slammed the bedroom door from the *inside.*

We really are going to be late, but I couldn't give a single fuck. My girl can take as long as she wants to get ready. She's nervous to meet my family today, and I honestly can't blame her. They're a lot to handle.

We've spent the past couple of days lounging around the house, getting to know one another. I've shown her around the property, making sure she knows how far the land stretches and where it is and isn't safe to explore. I want her to feel comfortable here, in her new home, but it's a lot different than what she's used to.

I took her out on the quad yesterday, promising to teach her how to drive it soon, so she can have her own to get around. We spent hours exploring. Porkchop trailing behind us the whole way, Tank tucked between us.

I showed her Arrowhead Lake, which is the largest runoff from the river. It's also the one with the waterfall, though it's too cold to be running at full capacity. I'll take her back in spring when it's full of fresh snow water. I showed her Stephen and Charlie's houses and how to navigate the back roads connecting our properties.

She squealed and screamed the entire time. Loving every second of the bumpy ride, which I may or may not have intentionally made worse by driving faster than necessary. What can I say? I love having my girl wrapped around me. I can't get enough of it.

Especially in our bed.

I've fucked Shiloh seven ways from Sunday on every single surface in our room. I even fucked her in the bathtub this morning. How? No idea, but I made it work. Her pussy is the single best thing I've ever had wrapped around my cock. Always will be, and that's a hill I'm willing to die on.

A few minutes later, I'm finishing up a text to Roman, making sure he's got everything covered for tomorrow. When he sends a confirmation, I quickly delete our text thread. I click over, seeing the alert that my packages will be delivered tomorrow morning while Shiloh's at the office. I grin.

Hell fucking yeah.

I'm tucking my phone into my pocket when I finally hear the creak of her feet on the stairs. My eyes dart up, finding hers almost instantly. My heart pounds in my chest as love and pride fill me rapidly.

"Shiloh," I breathe, taking her in. She's wearing a long, white dress that flows around her body in a way that has me wanting to drop to my knees, crawl across the living room floor, and worship at her altar. The dress has sleeves that lay loosely around her biceps. The neck drops to a V, showing off her perfect tits. There's a tight part just below that, accentuating her curves. Her hair is down and curled. Her golden tan skin pops next to the light color of her dress.

She looks like a literal fucking Goddess.

She's perfect.

I want to tell her that. Tell her she's beautiful. Stunning. The woman of my goddamned dreams. But...my head can't get past the fact that it's long and white.

It's white.

"You look like a bride," I say dumbly instead. She pauses, her hand wrapped around the banister, her foot stalling mid-step. Charging forward, I take her face in my hands before she can think a single negative thought. "Marry me. Today. Wear this. We'll go to the courthouse right the fuck now."

Her face breaks out in a mega-watt smile. One I've noticed more and more every day since we met. She has a tiny dimple on her chin that I want to lick. No... I want to fill it with my cum. Is that weird? Fuck it. Doesn't make it any less true.

She scoffs, rolling her eyes. "It's Sunday, Logan."

"So?" I drawl, my eyes raking over her gorgeous body. My dick is so hard, it's already leaking in my jeans. How can that be possible? I've cum inside her so many times in the last few days I've actually lost count. I'd assume my balls are empty at this point. Guess not.

She presses a hand to my chest, pushing me back as she steps off the stairs. "Courthouse isn't open today, baby."

God, I love her. "That's not a no," I murmur, watching her ass swish back and forth as she steps around me. Reaching down, I adjust my aching dick, already knowing it's useless. Jeans are becoming a real problem for me at this point. Maybe I should switch over to sweats permanently.

"I thought you said we were late," she calls, winking at me over her shoulder. Groaning, I jog past her, slapping her ass as I go. She screeches, and I smile.

"Grab Tank. I'll load the beast."

"Stop calling our dog a beast!" she screeches, scooping Tank up into her arms with all the care in the world as she coos at him.

Our dog.

Fuck. Will it ever stop being so perfect?

I hope not.

"Oh my god! He did what?" Shiloh cries as she wipes her tears of laughter away. "Are you serious?"

Charlie nods, taking another drink of his beer. "Yes, and he wore it like that for months."

"It's not my fault," I bark, running my fingers through my wayward hair. I tug on the strands, making sure it's all intact as awful memories of me with a mohawk flash before my eyes. "He dared me!"

"You didn't have to do it!" Charlie shouts, his hands flying up as if to defend himself. "Just because I dared you to shave your head doesn't mean shit!"

"Language!" Mom chastises, but the smile behind her glass of iced tea gives her away. "And your brother is right, Lo. A dare or not, that was a terrible decision on your part."

"What did you expect me to do? Its code. Don't crap out on a dare, or the next one will be ten times worse." I say vehemently, knowing that's exactly what would have happened if I'd chickened out.

Shiloh looks at me, a wide smile on her perfect, round face. She's barely wearing any makeup. Just some black stuff on her eyes that makes her lashes look big and long and some pink lipstick that makes her full lips damn near pornographic.

"I don't understand," she mumbles, her brows pinched together adorably. My thumb sweeps across her neck, loving the feel of her skin beneath mine. She shivers. I smirk. She rolls her eyes. "If he dared you to shave your head bald, how did you end up with a mohawk?"

"Because he was a pussy," Charlie cuts in unhelpfully.

"Charles Robert Huxley! I'm going to put you in the corner for a time out if you keep talking that trash!" Mom shouts. All three of us boys cringe, knowing she absolutely has the power to do that, even if we're all in our thirties.

He drops his head, a picture of apology. "Sorry, mama."

"Anyways," Stephen drawls, bringing us back to the ridiculous topic. "He started shaving his head but freaked out halfway through when he heard mom and dad come home. He threw all his hair down the sink drain and wore a beanie for a week."

"Clogged that sink, too," Dad grunts. "Had to rip out the whole pipe."

Shiloh falls into a fit of giggles. The sound is both angelic and boner-inducing. Fuck. I'd barely just gotten the thing to chill out. "You're just lucky you started on the sides instead of the middle."

I groan, sinking deeper into the couch cushions. I tighten my arm around Shiloh's shoulders, tugging her into my side. She laughs again, listening as Stephen prattles on about some other stupid bullshit dare they gave me when we were kids. My heart fills near to bursting as I watch her interact with my family.

She fits in perfectly.

Looking up, I find my Mom's watchful stare, a proud, emotional smile on her face. She subtly tilts her chin toward the kitchen. I jerk a nod.

"I'm going to go get another round of drinks. Logan, come help me." She stands, patting my dad on the shoulder as she passes through the living room. He looks up, smiling at her like she's his whole world. My dad has looked at my Mom that way every day of their lives together, I have no doubt. He loves her more than life itself.

Looking at Shiloh, I can understand the feeling.

Leaning in, I tuck my face in her neck. I breathe in her sweet, frosting scent and barely stifle a moan. "Be right back, Babydoll," I murmur, pressing my lips to her neck. She shudders, then nods.

"Jesus, leave the girl alone, Logan," Stephen grunts. "She'll be fine for five minutes."

"Yeah, fuc—I mean—frigg off. I have pictures to show her in your absence." Charlie sends me a wink promising maximum embarrassment. I send him a scathing glare, promising maximum pain.

Shiloh shoves me away and claps her hands. "Oh my God! Is it the mohawk? Please tell me it's the mohawk!"

Smiling, I shake my head at her excitement and stand. I start to walk away but can't...not yet. I bend down and capture her smiling mouth in a searing kiss that is *way* too inappropriate for the present company, but I don't give a shit. She's mine, and this is me claiming her in front of the whole lot of them. If I could, I'd claim her in front of the whole world.

When she's pregnant, everyone will know.

I groan into her mouth, visions of her belly big with our baby filling my head instantly. I have to forcibly pull myself away before I throw her over my shoulder caveman-style and fuck her against a tree.

"Be right back," I whisper. She looks up at me, her eyes heavy with lust. She blinks. Blinks again, seeming to come back to earth. Her cheeks turn bright pink as realization washes over her. She glares at me. I smile, booping her nose.

Who am I? I don't boop.

Shiloh bats my hand away. Chuckling, I leave them to it and head to find my Mom, who is most definitely not in the kitchen. A few minutes later, I find her in Dad's old office. She's sitting on one of the large, leather wingback chairs across from the fireplace, twirling something around in her hands.

"Close the door," she murmurs. I do, clicking it shut. She juts her chin at the chair next to her.

"What's this about, Mom?" I ask, taking a seat. The old leather creaks beneath my wide frame. The nostalgic feeling of sitting exactly as I am, years and years ago with my Dad, bring on an unexpected wave of emotion.

God. I spent hours here, with not only him, but my brothers as well. He'd tell us all about life and business. Relationships and love. Hell, he even gave us all the sex talk in this room. My lips lift in the ghost of a smile. This room reminds me of Liam.

"How are you, Lo?" she asks softly, pulling my attention back to the present.

My brows furrow. "What do you mean?"

My Mom's head tilts to the side as she considers me. I fight the urge to twitch under her knowing gaze. "She's very sweet."

I smile then, unable to help it. Nodding, I say, "I know. She's amazing."

Her smile grows, causing her wrinkles to deepen. "She's the one."

"She is," I agree, not missing a beat. I'd had a feeling this was why she'd called me in here. No doubt, she knew about Shiloh even before I did. "I'm going to marry her as soon as she'll let me."

My Mom's eyes gloss over seconds before the tears begin to fall. She's still smiling, though. Beaming, actually. "I'm so happy for you, Lo. She fits in well with the family." I nod, my eyes catching on the object in her hands. "I've held onto this for you. For when the time was right."

She bends her tiny body over, reaching across the space between us as she passes me the box. My eyes widen, but my heart stays steady in my chest. I have no doubts, no concerns, or questions. Shiloh's it for me.

I flick the box open, finding the most incredible engagement and wedding band set I've ever seen. It's rose gold, which makes my heart skip a beat. *It's her favorite.* I glance up at my mom, and she smiles, her shoulder lifting in a shrug. I chuckle, shaking my head.

In the center sits an oval cut diamond in a split-marquis setting. It flows into a diamond band that looks like vines wrapping around each other. It reminds me of the vines that hang from the cave beneath the waterfall at Arrowhead Lake. It's vintage yet modern, weaving together old and new with a hint of nature. The matching wedding band is also the vined pattern, but it fits against the engagement ring seamlessly, sealing them together and making them one.

It's perfect. Not too flashy, but big enough to show the world she's taken.

Pulling my gaze from the ring is harder than it should be. It's just a ring, not a wedding, but still—

Looking up at my Mom, I'm not surprised to find her crying. I have to blink black a tear myself. "Where did you get this?"

She laughs, wiping her face. "It was your Grandmother's." My forehead wrinkles in confusion. She laughs again. "I know. She was never married. I have no idea why or where she got it, just that she told me my oldest son would need it someday."

"But grandma died before I was born."

She nods, saying nothing. A knowing grin on her face. Sighing, I release a shaky breath. Wild, psychic women in this family, I swear.

"I really am happy for you, Logan. We all are." She pauses, her smile widening. "She wants kids?"

My heartbeat picks up. "*We do.*"

"Good." Her eyes twinkle in that way of hers, and my heart practically leaps from my chest.

"Mom?" My heart moves its way up—up—up. She smirks. It's in my throat now. "Mama?"

She lifts a shoulder as if to say, *sorry, bucko, that's all you get.* "I think I prefer Gigi."

I fly from my chair, passing the ring box back to her for safekeeping. "I'll come back for this." She bursts out laughing but takes the box, tucking it in her lap.

"Don't go leaving, Logan Huxley. We haven't even eaten yet."

Oh, I'm about to eat, alright.

Turning, I bolt from the room, calling over my shoulder, "Just wanna show her around." I make it to the living room in record time, needing to have eyes on my woman. I find her huddled up on the couch, Stephen on one side, Charlie on the other. I grit my teeth, not liking *that* at all. I ignore everyone as I circle the couch and pull her to me. A stack of photographs goes flying, but I'm too happy to care.

"Logan!" she shrieks. I barely, *just barely*, resist the urge to throw her over my shoulder. The only reason I don't is that I don't want her to feel embarrassed. Grabbing her hand, I yank her after me as I bob and weave through various pieces of furniture.

"We'll be back. Carry on," I bark as my pace picks up. I practically drag Shiloh upstairs, needing to get some distance from everyone else. Needing to get my girl alone. "Wanna show you my old room," I grunt, sounding more caveman than anything.

I pull her into the room, catching her as she stumbles behind me. Her eyes dart around, taking in the space that's practically a time capsule of my formidable years. I kick the door shut with my foot and push past her. I stop next to the bed and turn, finally finding her eyes. I'm breathing so hard; I'm basically panting like a dog.

My gaze trails down her body, homing in on the swell of her belly. It's not round from our baby yet, but it will be—*soon.* I don't know what my mom meant exactly, but I have an idea. Shiloh's on her way to being pregnant. Either my seed's already taken, or it will soon; only time will tell. I know there's some sort of delay with these things. Doesn't matter. All I know is that it's happening, and when it does, my woman's going to be happier than she's ever been in her life.

We're having a fucking baby.

A tidal wave of possession coats my body like a second skin, overpowering me until it's all I see, all I feel.

Mine. Mine. Mine.

My cock is so hard just thinking about it that I'm pretty sure I'll blow my load the second she touches me.

"What are you doing?" she murmurs, her eyes flaring as they rake down my body. Much like I'd zeroed in on her belly, she's locked onto my cock as it practically pokes a hole in my jeans. "We can't do this here."

Ignoring her, I rip my shirt off my body and toss it somewhere over my shoulder. "Shut up, take your panties off and sit on my fucking face, Shiloh," I growl. I've never been more thankful than I am right now that my girl is obsessed with dresses.

I see the moment it happens. The exact second, her nerves turn into something else. Something darker. Deep, carnal lust.

Her voice becomes a throaty purr as she slides the lock in place. The click sounds like a gunshot in the silent room. "Are you going to breed me, Daddy?"

God-fucking-damnit.

I drop down onto the bed, tucking my hand behind my head as I watch her. She saunters toward me, swaying her hips as she goes. Tugging her fat bottom lip between her teeth, she grabs her dress and bunches the material up in her fists.

Up...up...up...

I groan, my eyes taking in the lacey booty shorts she's wearing beneath her dress. *They're white.* "Are you trying to fucking kill me?" I grunt, thoughts of our wedding night filling my brain. "You better wear those when we get married."

She chuckles quietly, sliding the lace down her thick thighs. "I'll buy new ones."

I smile, loving the way she's openly acknowledging this. Talking about our wedding night like it's a foregone conclusion. Good. She better be ready. It'll be happening way sooner than she thinks.

Shiloh tosses the panties next to my shirt and steps forward, her knees touching the bed. Her hands twitch, still holding the dress rucked up around her hips. It's dipping over the crease of her thighs, hiding my view of her perfect, pretty pussy, and I find myself quickly getting angry at a piece of clothing.

"Come here," I growl, shifting my body, so she has room to straddle my face. Her eyes dart back to the door as she hesitates. "It's fine, Babydoll. You'll just have to be quiet. You can do that, right? Be a good girl and keep your mouth shut?"

Her head flies in my direction, her pupils blown wide. Damn...what exactly did I say to cause that reaction?

I wanna do it again.

"Come here, Shiloh," I grunt. Reaching out, I fist her dress and yank her forward, tired of waiting. She falls to the bed, colliding with my chest. "Climb on my fucking face and let me eat you."

"Logan," she whispers, shaking her head. "I can't."

"Why?" I grunt, narrowing my eyes. She looks down at her body, and it clicks. "What did I tell you before, Shiloh? What did I say about exactly *this?*"

She thinks for a moment, then gasps. "You said you look forward to the day when you can have my thighs wrapped around your head while you eat me. Then something about being buried so deep inside me that you—" she breaks off, her face beet red.

"That I what?" I groan, adjusting my cock. I want to fuck her so bad right now; my cock is practically weeping.

"*Suffocate,*" she whispers.

Nodding, I yank her closer and slap her thigh. "That's right. Hop on and give your man what he wants."

It takes a little shifting, but I finally get her where I want her, her thighs spread wide on either side of my head, her long dress yanked up, giving me a perfect view of her lush body. I don't give her a second to rethink or object before tugging her down, so she's sitting on my face instead of hovering. I wasn't kidding when I said I wanted to suffocate between her thighs.

I inhale deeply, taking in her musky, sweet scent. Her pussy's already dripping for me, and I know it won't take long to get her off, but this isn't for her; it's for me.

Yeah, I want to make my girl cum. I want to make her cum one hundred times a day, but this right here? This is purely for selfish reasons. My possessive instincts when it comes to her are insane, and right now, I need to be covered in her scent. I need her cum all over my face and chest. I need her to mark me the way I've marked her.

How much more seed do I need to put inside her to make sure it takes? Is it like a one-and-done deal? If I keep stuffing her full, will she have twins? Triplets?

Fuck.

My tongue lashes out, licking up the juices dripping steadily from her core. I groan at the first taste of her as it explodes in my mouth. Perfect. She's perfect. She whimpers, her hips twitching. I wrap my arms around her thighs, and then *I feast.*

I eat Shiloh's cunt like I'm a dehydrated man in the middle of the desert. I lick and suck and bite. I ravage her, licking her from taint to clit before repeating the process. I lick long strokes up and down, then suck her clit into my mouth. Biting down on the tiny, hard nub. I spear my tongue into her cunt, fucking her like it's my cock, then swap it out for my fingers.

I fuck her with one then two. Curling them until I'm massaging her g-spot. The spot I know makes my woman squirt every damn time. I add fingers until I'm practically fisting her, knowing she loves the stretch.

I don't stop, even when she's shaking and whispering her protests.

I don't stop, even when she's clenching out her release.

I don't stop, even when she cries out, making more noise than she's supposed to. Instead, I tilt my head, biting her fleshy thigh in a warning. She grabs a pillow, muffling her cries with it. I rip my mouth away from her cunt, praising her.

"You're such a good girl, Babydoll." She whines a low, drawn-out sound. Another release barrels through her at nothing but my words. She gushes, cumming all over my face and chest.

I smile.

Guess I know what set her off earlier.

I clean her up, licking every single drop from her pussy and thighs. She trembles, her poor cunt oversensitive from all the action. I release her and rub slow, soothing strokes down her back while she comes down from her high. She exhales a ragged breath and shifts down, moving off my face. She goes to stand, but I grab her hand, tugging her down next to me.

Shiloh's eyes widen when she takes in the state of me. Her face flushes, but then she leans in and cleans her cum from my face and chest. Licking me clean.

I groan as my cock twitches out a spurt of cum at the sight. "You're so fucking perfect," I grunt. Shiloh looks up at me, her tongue dragging up my throat. She grins, licking her lips clean. I grab her face, smashing our lips together.

We make out like teenagers, on my childhood bed, for I don't know how long. The entire time, thoughts of my younger years spiral through my mind. When I was struggling, not knowing what my future held or where I'd end up. I never lost the dream of a family of my own. Never. No matter how depressed I was, I held onto that.

But never in a million years did I think I'd find a future so goddamn perfect.

"I love you," I breathe, meeting her chocolate eyes.

She smiles, digging her head into the crook of my neck. I've noticed it's her favorite place to be. She inhales deeply, as obsessed with my scent as I am with hers.

She lets out a happy little sigh. "I love you, too."

IT'S MY CHOICE

BE PATIENT WITH YOURSELF

Unapologetic MYSELF

BE Bold

love yourself

beautiful

yes you can

Fearless

IN CONTROL

LOVE yourself

HERE TO STAY

you're enough

FEEL DEEPLY

YOUR POTENTIAL IS ENDLESS

be kind to yourself

it's my choice

Brave

I am exactly where I need to be

you are worthy

I am capable

YOU ARE enough

breathe Perfect

Shiloh

Eighteen

"Holy effing shit. Is *the* Shiloh Dominguez seriously FaceTiming me?" my bestie gasps, feigning a healthy dose of shock. I scoff, shooting the phone a scathing glare. Rayvn falls into a fit of tinkling laughter. "Alright, alright. No need to get all psycho on me."

"You're one to talk! You're way crazier than me!" I screech, hefting another box into the office. She gasps, pulling my attention away from my pile of cardboard. Glancing up to the bookshelf where my phone's propped up, I meet her stare. My brows lift. "What?"

"I thought you were at work," she grunts, her voice laced with disapproval. Leaning forward, as though it will give her a better view, her eyes scan my body. "Why are you dressed for the gym?"

I shrug, turning back to my project. Opening the box, I start to pull out various décor items I collected on my trip this afternoon. "I can wear whatever I want to work, *for now.* Hopefully, soon, Logan will have a full office staff running the place. When that happens, I'll go back to my dresses, I guess."

"But you love dresses," she mumbles, her mouth latched onto a straw. "I don't understand what's happening here."

Pausing, I stare up at her, my eyes narrowing on her tiny little face. "What are you talking about?"

"You love dresses," she says again, pointing an accusing finger in my direction. It has little effect on me since she's hours away and chastising me through a 3-inch screen.

Of course, she'd point out my less-than-professional outfit. Rayvn is *always* dressed to the nines. Like right now? Her black hair is pulled back into a tight, ballerina bun. Her dark skin has the perfect amount of makeup to accentuate her natural beauty. She's wearing a pink custom suit that pops against her brown skin. She looks effortlessly stunning, and it's noon on a Monday.

A Monday! No one has the right to look that good this soon after the weekend. Shit, I still look half-asleep.

Ray says she has to dress a certain way because she's a lawyer, which is true, but it's not just that. She's the most well-put-together, stylish person I've ever met. Always has been.

We've been besties since we were placed together as roommates at the University of Colorado. We stayed to-gether all four years, then were forced to separate when she went on to law school, and I moved to be closer to the school I interned at.

Ray and I found a way to make our long-distance friendship work. She's the closest thing I have to a sister. *I mean—besides my sister.* We tell each other everything. She knows every sordid detail of my relationship with Cole, and I know all about her dirty, nasty, kinky ways. Not that I'm one to judge. She may want to be chased through a forest and fucked on the ground like an animal, but I have fantasies of *actual* werewolves railing me with their massive, knotted cocks, sooo....

Grunting, I drop to my knees to sort through everything. I only have a few more hours before I'll be off for the day and Logan will expect me home. Apparently, we're going on a date tonight. I smile at the thought.

He dropped me off this morning since my car is still parked here. He's been busy all day with meetings, and though we've been texting back and forth whenever he has a free moment, it's not the same. I know I've only worked here for a month, but I've gotten used to spending our days together in our quiet little world.

"Yes," I sigh. "I love dresses Ray, but it's winter. Snowy and cold. Not to mention, there's no point in me dressing up if I'm just sitting on the floor and sorting through crap all day."

She lets out a sound of disgust and drops back into her office chair. "That sounds horrendous. Why haven't you demanded that prick gives you a desk?"

My heart nervously thuds in my chest, even as irritation fills me. No one's allowed to call my man a prick but me. It's not her fault, though. I haven't exactly told her what's going on yet. "Yeah, about that..." I groan. "Logan's not a prick, for one. For two, I like the floor. I sat on it for years when I taught the littles. It's comfortable. For three..."

I glance up at the screen, cringing when I find her wide eyes staring back at me, anticipating my next words. She's too observant for her own good. "Tell me" she all but screams.

Rolling my eyes, I shake my head, tearing open the packaging on the new curtains I picked up. "Logan and I are—" I break off. What do I say? In love? Living together? Trying to have a baby? Moving way too fast but unable to stop it? Jesus, she's going to have me committed. Actually, knowing her she'll come down here kick his ass, and then drag me home for an intervention.

"Tell me!" she squeals. A loud bang reverberates through the phone speaker, drawing my attention back to her. The screen goes black, then wobbly, before she finally returns. "Sorry! I got so excited I dropped my phone. You're fucking him, aren't you? Oh my god, please tell me you're fucking your boss, Shiloh!"

Feeling my cheeks heat, I shrug, unable to stop myself from grinning like a fool. Rayvn screams, then slaps her hand over her mouth, her wide eyes shooting toward her office door. "Fuck," she whispers. I bark out a laugh. "All the details. Now."

"Fine" I murmur, sighing my defeat.

I spend the next thirty minutes talking Ray through the last unexpected month of my life. It's a wild ride, that's for sure. I hadn't realized how nuts it all sounded until I told the story from beginning to end, all in one sitting. All the while, I work on my project, excited to see what Logan thinks when I show him. I hope he likes it. I spent *way* too much money on supplies for this to have been a bust.

When I've finally finished, I drop to the office chair. My phone now in hand, and stare at my best friend. She stares back. We sit in awkward silence for what feels like forever but is likely only a few moments.

"So," she breathes.

My phone slips from my sweaty grip. *Shit.* What if she thinks I'm crazy? *Her*, out of all people. Rayvn Porter; the woman with a kink list longer than the Declaration of Independence.

The woman who wants her blood to be sucked like she's Bella freaking Swan. The woman who wants to basically be abducted, *consensually*, and fucked like a hostage. Point is, her fantasies and mind are a crazy place to be, and if she finds *my* actions to be insane then they probably are.

"So," I say, biting my bottom lip as I wait her out.

Finally, *finally*, her face breaks out into a massive smile. "When can I meet him?" Oh, thank fuck.

We spend the next hour catching up. She promises to make some calls to get me out of my lease without any penalties, lamenting about *shitty-self-right-eous-skeezy-bastard-landlords.* By the time we get off the phone, I've just about finished decorating around one office, but I have a good few more days of work ahead of me, maybe more. We hang up with promises to chat again this weekend.

I hate to admit it but having Ray's approval of mine and Logan's whirlwind relationship solidifies my decision to jump into the deep end with him. A wide smile spreads across my face, feeling lighter and more positive about the future than ever before.

"Honey, I'm home!" I call out, grinning ear to ear. Stepping into the living room, I pause when Logan doesn't respond. My face scrunches up. That's weird, his truck's in the garage.

Pulling my phone from my pocket, I check for any missed calls or texts but find nothing besides his message saying to *meet him at home at 6:00 pm* and to *be ready.* I have no idea what he meant by that, but it's now fifteen after. I'm home, and he's nowhere in sight. Unsure of what to do, I slowly make my way through the house. It's awkward being here, especially alone. I may have agreed to move in, but the house still *feels his*.

I search the bottom floor and come up empty. "Logan?" I call out. Again, silence. *Where are the dogs?* There's a creepy, quiet feel to the house that has my spine stiffening. "Logan! Seriously, where are you?"

I jog upstairs, loathing how large the house is for the first time. He could be anywhere. "I swear to Sky Daddy, if you pop out in a mask, I'll punch your dick." The whole *scared* thing is Ray's kink, not mine. I fucking *hate* being scared.

I open door after door, finding nothing but empty rooms. Every bedroom, including his—*ours,* show no sign of life. I even checked the closets and—and the someday nursery.

Yanking my phone from my pocket once more, I click his name, ready to chew him out for fucking with me. I'm just about to press *call* when a loud, masculine curse comes from the backyard.

Why is he outside?

Beyond irritated from spending the last twenty minutes searching for him, I run back downstairs. I narrowly avoid breaking my head open when I trip and stumble down the last five steps. Forcing myself to slow down, I make my way to the backdoor. Slow is better. That way, I have time to calm down, so I don't chew him out.

Flinging the door open, I stomp onto the deck and come to an abrupt halt. My eyes feel as big as saucers as I take everything in. There's so much to see, I can't even figure out where to look first.

What and the ever-loving-holy-he—

"Babydoll?" Logan's voice trickles in through my shock. I'm pretty sure that's what it is. Could be a stroke. At this point, I'm honestly not sure. "Shiloh?" His voice is much closer now. Still, I can't tear my eyes away from the scene before me.

What did you do, Logan?

"Shiloh." And then, his hands are on my face, and he's standing in front of me, effectively cutting off my view. My eyes dart up, meeting his. The world returns to focus, and finally, my brain works again. "Are you okay?" he grunts, his thumbs rubbing a soothing pattern across my cheeks.

No. He's not soothing. He's wiping away tears. Am I crying? I hadn't even noticed.

"Babydoll, please say something. You're starting to freak me out."

"I think I might be dead," I choke out. Logan's eyes widen. He stares at me, confusion written all over his stupidly perfect face. He barks out a loud laugh, his cheeks pinkening in that adorable way I love so much.

I stare.

Stare at the tiny dimple that peaks out from beneath his beard. Stare at the curly, red beard that looks freshly trimmed and neatly groomed. My eyes flick to his hair, finding the same situation up top. My brows furrow. My eyes drift down his body, taking in his whole appearance for the first time since I arrived.

He's wearing—*what the hell?* He's wearing a suit.

"You're not dead."

"You're wearing a suit," I say dumbly, my gaze still caught on the expensive-looking material, hugging his every mas-culine curve. His thighs look like they're about to bust from the dark fabric. The jacket looks as though it'll need to be cut straight from his body when he wants to undress. His shoes are shiny, pointed, and unlike anything I've ever seen him wear before. He looks handsome. Unbelievably so, yet, it's weird seeing him like this.

He doesn't look like *my* Logan.

"I am," he grunts. "Is it—do you not like it?" My head jerks up, realizing that had come off as rude.

"Shit, I'm sorry," I choke out. "I think I'm in shock. You look amazing. So, *so*, good. I just—I don't understand what's happening right now."

His hands flex on my cheeks, his smile returning. He drops his hold on my face, and one of his large hands wraps around mine. He tugs me toward the center of the large deck and stops. Turning back to face me, he grabs my sweatshirt, using the material to pull me into his body. I trip, stumbling over my feet as I crash into him. His mouth finds mine in a searing kiss that's so possessive, *so feral*...it takes my breath away.

It seems to be exactly what I need to shake me from my shocked state. I kiss him back, putting as much love into it as possible. My heart is racing so hard and so fast; I'm surprised I haven't passed out. He pulls away, and finally, *finally*, I'm able to comprehend what I'm seeing.

There are hundreds, no, *thousands*, of fairy lights covering the deck. They twine around the pillars and drape down from the beams, lighting everything in a soft glow. Multiple space heaters are warming the area. A firepit sits to the right, matching Adirondack chairs on either side. There are candles and flowers on every available surface, in all of my favorite colors.

It's beautiful. Absolutely incredible.

But what has my attention is the huge makeshift bed in the middle of the deck, next to where we're standing. Cushions cover the ground, raising the comfy space by at least a foot. It might even be an air mattress, but it's hard to tell with all the pillows and blankets. *Tons* of blankets in a variety of prints and textures.

"What is this?" I whisper, dragging my eyes back to his. Logan smiles, looking down at me like I'm his entire world, his universe. I suck in a sharp breath, suddenly dizzy at the sight.

That's the way I've always wanted someone to look at me.

He bends down, pressing a soft, lingering kiss to my forehead. We both exhale at the same time, seeming to find peace when were wrapped together. "Let me show you," he murmurs.

And then, he drops to his knee.

My mouth opens, then closes, then opens again. So many things fly through my brain all at once that I actually short-circuit to the point that nothing exists beyond him. It's like my world narrows down until there is no one and nothing outside of our little bubble. It's just him and me in the middle of a blank void. I hear nothing, but him. I see nothing, but him. I feel nothing, but *him*.

Logan.

"Before we met, I was nothing. I wasn't living. Hell, I was barely existing. I hated everyone and everything. Still do," he grunts, running a hand through his polished hair, mussing it up. I chuckle, my hands trembling. "I didn't want an assistant. I sure as fuck didn't want one that looks like you. I knew having you around would shake up my world, and I didn't want that." He pauses, and my heart gives a painful squeeze, unsure where he's going with this. Logan barks out a laugh, shaking his head. "I'm fucking this up."

His head drops, tucking into his chest. I don't like that. Logan Huxley looks down for no one. I take a step forward and drop to my knees before him. In a move I learned from Logan himself, I grip his chin, beard, and all, and lift his head. Our eyes meet, and he inhales sharply at what he sees.

I show him everything.

My appreciation for him. My possession over him. The way I want and need him more than anything else in this world. The way he's not only completed me, filling a void I didn't think was fillable, but also the way he's fixed every crack and fissure that was created before him. Seamlessly, simply and without question. He repaired what someone else broke.

I show him that and so much more. I show him that I, Shiloh Huxley, will love him with every breath in my body until the day I die.

"I didn't mean to find you. I didn't mean to keep you. I didn't mean to need you, and I didn't mean to love you," he murmurs, his voice thick with emotion. "But I did. I found you. I'm keeping you. I need you more than you know, and I love you more than you'll ever understand." Reaching into the front pocket of his suit jacket, he pulls out a ring. Lifting my hand, he glides the single most incredible piece of jewelry I have ever seen onto my finger. "Marry me."

A demand, not a question.

Leaning forward, I press my lips to his, nodding and crying as I do.

We fall into each other. Kissing and touching, exploring, and memorizing. His body drops back onto the bed and tugs me down with him. The blankets are warm from the heaters, and for some reason, they all smell strongly of rain and forest and earth. It soothes me all the way to my bones. I feel so wrapped up in him, consumed by him that it coats me like a safety blanket.

There on that bed, in the middle of nature, beneath the starry night sky, I give myself to him completely. I give him everything. My dreams, my goals, my heart, my soul. I give him my past, present, and future, promising never to take them back.

He's mine, and I'm his from this moment on.

Slowly, we pull each other's clothes off, devouring every inch of one another like we have all the time in the world.

We do, I realize. We have forever.

Logan worships my body, and I his. I kiss every one of his scars, showing him my unending gratitude for his sacrifices. I kiss his freckles, tracing my tongue from one to another until he's panting and writhing beneath me. It's a heady feeling. Having someone so strong and demanding, begging for more, for mercy, for pleasure.

I grin against his flesh, nipping and sucking his delicious flavor into my mouth as I work my way down his body. He groans, threading his fingers through my hair.

"Babydoll, I'm dying here," he murmurs, thrusting his hips up in a not-so-silent demand. His rock-hard cock bobs against his abs. The sight makes my mouth water. "*Suck.*"

I smile, more than happy to oblige. Bending over his body, on all fours, completely naked and on display, I suck my fiancé's cock into my mouth, not stopping until he hits my throat. I gag, stretching to accommodate his size, but refusing to give up. He groans, tugging my hair in a tight grip. His hips thrust forward; his eyes locked on mine. In them, I see nothing but lust and adoration.

Gone are the days when a man who was supposed to love me endlessly, no matter what, cringes away from my body. Gone are the days when a man refuses to touch me, only fucking me in the dark, with most of our clothes on.

Never again.

Here, in the moonlight, with all my imperfections on display for him, I feel so, utterly *perfect*. I've never hated my body, but *until now*, I'd never fully given myself permission to love it.

"That's it, baby," he grunts, picking up pace, using my mouth and body to find his pleasure. "God-fucking-damnit, Shiloh. *Shit!*" Using my hair like a leash, he yanks me away. Spit and drool sting from my sore mouth to his cock. I moan at the sight and flick my tongue out to clean up the mess. "Don't wanna cum in your mouth," he pants, releasing my hair.

I wipe my face with my hand as I sit back on my knees. Logan's eyes rake down my body so intensely, I shiver.

"Spread your thighs," he grunts. I do, widening them until he can see all of me. "Touch *my* cunt. Play with *my* pretty pussy."

I moan, my head dropping back as my fingers find my sopping wet core. I do as he says, following his instructions word for word, speeding up when he demands it, pausing when he says to. I flick my clit until I'm shaking. Finger myself until I'm a trembling, whining mess.

"*Lo—*" he tuts, interrupting me. "*Daddy, please.*"

He shakes his head. "Not yet, Babydoll. I want you covered in your slick," he murmurs. My hazy eyes snap up to meet his, my fingers stilling knuckle deep inside myself. "You need to be sopping wet to be able to take my knot."

"Excuse me?" I choke out. My pussy flutters around my fingers as a fresh wave of pleasure courses through me. "Your—"

"My knot," he nods. Reaching over, he pulls a cloth bag from beneath one of the many pillows. I lean forward, my hand slipping from between my thighs. He shakes his head, tutting me again. "No. Not until Daddy says. You're not wet enough yet." I whimper in protest. "Not until I hear the sloppy sounds of your slick dripping down your sweet cunt."

Jesus Christ, have mercy on me and my vagina.

Leaning back, I spread my thighs once more, doing everything Logan says until I'm practically sobbing. Again and again, I get close enough to combust. Again and again, he makes me stop. Like a King on a throne, he lays before me. One hand tucked behind his head, the other idly stroking his cock while he destroys me with his words alone.

"That's it, omega. Fuck your pussy. Imagine how good you'll feel when I stuff you full of my knot."

"Do you want that? My cock and my knot, so deep in you I split your pussy in half?"

"Say it, Babydoll. Tell me you want my knot. Tell me you want me to fill your pussy with my seed. Tell me you want your Alpha to breed you."

Again and again and again.

"Please, Daddy," I beg, my body shaking so hard I can barely stay upright. "*Please.*"

Logan pauses his stroking, his eyes barely open with how hooded they've become. "Please, what?" he grunts, his voice a thick rasp. "What do you need?"

"Please—" swallowing, my eyes dart to the bag sitting on his chest. I can't believe I'm actually saying this out loud to another human being. "Please, *Alpha.* I need your knot."

Please, please, please let there be a real-life knot in that bag, I pray, murmuring my silent pleas to whoever will listen.

Logan bolts upright, releasing a feral as fuck growl. He empties the contents of the bag on the blanket before me. "Pick."

Ohmigod, ohmigod, ohmi—

"Hurry up!" he grunts. Apparently, five seconds wait time is too long. Grinning, I lean forward, inspecting his haul. *Sex toys!*

He bought four silicone cock rings that are shaped like knots. All four are different sizes, giving options for stretch. Two are smooth and veiny. One is covered in textured bumps, and the other in soft *spikes*.

Logan lets out a loud groan of impatience, and my hand darts out, grabbing before I can debate any longer. I end up picking the largest of the four, a smooth, veiny pink one.

Leaning forward, I place a hand on his chest and push him backward. He softly hits the pillows, his eyes narrowing on me in suspicion. I smile, saying nothing as I crawl up his body. With my thighs spread wide, I hover my dripping pussy over his cock.

"Daddy did such a good job," I whisper, praising him for his sweet gift, my fingers trailing up his abs. Logan's body shudders. I drop down, sliding myself along his length. We both groan. "I have to cover your cock in my slick, don't I?"

"*Fuck, yeah,*" he snarls, sounding more beast than man. His hands grip my hips, forcing me to move faster. My orgasm hangs just out of reach, getting closer and closer every time his cock bumps my clit. "Stop," he grunts, squeezing my flesh hard enough to bruise. "Put it on. Now."

I gasp at his harsh tone and jump to do as he commands. It takes a few tries but eventually, I get the knot in place. It fits snugly like a large, bulbous cock ring around the base of his dick, and the sight of it nearly has me cumming on the spot.

"Oh my god, Logan," I choke, entranced by the sight.

He growls, tossing me from his body and onto the bed. Seconds later, he's thrusting inside me, shoving his cock as far as it can go, leaving the knot out for now. I have a moment of panic as I adjust to his thickness. He's already so massive. I don't know how I'll be able to take anything more than this, especially with how wide the knot is.

We both pause, breathing heavily, our eyes locked on to one another as we adjust to the sensations coursing through our bodies. His forehead drops to mine, and we share a moment of intense emotions, our bodies connected in every way.

Logan's mouth drops to mine. He kisses me slowly, lovingly. His tongue licks my lower lip, requesting entrance. I open for him, sucking him into my mouth. We breathe in one another as we lazily take in this moment.

Sitting up, he murmurs, "Ready?"

I nod, tugging my lip between my teeth. Logan groans, his eyes tracking the movement. Sitting back on his thighs, he grips my knees and bends my legs, opening me up for him. Like this, nothing is hidden. He can see every part of me, and judging by the way his cock jerks inside me, he likes what he sees.

His hips thrust forward, pressing every perfect inch of his hot flesh deep inside me. I feel him bump parts of me that no one's ever reached before as his cock fills me to the brim. He pulls out slowly, then slams back in. He repeats the movement, again and again, fucking me so hard that he shoves me up the bed with every harsh snap of his hips.

"Take it, *Omega*. Take my cock, all of it," he grunts, fucking harder into my aching pussy. The knot smacks against my clit and taint with every agonizing movement.

Shit, shit, shit. I'm so close.

"Not yet," he barks.

I groan, realizing I'd said that out loud, proving how lost I am, how delirious he has me. My head tips back, my eyes gaze up at the stars as I commit every second of this undeniable pleasure to memory. His mouth drops down to my neck, and he gently bites the flesh below my ear. A shiver wracks my body at the feeling.

"You want me to claim you? *Mate you?* Are you ready for it, baby? Me and you, forever." *Oh, shit. He's pulling out all the stops right now.* I don't even think twice as I nod, moaning loudly. I want it so bad. "I'm gonna keep breeding you again and again." His thrusts pick up, and his huge dick pistons into me so deeply I can feel him against my cervix. "Keep your belly big and round with my babies. Keep you filled with my cum every fucking day for the rest of your life. You want that?"

"Yes!" I scream, my orgasm crashing into me like a tidal wave, brought on by the impact of his words. I want his babies so bad that it hurts. I want him to breed me, mate me, more than anything...except— "I want your knot, Alpha, please!"

"Shit," he shouts, shoving his cock deep, forcing his thick knot past my sopping entrance. It hurts, but it's the best thing I've ever felt. The stretch is unlike anything I could have ever imagined. "Shit, Babydoll, your pussy's strangling me. Let me in. Take my knot. I need to fill you up, split you in two."

I relax, letting him in. It takes some work, but I'm so soaked that the knot finally enters me with a pop. I scream, tipping my head back and presenting my throat. Logan groans, shifting his hips and locking us together seconds before he's filling me with his hot seed.

"Take my cum, Shiloh. All of it. I'm gonna knock you up. Fill you with so much fuckin' cum. Want it dripping down your thick thighs for days." Then, his teeth are sinking into my neck. The sharp burst of pain is quickly washed out by the overwhelming euphoria of another climax washing over me. I cum, and cum, and cum. I cum so hard, I black out.

As I come back down to earth, I find us turned on our sides face to face, my thigh pulled over his hip, his cock still wedged deep inside my pussy, knot and all. As we lay there in each other's arms, breathing heavily and enjoying the endless night sky, one thought continuously swirls through my exhausted brain.

He's mine. Mine for life. Mine forever. Soulmate.

"Did you like it?" he whispers. I smile, thrusting my hips forward, and grinding against him. He groans, slapping my ass and stilling my movements. "Are you okay? I didn't hurt you, did I?"

"I'm perfect," I sigh. Looking down, I take in my ring. The events of the last hour fill my heart near to bursting. "We're engaged."

"We are," he pauses, wrapping his arms around my body. His head drops to my neck, "but it's not enough." I groan, rolling my eyes. He slaps my ass again. "It won't be enough until you have my last name and my baby in your belly. You know that, right?"

Swallowing down my emotions, I nod. "I do." We lay there like that, lost in each other, enjoying the feeling of being in each other's arms for so long; I start to fall asleep. "Are we going to sleep like this?" I murmur, squeezing my pussy for emphasis.

He groans, rutting his hips into me. "I don't know what the protocol is. I didn't get that far in your books."

"I can't believe you did this," I say softly. "I thought Logan Huxley was against sex toys."

He barks out a laugh, his body shaking with the movement. "Only when you're using them without me, but after this, I think I could be persuaded to bring your toys into the bedroom."

I grin, tucking my head into his chest. "You have no idea what that Dragon Dong can do." Logan slaps my ass, once, twice, until I'm moaning and clenching around him.

"Goddamnit, Babydoll," he grunts. "I'm gonna end up fucking you all night, aren't I?"

"Is that a problem?" I ask, completely serious.

He pushes me onto my back, his knotted cock still lodged deep inside me. "You're insatiable. Is my little omega in heat?" His voice is a breathless pant as he slowly rolls his hips.

My eyes widen. Turning my head to the side, I take in everything he did. He didn't just make an adorably sweet place to propose and make love; he made—

"You made me a nest?" I gasp, my eyes burning as emotion clogs my throat. Holy shit, he really is the perfect man.

Bending down, he blankets my body with his, rutting his cock deep in my body. "I'd do anything to make you happy, Babydoll. *Anything*."

And as he slowly makes love to me beneath the stars, I know without a shadow of a doubt that I'll be happy for the rest of my life.

IT'S MY CHOICE

BE PATIENT WITH YOURSELF

Unapologetically MYSELF

BE BOLD

ALL BODIES ARE GOOD BODIES

LOVE yourself

beautiful

HERE TO STAY

IN CONTROL

I am enough

FEEL DEEPLY

YOUR POTENTIAL IS ENDLESS

be kind to yourself

be Brave

IT'S MY CHOICE

I am exactly where I need to be

I am capable

YOU ARE enough

glowful

breathe

Perfect

Logan

Nineteen

"Okay, okay," I grunt. "I'm coming."

"Are your eyes closed?" Shiloh asks, her voice a few octaves higher than usual. "You can't see, can you? I swear, Logan, if you ruin this, I'll punch you in the dick."

"Stop threatening my cock, Babydoll," I growl, wishing I could slap her cute ass.

She yanks my hand, pushing the glass double doors open for the both of us. "Shut up and answer me! Are your eyes closed?"

"Yes." I chuckle, grinning at her excitement. Letting her be my guide as she drags me through the front door of Huxley Homes shows how much I trust her. Especially when Porkchop barrels past me, nearly knocking me to my knees. Tank runs along right behind her, his wheels squeaking from the speed. I grunt, squeezing Shiloh's hand harder. "How much further?"

She groans and stops abruptly. I smash into her back, sending her forward a few steps with the impact. "Damnit, Shiloh," I growl, blindly tugging her into my body. I pat her down, making sure she's okay. She bats me away with a scoff.

"I'm fine," she growls. Still, my hands reach out, patting her belly. *Just in case.* "Logan!" she barks. "Enough!"

"Babydoll," I snap. "Take this blindfold off. *Now.*"

Did I mention I hate surprises? Like, really fucking hate them? It's been two weeks since I proposed, and every single day, she's figured out ways to keep me from the office. She doesn't know I caught onto her little plan a few days in, but I did, and it's been killing me ever since.

Day one, I actually had to be on a job site and couldn't be in the office, so she got lucky.

Day two, Stephen called me with an emergency at a different job site.

Day three, my mom needed help with a project that, apparently, couldn't wait.

By day four, I knew there was no way that everyone suddenly needed me all at once. What really solidified my theory was the way my girl basically shoved me into my truck every morning, making sure to remind me that *I wasn't needed at the office.*

So, now, here we are. Standing in the reception area of the HH building, a silk purple blindfold wrapped tightly around my eyes and my woman jumping up and down with glee.

"Okay," she breathes, a manic quality to her voice. I don't like it. "Okay. This will all be fine."

"Stop talking to yourself. I'm taking it off." I don't wait for her to respond, ripping the sash from my face. I tug it into my back pocket for safekeeping. Definitely using that later. "So?" she drawls, her hands clasped tightly beneath her chin as she gazes up at me with wide eyes.

Reluctantly, I drag my gaze from her perfect face and look around. *Holy shit.* Spinning in a circle, I slowly take in what was once a simple, plain room that has now become a beautiful, professional office space.

She's hung curtains on all of the windows that add color and texture without blocking the natural light. Throw pillows sit on the couches and lounge chairs in the waiting area. Magazines, books, and flowers adorn the tables and reception desk. There are rugs and various pieces of artwork. Everything still *feels* the way Huxley Homes does. Warm, rustic, inviting, the way it was meant to. But with her additions, it feels like a real, operating business now.

"Wow," I murmur, trying to absorb everything at once. Not only did she decorate the space beautifully, she cleaned the fuck out of it, too. "You did all this?" Meeting her eyes, I find her nodding softly. She tips her shoulders in a nonchalant shrug like it's not a big deal.

It is, though. It's a huge deal. Little does she know; she's turning a building that I despised for so long into a place I actually enjoy coming to. She's swapping out old, painful memories for new, happy ones. It means everything to me.

"Shiloh, I don't know what to say," I murmur. She grins. Grabbing my hand, she pulls me toward the back end of the building. To the left are our offices. To the right is another door that leads to the meeting rooms, public bathroom, and breakroom.

She pulls me to the right, glancing over her shoulder every few steps as if to ensure I'm still with her. I chuckle, elation filling me at an unnatural speed. I love seeing her so fucking happy. I'd do anything to keep that big smile on her beautiful face.

Shiloh leads me through the building, showing me all the small touches she's added to every single space. She left nothing out, even making sure to decorate the bathrooms. The whole time, she claps her hands and bounces around like a toddler. Her eyes remain locked on me, eager to see my reactions. If I could, I'd bottle this feeling up for her. I'd keep her this happy every goddamned day.

When we round the building, nearing my office, she pauses, tugging her lip between her teeth. "I hope you like it. If not, it's totally fine. We can change anything you want."

Bending down, I kiss her hard, backing her into the wall as I have my way with her. I shut her up in the way I know works best. My mouth on hers, my tongue in her mouth, my thigh between hers. Never fuckin' fails. When I finally pull back, she's cum twice and is panting and slightly delirious.

"What about you?" she rasps. I grin, shaking my head.

"You already know the answer to that." Since that night I used the fake knot on her, neither of us has been able to get enough. I've welcomed all her toys into our bed. My favorite is the tentacle. It fits in her tiny, tight ass perfectly while I knot her cunt. My girl loves to be stretched around my cock, and I love feeling it around me. *Fuck.* "Gonna knot your pussy when we get home," I grunt, grinding my dick against her.

Pulling away, I leave her breathless and panting against the wall. I smirk, stepping around her and into my office. I come to a halt, my eyes widening in surprise.

Everything, *everything*, is different. My father's desk is gone and replaced with a newer, more modern version. Same with the chair. There are curtains along the window wall and a faux cowskin rug beneath the seating area. She even painted. What were once plain white walls are now a dark gray that matches the walls in our home. In fact, everything matches our house.

But what has me stalling, unable to move my feet, are the *pictures*.

So many pictures.

The entire wall behind my desk is covered in framed, black and white photos. Big and small, arranged artfully. Photos of my parents. Their wedding day and various birthdays. Pictures of Tank and Porkchop, who have now become inseparable. Pictures of Shiloh and I, more of her than of me. I recognize a bunch of them as ones I've snapped on my phone, dating back to the day I found her asleep in the breakroom. There are photos of my brothers...

And photos of Liam.

Liam.

My heart slams to a stop.

Liam.

I haven't let myself remember him, let alone look at a photo of him, in years. No. Longer than that. Not since his funeral.

Liam.

Fuck. I can't...I can't look at him every day. I can't remember.

Liam. Liam. Liam.

As if to prove me wrong, memory after memory comes crashing down, plowing into me with the force of a semi. My knees buckle, and this time, I let them, barely catching myself on the wall before I go down. No, not the wall. On Shiloh. She's here, holding me up, her face a mask of pure horror.

I want to say something. Anything. But—

Liam.

"We're so sorry to have to inform you, but your brother, Liam Huxley, was killed last night. He was caught in an air raid. He—"

I never did hear the rest of the officers' words. Never heard the rest of what he'd been saying as he explained how my baby brother lost his life. Bits and pieces trickled through.

"Seven soldiers were wounded."

Blank.

"Three died."

Blank.

"Sending him home."

Blank.

Blank.

Blank.

"Casket."

Blank.

"Flag."

"Honor."

"We're sorry."

"Sorry."

"Sorry."

Blank.

Blank.

Blank.

Snap.

"Why?" I shout, my head spinning so hard I feel drunk. I feel so fucking drunk that I actually think I might be dying. I feel sick. So, so sick.

I see nothing, hear nothing, as my head continues to spin.

"Why did you do this?" My fist slams against the wall. Drywall explodes, shattering around me. "Fuck!"

Why Liam? Why did you have to follow me? Why couldn't you have just listened and stayed the fuck home and go work with dad, like you were told? Why did you look up to me? I didn't deserve that. Didn't deserve his respect. Didn't deserve a little brother who loved me that much.

I don't realize I've left until I find myself in my truck, pulling into the vista point by the river down the road. A place I haven't been to in years. *Years*. A place I used to come to with my brothers. With Liam.

Shit, shit, shit.

Shiloh.

"Fuck!" I shout, patting down my legs as I search for my phone. Shit, I hadn't even realized I'd gotten in the fucking truck. What if I hit someone or crashed? What if she'd been with me? Panic swirls in my gut so fast that I barely have time to get out of my truck before I double over, emptying the contents of my stomach.

I vomit until there's nothing left, and I'm just dry heaving. I stagger forward, finding the river's edge, and drop to my ass in the dirt. I have to get my head right before I drive again. I have to get it right so I can go to her and fix this.

My head drops into my hands as I attempt to put everything back into place, back where it belongs. Stuffing emotions and memories way down deep where I can't find them. I'm better that way. Everything is better when I forget.

Forget the military. The friends I lost. The warzones. Explosions. Gunfire. *The screams*. I have to forget.

Pull it back, Logan.

It's better when I forget Liam.

Liam.

"Damnit, Liam," I mutter, saying his name out loud for the first time since that day I'd told Shiloh about him. Even then, I'd been brief. Outlining the details vaguely, barely saying his name above a whisper. "Damnit, Liam," I say louder. "Why? Why did you have to fucking follow me? You motherfucker!"

He says nothing back, of course...because he's dead.

Groaning, I rub my face roughly and yank my hair. "I miss you, bro. I miss you so fucking much; it kills me." I choke out a sob.

For the first time since it happened, I cry for the baby brother I lost.

There, in the place we used to love, my ass in the dirt, my face in my hands, I cry. I release every single pent-up thought. Every bit of heartache. I release it all. I shout until my voice is nothing but a raspy husk. I cry until I have no tears left. And I talk until I lose my voice.

I tell Liam *everything*.

"You'd love her. She's so fucking perfect. Beautiful, too. Thick and curvy. Perfect ass and tits." I chuckle, shaking my head as I look out onto the river. "She's funny and sweet. So fucking kind, too. Like shit, her heart? Man, her heart's *huge*. You should see what she did to the Huxley building. It's awesome. You'd probably laugh if you saw me now. Tell me I'm pussy whipped." I scoff, rolling my eyes. "You'd totally be right, but fuck, it's so worth it. *She's* worth it. She's everything." I pause, exhaling heavily. "Wish you could be at our wedding, meet your nieces and nephews. *Fuck*."

After a while, I stand, dusting my jeans off. "I love you, Liam. I promise to visit more." With one last look at the river, I turn to head back to my truck, more than ready to apologize to my woman.

"Shiloh?" I breathe, finding her sitting only a few feet behind where I'd just been. Her face covered in red splotches and tears. She takes one look at me and breaks into a harsh, heaving sob. "Shit, baby." Closing the distance, I drop to my knees before her. "Shit, fuck. I'm so sorry, Shiloh. So, so, sorry."

I move to wrap my arms around her but pause, worried that she might be afraid of me. She leans forward like she's trying to throw herself at me but physically can't. Grunting, I pick her up, my arms banding around her body as I drop onto my ass, holding her.

She cries hard, digging her face into my neck. Her body trembles and shakes from the force of it. I hold her tighter, doing everything I can to calm her down.

"I'm sorry," I whisper, rubbing her back. I repeat the words again and again, praying they soak through soon. "I'm so sorry, Babydoll. I didn't mean to yell and scare you. I'm so fucking sorry."

She pulls away, sniffling and gasping. She shakes her head, her poor face swollen and irritated from crying. "No, I'm so sorry. I shouldn't have done that. I shouldn't have messed with your stuff."

"Baby, no," I sigh, gripping her tear-stained face. I drop my head, bringing us face to face. "Shiloh, it wasn't your fault. It was—" taking a deep breath, I press on. "It was Liam. I haven't seen his picture since he died. It was just a lot. I had a—" Again, I have to take a deep breath, steadying myself. I have to be stronger. Stronger than my demons.

Stronger for *her.* "I had a flashback, Babydoll. It was not your fault, I swear."

She takes a deep breath and releases it with a shudder. "You're not mad at me?"

Shaking my head, I shove down the self-deprecating thoughts at how royally I fucked this all up so quickly. "*No,*" I say adamantly. "Absolutely not. You're perfect, Shiloh. What you did back there meant the world to me."

"So—" she murmurs, her face scrunched up adorably. "You still want to marry me?"

Now it's my turn to be confused. My head jolts back like she's slapped me. "What?"

"Do you—do you still want to marry me?" her brows furrow, and her eyes gloss over again. Shit. I'd just gotten the tears to stop.

I readjust us so she's straddling me, bringing our foreheads together. "Of course, I do. Why would you think I don't want to marry you?"

She sucks in a sharp breath. Her hands come up to rest on mine over her cheeks. They're shaking. "Because you were so mad, and when you left, I thought you were done, that you didn't want—"

"Shiloh," I murmur. I don't want to bring this up, but I need to know where this is coming from. "Baby, did your ex do that? Did he walk out on you when he was mad?"

She shrugs, releasing a tiny whimper. It goes straight to my heart, breaking it in two.

"Your relationship with him was nothing like ours. You see that, right?" I say slowly. She nods, her head moving against mine. I squeeze her cheeks, rubbing her tears away with my thumbs. "We will *never* be like that. I will never treat you like that and if I get mad or upset, or need a minute, just know that I will *always* come back."

"How do you know?" she whispers. "How do you know we'll never turn out badly?"

Gripping her cheeks, I press my lips to hers, stopping her panic in its tracks. Pulling away, I murmur, "Because you can't build a house on a cracked foundation, Shiloh. Ours is solid. It's built to last. I know without a shadow of a doubt, down to my very soul, that we won't break. Our house is strong."

She grins. A tiny giggle makes its way through her lips. "Did you just use a construction metaphor for our love life?"

I tip my shoulder in a shrug and nod. "Why not? It worked, didn't it?"

She laughs again, this time louder. The sound is a husky rasp that goes straight to my cock. "So, you're saying," she mumbles, her lips moving against mine. "That you still want to marry me, and our relationship will last as long as a log cabin?"

I slap her ass playfully but laugh, my mouth never leaving hers. "Yep," I mumble, grinding my cock against her. She groans.

"That's good to know," she pants, rubbing her pussy on me like a cat in heat. She's been insatiable lately. I don't blame her. I'll never get enough, either. "Hope it's a big cabin."

"Oh yeah? Why's that?" Gripping her hips, I thrust up, seconds away from ripping her clothes off and fucking her in the dirt.

Leaning forward, her teeth latch onto my ear and tug. "Because," she breathes, her hot breath fanning across my cheek. "*I'm pregnant.*"

And just like that, I cum in my jeans.

And now, an extended Epilogue for your enjoyment....

IT'S MY CHOICE
BE PATIENT WITH YOURSELF
Unapologetic MYSELF
BE BOLD
ALL BODIES ARE GOOD BODIES
love YOURSELF
beautiful
yes you can
Fearless
be happy
IN CONTROL
LOVE yourself
HERE TO STAY
I am enough
FEEL DEEPLY
YOUR POTENTIAL IS ENDLESS
be kind to yourself
IT'S MY CHOICE
I am exactly where I need to be
be BRAVE
you are worthy
I am capable
love you
YOU ARE enough
glow
breathe
Perfect

Shiloh

Thanksgiving

"**D**o you really think this is enough food?" Charlie groans, dropping a heaving bowl of mashed potatoes on the table. "We're going to starve. Maybe we should have gotten another pie."

Even from the living room, I can hear the sarcasm in his voice. A giggle escapes me, and I quickly cover my mouth when Logan shoots me a glare. I roll my eyes at the over-possessive dork. He's been this way since the very beginning, so it's nothing new. However, since we found out about the baby, he's been....

Well—let's just say I'm surprised he allowed me out of the house today at all. It was a close call there for a minute when I was trying to get in the truck. I'm pretty sure the only reason he didn't strap a leash around my throat and tie me to the bed is that it's Thanksgiving.,

A surge of arousal pools low in my belly at the thought.

A leash? That might be fun.

"What has you looking like that all of the sudden?" he murmurs, his hot breath fanning over my cheek. "Better not have anything to do with my brother."

"Christ, give me the strength," I mutter, my words barely above a whisper.

Logan tugs my earlobe between his teeth and bites down, sending another wave of need coursing through me. At this rate, we'll have to visit his old room before the turkey's even on the table.

"What was that, Babydoll? Are you looking for another punishment?" My eyes widen at his words. My head jolts back, causing his teeth to drag along my lobe painfully, and I barely stifle a moan.

Ever since I conceived, I've been like this. Ready to jump my man at any given moment. Though, honestly, that could just be because he's...*him.*

My Logan. My fiancé. My baby daddy.

The thought has me giggling again. His obsessive need for me to refer to him as Daddy hasn't changed in the last week. However, he's added a caveat.

When we're naked, I call him Daddy.

When were dressed and alone, in our own little world, it's: *baby daddy.*

Logan leans back, taking me in with narrowed eyes. "What?"

I shrug my shoulder, taking a slow sip of my orange juice as my eyes rake down his perfect body. "Nothing...Baby Daddy," I mouth, making sure no one else can hear my words. He grins, and I swear, I can see his possessive instincts growing instantly.

"Say it again," he whispers back, his voice a husky rasp.

"*Ba—by—Dad—dy*." My words are so quiet; there's no way anyone can hear them besides us as I drag them out, making sure to enunciate every syllable. His body visibly shudders. His eyes close as he releases a heaving breath before smiling a mega-watt smile, just for me.

Since I'm only about six weeks along, having likely conceived that fateful night in my *nest*, or at least that's our best guess, we've decided not to tell anyone yet. Logan knows how terrified I am to lose this baby, and while I don't believe telling people will jinx the pregnancy, I do think that if something goes wrong, having to break the news to our families would kill me.

If I've learned anything in my infertility journey, it's that there is no 'safe point' in creating life. Anything can happen to anyone at any point in their lives. The same goes for pregnancy. Logan and I have celebrated every step of this baby's life so far and will continue to do so. But for now, we're celebrating quietly.

Bending, he brings our foreheads together, something we both love. We share breath, enjoying our secret. "I love you, Mrs. Huxley," he sighs, pressing his lips to mine.

"You're making me lose my appetite," Stephen grumbles. Logan and I pull apart, both of us with dopey smiles across our faces. "And I cooked that food, so I know it's fucking phenomenal."

"Shut it," Logan growls, though he never takes his eyes off of me. "You're just jealous."

A stilted, awkward silence follows his statement, and an immediate pang of sadness fills me. I pull my gaze from Logan's, finding Stephen a few feet away. He swallows with enough force; I can see his Adam's apple bob from here. I still have no idea what's going on between him and Dom. The few times I've asked, Dom has moved us from the topic, refusing to comment either way. I don't blame him. We hardly know each other. *Yet.*

Then and there, I make it my mission to spend more time with him. He doesn't need to tell me everything right now, but I at least want to give him the option of someone to talk to. It's the least I can do with how much he's sat and listened to my drama.

"Shit," Logan murmurs. He runs his fingers through his hair, shooting an apologetic look toward his brother. "Sorry, man."

"Well, that was heartfelt," I mutter. Apparently not quiet enough when both men shoot me surprised looks. I should feel embarrassed or sorry, at least, but I feel neither emotion. Instead, I shrug. "What? All men are ridiculous."

"Jesus," Logan groans. "Less than two months in, and I've already been lumped with *all men*? Give me a few more before you throw me to the wolves."

Grinning, I push myself from the couch, tired of being treated like a spoiled pregnant fiancé, even if that's exactly what I am. No one here knows either of those details, so I can only imagine how I look sitting on my ass while everyone rushes to prepare a massive spread.

Stepping past Logan, I shoot him a wink and dart out of his reach when he tries to pull me back. I ignore his frustrated, worried glare and make my way to the kitchen.

"Mrs. Huxley, please tell me how I can help," I insist, washing my hands thoroughly at the sink. She whirls on me, spatula brandished between her hands like a weapon.

Shaking her head, she glowers at me with all the force of a savage beast. "Do *not* call me that."

My head jolts back, surprised by her vehemence. "Umm, okay—" swallowing, I try to figure out what the right answer is here. "Dolores?"

She shakes her head again. This time, a smirk crawls up her tiny, little face. "I prefer mom or mama." Her eyes dart down to my belly, a knowing twinkle in her green eyes. "Or Gigi."

I barely stifle a gasp. Anger quickly fills me. Anger and panic. *A lot of panic.* My head shoots in Logan's direction, ready to tell him off for going against my wishes. Especially when he knows why I feel as adamant as I do. Dolores halts my tirade before the shout's even left my throat.

"Don't get mad at him, Sweetheart. He's said nothing. I just," she shrugs, stepping into my space. "I just know."

"You just—know," I say dumbly, drawing the words out, my brows pinched. She nods, her grin growing. Her eyes flick to the pocket of my dress, where my ring is tucked away for safekeeping until we make our announcement.

Her smile widens. "Well, shit," I breathe before quickly slapping a palm over my mouth.

I steel my spine, completely ready to be called out the way the boys always are for swearing. Dolores surprises me once again when she falls into a fit of loud, boisterous laughter. She takes in my shocked expression and laughs even harder. "What? Did you think I'd yell at you?"

I smile and nod. She barks out a laugh so loud she draws everyone in the vicinity's attention. Logan's face scrunches up, his eyes bobbing between the two of us. I give him a confused look. I have no idea what's happening here. He steps forward as if to rescue me but halts when Dolores closes the distance between us, wrapping me in her warm embrace.

"I'm so happy for you both," she murmurs, her words barely above a whisper. "About all of it. You're going to be incredible parents."

My eyes cloud over as I hug her back, her words meaning more than she could ever imagine. We stand there, in a tight embrace, for countless moments. I peel my watering eyes open and find Logan standing just behind his mom, his own eyes glossed over as he takes us in.

"I love you so much," he mouths. My responding smile is so wide my cheeks burn.

Pulling away, Dolores pats my arms. "And I don't care if you curse, Sweetheart. I just like to fuck with the boys." Logan's mouth drops open in shock, having heard his mom's secretive declaration. This time, I can't hold in my laugh.

"Dinner is served," Stephen calls, settling the huge turkey in the center of the table. My eyes grow impossibly large as my mouth begins to water. My stomach gives a responding, *loud* growl.

Logan grins, closing the distance between us. He wraps his arms around me from behind, holding me tightly against his chest. "I love you more," I sigh, finally finding my voice. Tilting my head back to look up at him, I mouth, "Baby Daddy."

He chuckles, pressing his mouth to mine for a quick, passionate kiss. When he releases me, I'm a little breathless and woozy. Looking back at the dining table, I find it surrounded by people. Excitement fills me when I realize Dom is here. He smiles softly, tipping his shoulders. Stephen leans in, murmuring something quietly in his ear. His cheeks turn an impressive shade of pink in response. Stephen stifles a laugh, pressing a kiss to Dom's cheek.

My eyes dart around the table, looking for any sign of disapproval. Though I can't imagine Logan's family being anything but supportive of their sons, I still don't understand why Stephen holds back with Dom. I find nothing but happiness from the remaining Huxley members as they laugh and chat with each other.

My heart fills full to bursting.

This. *This* is family.

Logan's hand slides into my pocket slowly, retrieving my engagement ring. "I thought we were waiting till dessert," I murmur. His beard brushes against my cheek with the shake of his head.

"Can't wait any longer," he grunts. Ah. My caveman is back. We both watch as he slides the ring onto my finger. My heartbeat pounds in response. God, my love for this man is insane. Completely and utterly insane.

Logan bundles me in his arms once more, my back to his big, strong chest. He kisses the top of my head, inhaling deeply. *"Cupcakes,"* he sighs, a sound full of happy contentment. Clearing his throat, he calls out, "We have an announcement—"

And just like that, I know...

Logan Huxley isn't just my future, he's my forever.

IT'S MY CHOICE

BE PATIENT WITH YOURSELF

Unapologetic MYSELF

BE Bold

ALL BODIES ARE GOOD BODIES

love yourself

beautiful

be happy

yes you can

Fearless

IN CONTROL

LOVE yourself

HERE TO STAY

I am enough

FEEL DEEPLY

YOUR POTENTIAL IS ENDLESS

It's my choice

I am exactly where I need to be

you are worthy

YOU ARE Enough

breathe

Perfect

beautiful

Christmas

LOGAN

"**B**abydoll," I murmur. "It's time to wake up. We have to get going soon, and you need to eat first." She grunts, letting out a sound that is zero percent seductress and one hundred percent angry cave beast.

Rolling onto her side, she digs her face into the mound of pillows that was once our bed. "No." That's it. Just one, pissed off, barked word. That's all I get from my fiancé. Yes, fiancé. Because she *refuses* to marry me while she's *puffy*. What the fuck is puffy, you might ask?

Well. Let me tell you. I have no fucking idea.

None.

She looks the same as before. No. Correction. She looks better than before if that's even possible. I don't know if it's just the fact that I'm aware my baby is growing in her belly. That my seed is so potent, it took that very first week we slept together, despite her years of struggles, before me. Knowing that my seed is far more virile than the average man.

Than her ex's. I grin at the thought.

My sperm is spectacular. Strong, brave, potent. It broke through whatever situation she's got going on inside and planted its way deep in her womb. It's so fucking spectacular that I did in less than a week what that stupid piece of shit couldn't do in ten years.

Knocked her up real fucking good.

She doesn't understand it at all. She tries to wrap her perfect, pretty head around how it's possible that it happened so quickly. I remind her again and again that it happened exactly how it was meant to. My heart breaks for what my woman's been through and for her loss, but I fully believe that everything happens for a reason. Things with her ex were shitty from the beginning, and it only got worse as they progressed. A baby can't fix a broken marriage.

"Come on, Babydoll. Don't you want to see our little one today?" I coo, reminding her that our first ultrasound is this morning. I was able to get the doctor to see us, despite it being two days from Christmas. I couldn't wait any longer. Neither of us could. "You can't see him if you don't get up."

"You don't know it's a him," she murmurs, rubbing her face in my pillow like a wolf marking its territory. I smile. I love her.

"Sure, I do," I grunt, yanking the blanket from her lush, naked curves. My cock instantly hardens at the sight. I'll never get tired of my naked-in-bed rule. Never. "Come on.

Your blueberry pancakes are getting cold." I grab her hip and roll her onto her back. She resists, refusing to look at me. My brows furrow. "Baby, what's wrong?"

When she still refuses to move, I crawl over the bed and straddle her thick thighs. My cock is leaking in my sweats, but I ignore the fucker so I can focus on my woman. When I finally dig her face from the mound of fluff, I find her cheeks pink and tearstained. She sniffles, avoiding my eyes. I grip her cheeks, forcing her to look at me. Her face crumbles, along with my heart.

"Shiloh," I whisper, my voice cracking. The power this woman has over me is mind-boggling. "Talk to me."

She shakes her head and tugs her lip between her teeth, biting down hard enough that I worry she'll make herself bleed. I pull the abused flesh from her mouth and kiss the hurt away. "Tell me," I murmur against her lips. She's been extra emotional the last few weeks, which is understandable. I know her hormones are a mess right now, but I thought she would be excited for today.

Shiloh buries her face in my neck and wraps her arms around me, banding me tightly against her soft body. She unleashes everything, then. Heaving sobs escape her, covering my skin in warm, wet tears. I drop down onto my back, taking her with me. I hold her tightly, letting her feel whatever she needs to. All the while, my heart is beating erratically in my chest, and my palms are beginning to sweat as worry consumes me.

Is something wrong with the baby?

I say nothing, giving her the silent support I know she needs right now. When she finally calms, her body shaking in my arms, she exhales a heavy breath. "What if—" she breaks off, another sob spilling from her body. I hold her tighter, refusing to let her go through these emotions alone. "What if he's not okay?"

Her words are barely audible, but I hear them nonetheless. My heart and guts give a painful squeeze. I'm worried about that, too, not that I would ever say it out loud. I will never diminish or belittle what she's been through, and I honestly can't even wrap my brain around the heartache she's experienced, but this time is different. She's not alone. She has me, and no matter what happens, we'll handle it together.

Doesn't mean I'm not worried.

"Everything will be okay," I grunt, my arms so tight, I'm worried I might hurt her. Her body tenses, and I roll my eyes at my own words. What a heartless fuckin' thing to say. "Everything will go how it's going to go. We can't control the future any more than we can change the past, Babydoll. Just know that no matter what happens today, I'll be with you. You aren't alone anymore, Shiloh."

Her body shudders. "I know," she breathes, nodding against me. "I know I'm not." I didn't think it was possible, but I love her more at that moment. She may have been married, but she was alone. It's taken a lot of work for her to get to this point, and it will continue to take a lot of work to keep healing, but she's doing it, and I couldn't be prouder.

"I love you, Mrs. Huxley," I murmur against her hair. She huffs a laugh at my instance to call her by her proper name. We may not be married yet, but she's still my wife.

Shiloh lifts her head, resting her chin on my chest. "I love you more, Mr. Huxley."

My grin is so wide my cheeks hurt. "Love it when you call me that."

She scoffs. "You do know that whether we're married or not, that's your na—" I slap her ass playfully, cutting off her words. Her lips tip up in a quick smile before she sighs and drops her head back on my chest. "I'm not alone this time," she whispers, talking more to herself than to me. "We'll get through this."

"We will," I say matter-of-factly. I may not know what the future holds, but I do know that much.

"Alright, Shiloh. Are you ready to see your baby?" Dr. Jacobs asks, a wide smile on her face as she prepares the ultrasound machine. "I hear this little one was a bit of a surprise?"

I grunt in response. "No, actually—" Shiloh squeezes my hand so tightly I hear my knuckles pop. Glancing down, I cock a brow in question. The glare she sends me is harsh enough to have my balls practically climbing back into my body. "Sure," I drawl. "We'll go with surprise."

The doctor tilts her head to the side, her lip twitching with the beginnings of a smile. "Oh?"

Shooting Shiloh a grin that's half-apology, half-cocky pride, I tell the good doctor *exactly* what I think. "It's hard for it to be a surprise when I've kept her stuffed so full—" Shiloh reaches up and socks me in the gut. My words cut off with a grunt.

The doctor surprises me when she barks out a laugh and quickly smothers it. "Okay, you two. Let's move on, shall we?" Shiloh sighs heavily and turns to look at the doctor. She readjusts her feet in the little kickstands that have her all sorts of sprawled out and nods.

"So, since we aren't totally sure when you conceived and how far along you are, we're going to do an internal exam." She rolls her stool between my woman's thighs, and only the knowledge that I'm about to see my kid for the first time keeps me from shoving her away. "How have you been feeling?"

"Wonderful," Shiloh immediately says. "Really good." She bobs her head up and down as if it makes her bald-faced lie more convincing.

"Actually," I grunt, rubbing my thumb across her palm when she tries to break my fingers again. "She's been extremely nauseous. She throws up at least five times a day."

The doctor's brows lift to her hairline, and she reaches over to jot something down in Shiloh's chart. Realizing that's apparently important and *new* information, I keep going. "She cries a lot too. Like...*a lot*. And she has really bad gas, especially at night. Oh! She also—"

"Okay, Logan!" Shiloh screeches. "She doesn't need to know all that. Those are normal pregnancy symptoms." She palms her forehead and rubs the space between her brows. "I would have told her if I thought it was relevant."

"Well," the doctor interjects. "The frequent vomiting throughout the day isn't all that normal, especially if you're unable to keep food down. We can prescribe you something for it if you'd like." Shiloh shakes her head, but I interrupt.

"We'll take it," I bark. Shiloh shoots a wide-eyed look my way. I cough, lowering my volume; I say, "We'll take it. If it will help you feel better, and help keep the baby healthy, then you should do it. Right?" She tugs that big bottom lip between her teeth and slowly nods, understanding what I'm saying.

"Yes. I'll take it. Whatever I can do, I'll do it. I just don't want to complain too much when this is such a miracle."

Bending forward, I close the distance between us. Smoothing her long hair from her face, I kiss her forehead, hoping to calm her nerves before they really get going again. "You can be happy and thankful and still miserable, baby. You don't have to be brave all the time."

The doctor stays silent, giving us our moment. When we separate, she smiles approvingly. "Okay. Showtime."

A few tense moments and some uncomfortable-looking prodding later, the most incredible sound I've ever heard fills my ears. It's a mix between a whoosh, like when your heartbeat is in your ears, and a horse galloping. My heart thumps at a rapid pace. My eyes burn as they fill with tears of unbelievable happiness before spilling down my cheeks. I let them. I couldn't give a single fuck how I look right now.

That sound? It means our baby is alive and healthy. Right?

The doctor's face pinches, and she leans in, peering at the monitor like it holds all the answers to life.

"What?" Shiloh murmurs. She tries to sit up, practically dragging herself closer to the screen. "What is it?" I drop down onto the bed and pull her back, settling her on top of my chest. I wrap my arms around her body, partly for comfort, mostly to keep her down so the doctor can finish her job.

"It's okay," I murmur, repeating the words softly even though my heart is in my throat. "It's okay, right?" I ask, my gaze meeting the doctors.

She gives us both a warm, happy smile. "It's amazing." Turning the screen, she points to a black bubble blob-looking thing and then some numbers. "I'd say your guess as to when you conceived is pretty spot on, though, in situations like this, it's hard to get a proper measurement. I'd say you're about 10 weeks, Shiloh."

"Situations like this?" Shiloh chokes out, ignoring the rest of what the doctor had said. "You mean because of my PCOS? Because my periods are irregular?"

The doctor smirks. "Well, that's part of it, but no, that's not what I meant." She lifts her finger again, pointing at the blob with one hand. She moves the *wand* that I'd previously thought was a massive dildo around, getting a better angle. "It's hard to get a proper timeline with twin pregnancies. This is baby A, measuring 9 weeks, 5 days. This is baby B, measuring 10 weeks, 1 day."

"*Twins?* As in—twins? As in...two babies?" I ask. At least, I think I do, though; I could just imagine the words. The doctor smiles, nodding in agreement. Okay, so I spoke out loud. That's good. Good. Great. *Holy. Shit.* "Twins."

"Twins." She nods again.

"Twins," Shiloh breathes. "Oh my god." She tilts her head back, finding my eyes. Immediately, she falls into another round of sobs, just like this morning. Except for this time, she's not crying in terror of the unknown, she's crying because instead of one miracle, *we got two.*

Goddamn. My sperm is potent. Twins? Does that mean I knocked her up and then knocked her up again? Shit. My cum is fucking magical.

Instantly, I'm rock hard beneath her. Thousands of visions of how I'm going to keep her full of my babies swirl through my head. What if I give her three babies next time? Holy shit that would give us five kids. That's a lot. Isn't it? No. No, definitely not. I'd be down with more than that. How many are too many? Ten?

"Logan?" Shiloh murmurs, her brows scrunched up adorably. Glancing down, I realized I'd spaced out staring at the screen. It's blank now, and an immediate wave of panic fills me. Fuck.

"Where are my babies? Where'd they go?" I ask my voice just south of frantic. "Did I miss it?"

The doctor chuckles, handing me a long sheet of photos. "No, you didn't. I recorded the ultrasound for you when I noticed you'd checked out and took some images for you to keep. I'll email you the recording. Congratulations, mom and dad. You're officially parents."

Looking at Shiloh, she continues on, giving her instructions and information regarding her prescription. Once again, I check out, my eyes zeroed in on the photos in my hands.

Two fucking babies.

Possession, fear, protectiveness, joy, and love...*so much love*...fill me rapidly. So many things. I feel so many emotions for these two tiny humans I've never even met. I will do anything, *be anything* they need, from here on out. Anything to make sure they are happy and protected for as long as I live.

Looking back at Shiloh, I feel the exact same thing for her. Anything. Anything and everything.

The doctor steps out, giving us a moment of privacy to bask in our life-changing news. We stare at the photos for a while in stunned silence. Finally, she looks up at me, still crying but now with a beaming smile on her beautiful face.

"We're parents," she chokes out. "Two babies, Logan. *Two.*"

I capture her mouth with mine, kissing the ever-loving shit out of my woman. When I finally pull back, I rest my forehead on hers, breathing in her cupcake scent. "Merry fucking Christmas, Babydoll."

IT'S MY
CHOICE

BE PATIENT
WITH
YOURSELF

Unapologetica
MYSELF!

ST
posi

BE
Bold

ALL BODIES
are
GOOD BODIES

be
happ

Love yourse

beautiful

yes
you
can

Fearless

IN CONTROL

LOVE
yourse

HERE
TO STAY

I am
enough

YOUR
POTENT
IS ENDL

FEEL
DEEPLY

be kind
to yourself

Ye
pre

Be
Brave

It's my CHOICE

I am exactly
where I need to be

You
are
worthy

I am
capable

YOU AR
enoug

glow

Love you

breathe

Perfect

Valentine's Day

SHILOH

Bending down, I slide the roast into the oven and grunt when I damn near topple over. This whole gravity thing isn't exactly my friend anymore. At 16 weeks pregnant with two lumberjack-sized babies, I'm an accident waiting to happen. I walk into things, bump things, knock things over...

Basically—me and *things* no longer get along. At all.

"Shiloh!" Logan barks as I push myself upright. I turn a narrowed-eyed stare at him, waiting for him to say something that I just know is going to piss me off.

"Yes, my love?" I say, blinking rapidly in a way that usually gets me things. Including grade-A dick and foot rubs. "May I help you?"

He scoffs, rolling his eyes. "That only works when you're naked." Leaning his hip against the island, he crosses his arms over his broad chest and glares down at me. "What did I tell you about putting shit in the oven?"

"That if I did, you'd punish me." I blink up at him again, tugging my lip between my teeth, hoping he takes the hint.

For the last few months, my hormones have been all over the place. The first month, I was insatiable. Literally. I could go again and again and again—okay, you get the point. It was crazy. I've never been so horny in my entire life. *Ever.*

Looking back, I'm glad, too, because as soon as I reached week 7 of my pregnancy, everything went downhill. My emotions, my sex drive, my ability to sleep through the night. After we met with the doctor, I was officially diagnosed with hyperemesis and put on meds that helped me tremendously. I finally stopped vomiting like a drunken frat boy and began to feel better. What didn't improve? My sex drive, which unfortunately tanked at week 11. More than likely due to exhaustion, nausea, random bouts of crying, hunger, and the never-ending need to pee.

Regardless, Logan never stopped trying to get me off, ignoring me when I tried to return the favor. He's been incredible. He dotes on me constantly. It's both wonderful and annoying, especially at times like this, when he won't let me cook a damn meal. Still, he's been the perfect fiancé and daddy to our babies, and it's time that I show him just how much I appreciate him.

Starting...*now.*

It is Valentine's Day, after all.

His brows lift as he zeros in on my mouth. "Oh, yeah?" he murmurs, his eyes transfixed. "Were you *trying* to be punished, Babydoll?"

I nod, licking my lips. Might as well keep him roped in while I've got his attention. Tossing the hand towel onto the counter, I sashay toward him, loving how he tracks my every step.

"I've been a *knotty* girl, Daddy," I whisper, my voice husky and thick with need. It's been too damn long since we've played with our sex toys.

Too. Long.

"Shit," he grunts, adjusting his already hard cock that's leaving an impressive outline in his jeans. His eyes dart up, meeting mine. "Are you serious?"

Smiling, I take the remaining steps between us and wrap my arms around him. He immediately cuddles me to his chest. "Yes," I sigh. "I miss you, Logan. I miss having sex with my fiancé." His title makes his brows lift, and his lip twitch. *Not good enough*. Leaning in, I drop my chin on his chest, never losing his eyes. "I miss having you inside me, *Alpha*," I purr.

Like a too taut bowstring, he snaps.

Logan loves to be called *baby* when we're being sweet. He loves to be called *fiancé*, especially in public. For him, it's an ownership thing, I think. Surprisingly, I love it. I love his possession of me. When we're naked, whether that be in the shower, bed, or in the middle of steamy sex, he loves to be called *Daddy*. And now that the word about us being pregnant with twins is out, he loves the title *Baby Daddy*.

But *Alpha* has become sort of a code word for us. The same with Omega. If we're feeling particularly freaky or in the mood for role play, we drop the title, and it usually sends the other person headfirst off a kinky cliff.

Like now.

I'm in his arms before I even realize what's happening. I tighten my grip around his neck, holding on tight as he dashes up the stairs. Gone are the days when I can wrap myself around him like a spider monkey. Not only does the bump get in the way, but Logan's terrified to *squish the kids.* It's sweet, it really is, but shit, I miss being in his arms.

He climbs the second set of stairs, the much narrower set I hadn't noticed before he showed them to me a few months ago. As part of my Christmas present, Logan made me a permanent nest in the large attic loft I never knew existed. Well, I call it a nest. Really, it's just a place where we do the extra freaky shit. He said we'd need a sex dungeon to escape to when our house is filled with babies. I simply smiled, completely loving his forethought.

Logan barrels through the door, back first, making sure to keep me safe at all times. He kicks the door shut and half tosses, half sets me on the massive mound of pillows and blankets. Similar to the one he'd set up the night he proposed, this *nest* is basically a huge mattress on the floor, covered in everything squishy, soft, and plushy you could imagine.

"Get naked," he grunts, barely sparing me a second glance as he literally *runs* to the drawers where we keep the toys. "Hurry!"

"Jesus, Logan," I murmur, rolling my eyes. "After a month without sex, you'd think you'd want to take this slow. Enjoy things. Savor it."

He grabs his selection and bundles them to his chest like a dragon with his horde. Spinning, he squints at me, his eyes raking over my still very dressed body. "Woman. My cock is so fucking hard right now, I'm probably going to cum the second I see your tits. Now take off your fucking clothes before I cut them from your body."

Holy shit-balls.

I pause, thinking his words through. I glance down, taking in my dress. It's new. Like, brand new. And really pretty. I bought it just for today. Do I really want him to cut it from my body? Crap.

"5," he barks, dropping the toys onto the bed next to me. Unable to help myself, I take in his choices. My eyes widen. Well, damn.

"4!" Looking up, I find him shirtless. Again, unable to help it, I find myself distracted once again. He's just so freaking perfect. His abs have softened slightly over the last few months, especially with how much time we spend lazing around in each other's arms, but he's still just as gorgeous as ever.

"3-2..." *Shit!* Scrambling onto my knees, I peel the dress over my head quickly, excited to see his face when he finds his surprise.

"Aww, shit, Babydoll. All day?" I grin and nod. I've been without a bra and panties all day for him. Waiting for this moment. "*Fuck,*" he groans. And then, he's on his knees, crawling across the bed. He's naked as can be, and I imme-diately zero in on the very hard, very angry-looking cock hanging heavily between his thighs.

Aww, shit is right.

"Perfect," he murmurs. "So, fucking perfect." My heart thumps in my chest as love and adoration for this man fill me.

I no longer question his words or declarations, knowing without a shadow of a doubt that Logan loves me and how I look. Not only that but so do I.

It wasn't just because Cole clearly didn't like my appear-ance that I struggled with my body image. Yes, that was part of it, but more than that, it was how *I* felt about my body. It's difficult to love something that is hell-bent on screwing you over every step of the way, and no, I don't mean my weight.

Getting pregnant finally didn't make me stop being angry with my body, but it did help me to stop blaming it. My condition is no one's fault and something I'll live with forever. It's a healing process, and slowly yet surely, I'm coming to love myself fully.

"Shit, Shiloh. I wanted to do so many things to you. So many fucking things, but I can't. I need to fuck you, Babydoll. I need to feel you again." I moan at his words. Dropping onto my back, I spread my thighs, letting him take his fill of my naked body.

Logan flattens himself to the bed, his face between my legs. He tosses them over his shoulders and leans in, in-haling me. I used to think it was weird, his need to smell me all the time. Now? Now it turns me on just as much. I can never get enough of his rain, earth, and forest smell, so who am I to judge?

He inhales again, groaning like a starving man at a buffet. "I need you," I choke out, thrusting my hips up in an attempt to entice him. Logan slaps my thigh in warning. I drop my ass back down and grip the comforter. "*Please, Alpha.*"

"I love when you beg," he murmurs, and then he devours me. Logan licks me from taint to clit, before tugging the little bundle of nerves between his teeth. I cry out, my body thrashing back and forth. Everything feels so fucking sensitive right now. One lick and I'm already on the edge. *What is this magic?*

Apparently invested in getting more of *that* reaction from me, Logan tightens his hold on my outer thighs, bringing me closer to his bearded face. He licks, sucks, and bites every inch of my pussy, before starting the process all over again. He finds what makes me shoot off the bed and then ignores the area, teasing me in a way that has me sobbing immediately.

"Please, please, please." My words become an incoherent jumble as I shake and cry. "Please, *Logan,*" I beg.

Finally, realizing I've dropped the scene, resorting to his name out of sheer desperation, he gives me what I need. Two fingers find my sopping wet entrance and thrust inside, curving to find my g-spot. His eyes meet mine over my baby belly just as he nips my clit. I practically fly off the bed, my hips thrusting into his face. I reach down, tugging his long curls and dragging him closer.

"Oh my god," I scream. He's relentless, fucking me hard with two fingers and then three. The burn of the stretch is good. *So good.* He's right; it's been too long. Fuck, this is going to be incredible. "Alpha!" I cry out as he pushes me into another orgasm.

Still, he doesn't stop. I know what he wants, what he's after. He won't stop until I've drenched his beard in my release. He always, *always* makes me squirt before we use the knot. I could suggest lube but *Fuck. That.* If my man wants to make me gush, who am I to stop him?

Again and again, he keeps up his relentless pace. He fucks me hard, his tongue never leaving my cunt. It doesn't take long to get me to the point of no return. My walls clench around him, and my breathing picks up until I'm panting and trembling beneath him.

"That's it," he growls. "Give it to me, Omega. Cover me in your cum so I can knot this tight cunt." Just like that, my fourth orgasm slams into me like a freight train. I cum so hard, I see stars. The room spins, and I get a little hazy, but I don't miss the sensation of liquid coating his face, my thighs, and ass.

Logan slows his movements before finally, he pulls his fingers free from my pussy. Sitting up, he locks eyes with me as he covers his cock in my release. I moan at the sight, ready for more even as my body twitches in pleasure from my orgasm.

"Ready?" he murmurs, sliding the knot into place. I nod, still breathing heavily. *Pregnancy perk.* "Play with your tits, and don't stop until I tell you."

"Okay, Daddy," I whisper with a smile. I can't help it. Sex should always be like this. Always. Fun and filled with love, respect, and safety. And with Logan, it always is.

He smirks as he knee-walks toward me, his hand stroking lazily over his knotted dick. "On your side," he murmurs, his eyes on my belly.

I could argue. Could tell him I'm fine just like this, but lazy, slow sex sounds kind of perfect right now, so I do as he says, my fingers never leaving my sensitive nipples. Logan slides up behind me and pulls my top leg up and over his thigh, giving him access to my pussy. He drags the head of this thick cock across my soaked core, and my body shivers in response.

Tilting my head back, I find his mouth, needing him as close as possible. He closes the distance immediately, knowing exactly what I want. His lips press against mine at the same moment he slowly presses his cock into me. I groan into his mouth, a sound he echoes as we reunite in such a way for the first time in far too long.

Slowly, *achingly slowly,* he fills me completely. When the knot bumps my entrance, he stops, pulling his mouth from mine. "I missed you," he whispers, his voice thick with emotion. "I'm torn, Babydoll."

My brows furrow as I lean back an inch, taking in his expression. "What do you mean?"

He smirks, but it fades quickly. "I want to keep you knocked up for the rest of our lives." His hand palms my belly, caressing it lovingly. "I want to keep breeding you, filling you with my cum. I already fantasize about doing it again as soon as I can, but shit," he murmurs, shaking his head. "I don't like not being able to be inside you, but more than that, I don't like you being so sick that I can't make you feel good."

A shudder wracks my body at his words. Logan's hips twitch in response. The knot bumps against my asshole, and I shiver again. "Let's just take it one day at a time, hmm?" I whisper, rubbing my ass against his crotch, a silent signal to *stop talking*. He chuckles, finally getting the hint.

His hand slides from my belly, finding my clit in an instant. He circles it slowly as he pulls out, leaving just the tip, and thrusts back in. He continues this slow, torturous pace until I'm practically trembling in his arms. My hand covers his, pressing harder, rubbing faster. His pace picks up in response. He tilts his hips, lifting my leg and holding it in the crook of his arm, using me for leverage.

And then...my man *fucks me*.

He pulls out fully, only to slam back in so hard, I jolt up the bed. He does it again, and again, giving us both what we need so desperately. He's a ruthless, savage beast, and I fucking *love it.* My nerve endings feel like I stuck my finger in a light socket. Everything tingles and pricks against my skin. I feel sensitive and on fire, like the moment before lightning strikes.

"Logan!" I scream, pressing down on my clit like the pleasure button it is. I shatter, squeezing his cock so hard he can barely move. He grunts, rutting his hips as I ride out my orgasm.

"Fuck, Shiloh. You're gonna snap my fucking cock off," he groans. Finally, I relax enough that he's able to move again. He wastes no time pressing forward and working the knot into my slicked core. "Take it, Omega. Take my knot like the good little girl you are."

My head drops back, resting on his chest as he rolls his hips. The knot breaches my entrance with a pop. Sharp, burning pain consumes me for less than a second before quickly sending me into another orgasm. My release sets Logan off, and then he's filling me with his hot, thick cum, coating my walls.

We both still, breathing heavily and enjoying the pleasure coursing through our bodies as we come down from the high. We stay locked together in all senses. If I had it my way, I'd stay like this with him forever. Wrapped so tightly in each other, it's impossible to tell where one of us ends, and the other begins.

"I love you, Logan," I sigh, nestling deeper into his embrace.

He drops his head, finding my neck with his teeth and scraping them along my skin. My pussy clenches at the feeling. His softening cock twitches, sending another wave of arousal through us both. "I love y—"

A shrill, blaring alarm fills the house, ruining our perfect moment. "Fuck! The roast!" I shout, moving to sit up. The knot tugs, preventing me from moving even an inch. Logan grunts, dragging me back down.

"Shit, Shiloh. Don't go breaking my pretty pussy when I just got her back." I groan but drop back down. He's not wrong. Logan chuckles and runs his tongue across my cheek in a move that's far more shifter than man. "Looks like we're ordering in."

"But it's Valentine's Day," I whine, irritated that I ruined the first home-cooked meal I've had the energy to make in months. "I'm—"

"Don't," he growls. "This is the best gift in the world and the only thing I need." He runs his hand from my belly to my breasts, before collaring my throat. "You. *Them.* It's all I need."

"Happy Valentines Day, Baby Daddy," I whisper, melting into a puddle of lust and happiness right there in my nest.

IT'S MY CHOICE

BE PATIENT WITH YOURSELF

Unapologetic MYSELF!

BE BOLD

ALL BODIES ARE GOOD BODIES

beautiful

Fearless

be happy

HERE TO STAY

IN CONTROL

LOVE yourself

I am enough

FEEL DEEPLY

YOUR POTENTIAL IS enough

be kind to yourself

be Brave

IT'S my choice

POWERFUL

you are worthy

I am exactly where I need to be

I am capable

love you

YOU ARE enough

beautiful

breathe

Perfect

The 4th of July

LOGAN

"**A**re you sure you want to go today?" I grunt, running a hand through my hair. Shiloh rolls her eyes, earning a hard slap on the ass from me. She squeals, attempting to dart away from me. I immediately feel bad when she teeters to the side. I catch her before she falls and hurts herself or the babies. "Shit, sorry."

"Don't be," she says softly, though it sounds more like a breathless pant. My poor woman is 34 weeks pregnant with our twin boys, who, as predicted, take after their father. Apparently, they're pressing on her organs or lungs, making it difficult to breathe. She's getting through it, though. Taking everything in stride, handling it like a champ.

My heart gives a squeeze.

As bad I feel for how miserable she's been, especially lately, seeing her big belly fills me with so much fucking pride and happiness that I could legit die from it. Shiloh is stunning. Hands down, the most incredible woman I've ever seen. With her thick long, brown hair, her chocolate brown eyes, and cherub face, she's beautiful. But like this? Her cheeks red, her forehead slight sweaty, her skin glowing, and her belly huge with our kids—she's *everything.*

Everything.

"Yes, I want to go. It's the 4th of July, Logan. Our first one as a couple, with both of our families, and our last big holiday before the boys get here. I want to see everyone." My eyes move from my woman to the nursery we're sitting in. Shiloh likes to spend most of her time here.

Apparently, she's *nesting* and not the kind of *nesting* I like. This isn't a kinky kind of nest. It's an OCD, never-ending, organizing, washing, decorating, moving shit, and moving shit again, kind of nesting. I'm not mad at it, per se, just annoyed. I want her to be happy. I'd do anything to make her happy. *Anything.* But how many times can you move the same picture before a person snaps, honestly?

A little to the left. No, the other left. Oh, that's no good. A little to the right. How about up? How about down? No, maybe I don't like it in here. Let's get a new picture. Oh, hey, Logan. Where's that old picture? I wanna put it up in the nursery.

It. Never. Ends.

My mom, the doctor, and Shiloh's mom, all said it would get better when the boys are here. But considering the fact that I have every intention of knocking her up again the second I'm allowed to, I have a feeling this is my new way of life.

Whatever. Totally worth it.

My eyes take in the room Shiloh and my mom put together for the twins. It's beautiful. She did it in the theme of the forest, which I had assumed was because of our surrounding property, but apparently, it has more to do with the way I *smell*. Whatever that means. Regardless, it's perfect. The room just off of ours is a bit small for two cribs since I'd never factored in multiples when I'd designed it, but we made it work.

As soon as they're big enough, we'll move them into one of the larger rooms down the hall that I'd built for exactly that purpose. I mean, come on. What did you expect in an 8-bedroom house with two Jack and Jill bathrooms? This house was built for a massive family.

At the thought, my eyes rake back down my woman's body, homing in on her big belly. Dropping to my knees before her, I press kisses all over the swell of her stomach.

"Hi, babies," I murmur. Shiloh chuckles but drags her nails through my hair as she relaxes on her cushy rocking chair. "Happy 4th of July. You don't know this because you're too tiny and can't see the world yet, but your mommy looks extra beautiful today," I tell them, meaning it completely. "She's grumpy sometimes, but she doesn't cry as much as she used to."

A hand softly lands on the back of my head, but I ignore the angry kitten.

"See what I'm talking about? Grumpy." Shiloh giggles. She may act annoyed, but she loves these moments between the four of us just as much as I do. Rubbing her sore, heavy belly, I continue to tell the boys all about our plans for the day, just like I do every morning. I like to keep them involved. Just because we can't see them doesn't mean they don't exist. They're part of our family.

When I've finished, I press my cheek to her stomach as if waiting for a response. It does as intended and earns a bark of laughter from Shiloh. *Good.* I move to stand up, but a kick under my palm stills my movement. The twins are active. Have been since around week 19, but lately, they've been practically breaking my woman's ribs.

"Shh," I coo, rubbing softly. "Give your mama a break, Asher." No doubt it's him. He's the bigger of the two. Has been from the get-go. "You're hurting her—" Another kick lands, this one from the opposite side of her belly. Shiloh groans, and I cringe. "And you're pissing off, Archer."

There's a lull in their attack on her insides, but it quickly ends with another round of kicks followed by a few well-placed punches. Then, one of them is twisting. In response, the other pushes and tries to flip. There isn't much room left inside my woman's belly, so I honestly don't know where they think they're going.

The doctor said she won't make it to full-term, which is normal for multiples, and that she could go into labor anytime in the next few weeks. If she doesn't, she'll be induced. But honestly, at the rate these boys are growing,

I wouldn't put my money on her pregnancy lasting much longer.

"Shh," she murmurs. "Please stop trying to kill your mommy." They ignore her, already acting like rebellious teens. Shiloh's eyes fill with tears, and my heart breaks at the sight. I wish there was something I could do for her.

"I'm so sorry, Babydoll. I'd carry them for you if I could," I say, meaning it completely. She ignores me, much like our kids did her, and continues to rub soothing circles across her stomach. I sigh, already knowing she's going to have my ass for this but oh well. Shiloh is mine to take care of. Mine to love and protect. Sometimes, that includes making hard calls. "We're not going today."

Standing up, I step back, putting some distance between us as I prepare for the shouting to start. Her angry glare snaps in my direction, just as expected. Her cute cheeks turn pink, and her knuckles are white from the death grip she has on the rocking chair. Her mouth opens as she prepares her tirade but then—

Then, her eyes widen, and instead of shouting, she whimpers. The sound goes straight to my motherfucking soul. "Babydoll?" I grunt, anxiety filling me in an instant. I step forward, right as liquid gushes from between her thighs. "*What the fuck?*"

"Oh my god," she screeches. Wide, terrified eyes meet mine, and it takes a second for it to click in my confused brain. My woman didn't just squirt for me. Her water broke.

Wait. Her water broke.

Holy. Shit.

Holy shit. We're having a baby. No, she's having a baby. No, again. She's having two babies. Two. There are two babies coming. Right here, right now. Fuck, I can't deliver a baby, let alone two. Am I supposed—

"Logan!" she cries, breaking me from my mental spiral. Her pained, nervous voice penetrates through my anxiety, and just like that, everything stops but her. I close the short distance between us in record time. Bending down, I grip her face, meeting her panicked gaze.

I take a deep breath and exhale slowly, trying to get her to follow my lead. She doesn't. She's holding her fucking breath like she's too scared to move or even breathe. I take another breath. It shudders when I exhale as more emotions than should be possible fill me. My heart races and my hands tremble, but I focus on *her.*

"I choose you, Shiloh Huxley," I murmur, repeating the words I gave her all those months ago in the bathroom. The words I committed to memory that very day, knowing they would be my vows the moment she lets me marry her. "I choose you as my friend, my partner, my wife. You *are* the mother of my children, my future. I choose you now, and I'll choose you, again and again, every day, for the rest of our lives."

The tears in her eyes spill over. She shakes as her gaze finds mine, and finally, she *breathes.* "We're having babies."

I nod, a massive smile spreading across my face as my world shifts once again. It begins, and it ends, with her, and now...with them.

"*We're having babies.*"

Also By Author

Bex Dawn

The Los Diablos world encompasses these three series (for now!)
For full reading order, please visit my website.
They are all still growing, but these are the books you can read/preorder now!

Los Diablos Syndicate (Unfinished)

Crash(Prequel)

Burn

Evolve

Resurrect

Prevail (Coming Fall 2023)

<u>The Trichotomy of New York(Unfinished)</u>

Violet Craves (Prequel)

Rough Love

Tough Love
Trust Love (Coming Fall of 2023)

<u>Sons Of Satan MC(Unfinished)</u>

Brass-Part One

**This series is a separate world. These are stand-alone, loosely interwoven, that take place in the town of Blue River, Colorado.
They each follow a different couple(or more) and their very specific kinks!
<u>Carnal Expectations(Unfinished)</u>**

Cracked Foundation

Primal Urges

Santa's Baby

Power Struggle

Dominate Me

<u>Divinity Falls Co-Write World with Haley Tyler</u>
Sin With Me (Coming Fall 2023)

For The Love Of Villains Anthology(Coming Fall 2023)
(This book will include a special bonus scene for Rayven and Wolfe from Primal Urges.

**Do you like Paranormal Romance or Omegaverse?
Check out my second pen name,
Phoenyx Saint and my upcoming book,**

Burning Wild!

<u>For updates, extras and more, subscribe to my newsletter!</u>

Thank You

So Damn Much.

My Team
Alpha/Beta Readers
Sensitivity Readers
Thank you for all that you do for me!
My author world wouldn't run as smoothly as it does if it was not for you two.
I appreciate and adore you guys more than you know!

MY PA!!!
Brittany—girl. I don't even know where to start!
You are an incredible human being and I am beyond thankful that you've come into my life.
You are my cheerleader, my weighted blanket (metaphorical, obvi), my team captain and so much more.
I am so fucking thankful to have you with me on this journey!

ARCS & Street Team

Basically....My hype squad

Thank you all so much for everything that you've done and continue to do for me.

Whether you've been a part of my team since the beginning, you're new to my team, or just here for this book....YOU ROCK!

ARC's, Beta's, and Hype members are essential to our careers as Authors.

You hold so much power in not only your opinions but your voice as well.

I adore and appreciate all of you more than you know!

My Mother-Fucking Readers
YOU-ARE-EVERYTHING!

About Author

Bex Dawn

Hey there Smut Sluts! Welcome to my world.

My name is Bex, and I am a 30-something biblio-phile from California. I love coffee, my five rescue animals, and the hundreds of books I collect like trophies. I have been writing since I could hold a pencil. My mom used to love to tell stories about the "books" I would write as a child. I would apparently scribble nonsense on paper and then proceed to "read" my books to everyone who would listen. Not much has changed since other than the fact that I've changed out the pencil and paper for a fancy laptop.

Writing and creative arts have always held a place close to my heart, but it wasn't until an extremely dark time in my life recently that I really pushed myself to fulfill my lifelong dream of publishing.

In the darkest days of my life, books saved me. Other people's written words dragged me out of my depression, kicking and screaming. And for that, I will forever be grateful. My dream is that my words will have a similar impact on even one person out there.

So, here's to sexy, possessive, alpha holes and kinky fuckery!

Follow me on social media!
www.authorbexdawn.com
TikTok: @bexdawnwrites
Instagram: @bexdawnwrites

Cover Photo Credit: Adobe Stock

PA/Proofread: Bound To Please PA Services

www.ingramcontent.com/pod-product-compliance
Lightning Source LLC
Chambersburg PA
CBHW070601300726
48975CB00006B/1678